She was a Vision. . . .
and a Summons to Compassion and Help!

The girl on the bench was not far from them, but she did not seem to be watching the birds. She had put her head down now on her arm across the back of the bench, as if she were too tired to watch birds or enjoy bits of parks.

Then suddenly as he gazed the girl slumped in a little crumpled heap and slid off the bench, as if she no longer had any power to help herself . . .

Startled he looked at the still form lying there on the ground, one arm thrown up and back the way it had slipped when she fell, the white face turned upward. Was he seeing aright? Or was this some illusion?

She was lying there as she had fallen on the ground beside the bench, and no one seemed to be doing anything about it. He was perhaps the only one who knew, and she might be dying if she were not dead already.

Greg sprang toward his door and raced down the stairs toward his fate. . . .

Bantam Books by Grace Livingston Hill
Ask your bookseller for the books you have missed

The Christmas Bride
Grace Livingston Hill

BANTAM BOOKS
TORONTO · NEW YORK · LONDON · SYDNEY

*This low-priced Bantam Book
has been completely reset in a type face
designed for easy reading, and was printed
from new plates. It contains the complete
text of the original hard-cover edition.*
NOT ONE WORD HAS BEEN OMITTED

THE CHRISTMAS BRIDE

*A Bantam Book / published by arrangement with
Harper & Row, Publishers Inc.*

PRINTING HISTORY

*Lippincott edition published 1934
Bantam edition / November 1981*

ISBN 0-553-20044-5

Published simultaneously in the United States and Canada

Bantam Books are published by Bantam Books, Inc. Its trademark,
consisting of the words "Bantam Books" and the portrayal of a
rooster, is Registered in U.S. Patent and Trademark Office and in
other countries. Marca Registrada. Bantam Books, Inc., 666 Fifth
Avenue, New York, New York 10103.

PRINTED IN THE UNITED STATES OF AMERICA

0 9 8 7 6 5 4 3

1

GREGORY STERLING rode slowly out of town toward his little shack among the hills. He had just come from signing the papers which gave over to the Blue Star Production Company full right and title to the land for which he had grubbed and starved and fought and almost died. He was going back to pack up and leave!

Ten years before, a mere lad with a sore heart and a great determination, Greg had come to the far west and taken up land, worked hard, raised a few cattle, striving against great odds year after year. Now suddenly within the last few months a rich yield of oil had been discovered, and the land which had been so hard to subdue had become worth millions. Actually millions!

Greg said it softly over to himself when he was out on the desert alone:

"I'm clearing out! I'm going back east. I'm going home *wealthy* just as I said I would!"

He set his grim young lips, gazed wistfully off toward the purple heights of the distant mountains and sighed.

"But it won't be home!" he added. "Not with Mother gone! There'll be nobody there I care about. Nobody left! Not even little Alice Blair!"

He was silent again reflecting how his mother had hated to have him going with Alice Blair! And then Alice Blair had run away with Murky Powers! Well, that was that! There wouldn't even be Alice.

He half closed his eyes and tried to visualize Alice as she

1

had been, a little pink and white and golden wisp of a thing with big blue eyes. Impudent eyes, his mother had called them. He hadn't thought of her for several years now. He had been grimly set on making a living. And now before he could have dreamed it possible, while he was still young enough to enjoy it, his fortune had come to him without any effort of his own!

He had never expected this thing. The utmost he had hoped when he first came out to these wilds, had been the right to do as he pleased, to hide his stricken young life after the death of his mother, to hide away from people who thought they were elected to manage him, and earn a meagre living through hard daily toil.

Then suddenly in a night he was rich! He was going back! Back to the place where they wouldn't lend him twenty dollars to start a newsstand down near the station. Back where they wanted him to be bound out to learn a trade!

He threw his head back and let out his triumph in a bitter laugh, the lightest that had passed his lips since his mother died and left him, a seventeen-year-old boy, with everybody trying to boss him. Well, now he could buy any house in town, pay twenty dollars for a single newspaper if he chose. *Rich!*

He laughed again that astonished mirthless laugh as if it were somehow a joke upon himself.

The thin old rackabones of a horse he was riding heard that unaccountable laughter, threw his head back in astonishment, gave a swish to his bobbed tail and a canter or two to express his interest. A squirrel whisked up into a tree and dropped the nut he had been so deftly manipulating, turning his head from side to side, taking in this most phenomenal sound on the wide open spaces. Guns he knew with their whistle of death; swearing he knew, and drunken calls; raucous singing he had heard at nighttime when cattlemen were riding home from a brawl. But this strange uncertain sound of mirth without joy was new, and there was a desperate wistfulness in it that even a wild creature would sense.

All the way back those monotonous miles to his shack Greg was staring ahead, not at the desert before him, but at his new life, trying to find a gleam. It must be going to be wonderful but he felt dazed when he should have been thrilled. He had been thinking so long in terms of cattle and feed and land and the bare necessities of life that his brain and imagination were numb. He could not seem to grasp the possibilities that were his.

He began to visualize his cabin on the mountain. A rude structure of logs and boards which he had built with his own eager inexperienced hands, a strong door, three small windows with wooden shutters. A sheet iron stove of ancient make, a cupboard with some tin dishes, salt pork, the end of a loaf of bread, a table against one wall made of a packing box. Two other boxes for seats, an army cot with gray blankets, and an old rheumatic couch of the kind known as "sofa" which he had bought from a settler about to move. Its decrepit springs were bursting forth like fallen soldiers from the old brussels carpet covering, faded and long since worn beyond all thought of its original pattern.

"Sometime when I'm wealthy I'll get you a new cover," he had promised it again and again when he had stretched his weary form upon its humpy inadequate dimensions. Well, now he was wealthy enough to buy him a new couch with great deep leather cushions, to build him a palace and furnish it throughout, and yet he found his heart turning wistfully toward a new cover for that poor old couch, the only real longing he had allowed himself during these barren years. He felt shy about going out into the world and hunting luxury for himself. In fact he had no standards of luxury. All he really longed for was home and somebody to care. His childhood home had been plain and simple, but it had been full of love and it was home! And you couldn't buy Home!

He had meant to build a fireplace some day in his shack, out of native cobble stones, and spread his big bear rug, the first trophy of his western prowess, before it. Draw up the couch with its bright new cover, sit and stare into the leaping flames as they bit into a great burning log, and heal his broken young heart. Now in his thoughts the couch seemed to rise in reproach at him as he rode along. He had sold it, couch, cabin, possibilities and all, and was going away forever!

He had planned to bring water down from the mountain spring above his shack and install a rude water system, to plant him a garden with vegetables and maybe a few of the flowers his mother used to love, just for remembrance, some day when he got time. He had meant to make the mountain side lovely too, and his dreams had even included a better dwelling there some day. But now that could never be. He had sold it

3

all and before long ugly disfiguring oil wells would spring up everywhere over his hillside site that he had selected so carefully.

Well, he was rich anyway, and there wasn't a soul to miss him. He had gone alone these ten long years, eaten and slept alone much of the time except for a few months when old Luke was with him, Luke a wanderer on the face of the earth dropping down for a little while, helping him work. But poor Luke was gone. Killed in a drunken brawl.

Even the dog that had companioned with him during the first few years of his exile had been wounded so badly by a wild steer one day that he had to be shot. There wasn't even a dog to care that he was leaving. No one out there in the west to care that he was not coming back.

The moon was shining when he reached his shack. He could see its silver light on the opposite hillside. His eye lingered on the wide expanse of sky, the purple mountains, the dark plumy woods, the river winding like a silver thread in the valley. Would he some day be homesick for all this quietness as he had longed for his home when he came out here?

Off there to the right was where the sun rose, bursting through bars of crimson. Off there to the left was where it set leaving tatters of purple and gold behind it. And there by the top of that tallest tree was the spot he watched when a storm was coming up and the tops of the tall pines bent with the wind. He sighed deeply and turned to his horse, touching the soft old nose with a lingering caress like a farewell. The horse was sold too.

When he went into the cabin he lighted his smoky oil lamp and looked around. There wouldn't be much to take with him. There were a few pelts fastened to the wall, skins of animals he had shot or trapped. His gun, he would have little need of that now.

He ate his supper and went to bed listening to the silence outside his cabin, wondering what the new life was going to be like.

It was a little past noon when he finished his packing and cleaning, for he took a certain pride in leaving everything immaculate. On the saddle were fastened two bundles, one sewed into an old piece of burlap bag, to be forwarded to himself in his home town, the other, crudely wrapped in newspaper containing a few necessities that he was taking with him. He had discarded most of his wardrobe. There was not much that would belong in his new life.

When he reached the settlement town and left the bony old horse with his new owner he found an uneasy regret in his heart at parting from him, and when he bought his ticket he stuffed it into his pocket with a strange distaste. He had a passing wonder why he had consented to sell his place and be shoved out again into the world when he was just getting a foothold here, and nobody out in the world wanted him. For just that instant if the Blue Star Company had offered to sell his place back to him, almost he would have been tempted to accept. Then he turned upon himself savagely and told himself he was childish, and walked away down the platform to "Jake's Place" where one could get a good dinner of liver and onions and baked beans with dried-apple-pie for fifty cents. But somehow he didn't feel like eating when he looked in the window. The pie looked tired, and there was a smell of burned fat in the air.

He walked back to the little station again and stood looking off down the track that gleamed red as two streaks of blood in the low rays of the setting sun, and presently out of the dazzle of it the train appeared, a dark speck, growing larger momently, and bearing down upon him.

An unanticipated shyness came upon him. A bear he had met, wild cattle in a stampede, a gun pointing into his face, the threatening angry growl of a group that outnumbered him, all without the slightest quiver. But that oncoming train that would carry him back into a world of civilization, brought a strange panic upon him. He waited while a bundle of papers and a mail pouch were thrown off, and a drummer's case of samples and a trunk were put on, then just as the conductor waved his signal to the engineer and the first slow revolution of the wheels began, he gravely stepped forward, swung himself aboard the lowest step, his newspaper bundle under his arm, and quite casually rode out of town into the great world.

Cautiously he opened the door of a Pullman and glanced inside. Here at once was a foreign atmosphere. Men and women of another world. Obviously he did not belong here. Swift as the vision of Adam and Eve after they ate the apple came the knowledge to him that his apparel was not right.

The porter approached him hastily from the other end of the

car as if he were a stray dog wandered in, to be hustled out as soon as possible.

"Common cah up the othah end of the train!" he said in an unmistakable tone of authority.

Gregory stiffened and lifted his chin haughtily. Here again was that same spirit of class distinction from which he had run away when he came west. He had not expected to meet it again at the first step of the way. He made a mental resolve that his wealth should never make him feel superior to his fellow mortals.

He looked the porter in the eye for an instant and then turned and stalked in the direction indicated, through another parlor car, a club car and a diner, on up through several common cars. He dropped finally into a vacant seat and settling down close to the window gave himself to watching the sunset, as much as he could see of it reflected in the clouds ahead of the train. Splendid flocks of pinks and blues and delicate pearly grays, like sheep being herded into the oncoming night.

Now and then the train took a slight turn and he could look directly into the west where were heaped up masses of velvety purple and midnight blue, rent here and there with heavy gold in ragged splashes.

Back there on his old hillside that mingled glory light would be still shining on the home he had left, touching with splendor his rude shack, laying bright hands on the far pile of stones that marked old Luke's grave, sailing silvery down the river in the valley.

As long as the display lasted he gave undivided attention to his window, until night pulled the curtain of twilight definitely down and pinned it with a star.

He sat with his head leaning against the cold window pane looking into the night. And presently he became aware of voices purposely raised across the aisle, three girls in a double seat. They were discussing his clothes, and Greg's anger arose again. Couldn't one wear what one pleased in this world?

Greg hadn't given much thought to what he should wear. Indeed he had little choice. Out there in his wilderness home it seemed a matter of very little moment. He was wearing khaki breeches stuffed into heavy boots, and belted with a cartridge belt over a flannel shirt of butternut brown. His short coat of khaki color was lined and furred with sheepskin.

His hat was a soft wide brimmed, weathered felt, and although he did not know it he made a picturesque figure sitting like a bronze statue against the brilliant changing sky.

As the girls' voices rose he turned and looked at them. He had scarcely noticed them when he sat down. They were gaily dressed, cheaply too, although he did not know that, and their faces were startling in their make-up. When Gregory came west nice girls didn't paint their faces. Even unnice ones did not go to such an extreme as these girls. They looked to him like the girls that came at intervals to "Jake's Place" and gave a show, and then danced and drank afterward with the clamoring cowboys who flocked to meet them. He had never cared much for that sort of thing. He had been too busy fighting for his land, too young when he first came west to feel the urge toward such brawls, and later too much in the habits of his hermitage to venture forth for an all-night orgy. Perhaps, too, the lingering memory of the clean, simple atmosphere with which his mother had surrounded his boyhood days was a strong element in protecting his life from such temptations.

So now as he turned a grave glance toward the three highly illuminated faces and took note of the impudent intimate challenge of their lawless eyes he judged them young women of no reputation and met their look with one of half pitying contempt. He would have been surprised to know that they were simply common ill-bred hard-working girls out to have a good time and eager to imitate a brazen modern world whose glamour had lured their souls.

The one in red began to laugh and suddenly addressed him mockingly:

"Why n't ya buy ya a haircut, Buddie?" she called across to him. "It would improve ya a lot."

Greg eyed her gravely an instant and then replied in a careless drawl:

"Thanks a lot! I was just thinking how much you girls needed a good facewash!"

Then he slowly straightened up, arose to his full height and turned his gaze down the car. He made a really stunning figure and the girls, catching their breath as one girl at his audacity, suddenly broke into embarrassed laughter mixed with a note of the hilarious. But Greg did not look their way again. He picked up his paper bundle and walked slowly away from them down the aisle and out the car door.

Back through the other common cars he went, looking to neither right nor left, through club car and diner, and Pullmans, studying the numbers of the cars as he made his slow progress, till at last he found the number he was looking for. As he paused beside it the porter whom he had at first encountered came hurrying nervously toward him from the rear end of the car.

Greg eyed him amusedly as he puffed up assertively and seemed about to speak. Then he said in his slow pleasant drawl:

"Sorry to disturb you, Brother, but this seems to be my seat," and he handed out the magic bit of green paper that gave him right to that place and sat down.

The porter eyed him incredulously, studied the ticket a moment and then looked at him sharply.

"Where d'you-all get this ticket? This yours?"

"Back there at the station where I got on," said Greg still in that calm half-amused tone. "Isn't it all right?" and he handed out a bill that made the porter stare and melt into smiles.

"Oh, yessah, yessah! It's all right, sah! I wasn't just shore where at this party was comin' on, sah? Any bags, sah?" and he eyed Greg's newspaper bundle questioningly.

"No bags!" said Greg grinning and stowing his parcel beside him.

The poor bewildered porter went on his way staring down at the greenback, and casting furtive glances about at the other passengers, and then entrenched behind his own special narrow sanctum at the end of the car, peered out and studied this strange crude-looking passenger who dressed like a common workman and threw ten dollar bills around so casually.

And Greg sank into his comfortable seat and mused on the ways of the world to which he had come back. He could sense that the porter was still troubled in spite of the tip, and he realized that his appearance was against him. Even money didn't count if one didn't dress the part. Well, he could do it now, but would it pay? Would it get him the kind of friends he wanted? Of course he meant to buy some new clothes when he got to a city. Perhaps he would stop off in Chicago and shop. He didn't want to go home looking like a wild man. But he registered a resolve never to dress conspicuously and never to judge a man merely by his clothes.

Presently one came through the train announcing the last

8

call for dinner, and Greg, with a furtive glance around, noting that most of his car companions were in their seats and had probably had their dinners, decided that it was late enough for him to venture into the diner. He found he was hungry enough to thoroughly enjoy the first well-cooked meal that he had eaten for several years.

Ten days later Gregory Sterling stood at the front window of the luxurious room that had been assigned him in the great new apartment hotel in his home town, looking out at the street that had been a meadow when he went away.

He had chosen the Whittall House from the list the taxicab driver had suggested because it seemed to be located out on the edge of town, and his soul was weary for the quietness and peace of his wilderness lodge. He had spent several days in Chicago shopping, having acquired what seemed to him a ridiculously large supply of clothing and several quite correct pieces of baggage. Porters and hotel clerks no longer looked at him askance. He was as well turned out as any modern young man could be. The home town had no need to be ashamed of him.

And now he stood at the window of his room looking out on the amazing changes that had come during his absence, identifying the bit of a park across the street as the very spot where his mother and he used to pick violets years ago, on the rare occasions when she had time to take a walk with him. His eyes suddenly filmed over with tears at the memory.

The street was wide, and the little park ran down the centre, making a boulevard of it. Traffic was whirling on either side, but the little park in the middle made a haven, a wide nice pleasant place to rest between the crossings. There were paths of cement wandering across the park, curving this way and that among the trees, and there were flowerbeds with late fall flowers in blossom, little button chrysanthemums, white and yellow, pompon chrysanthemums flaring red, orange, yellow, russet brown and flame color, growing rankly with bright ragged heads in spite of the touch of frost there had been the night before.

There were trees too. Tall pines and oaks and maples, still clinging to their brilliant foliage, for the street there was sheltered by tall buildings, apartment houses and hotels. And was that an old gnarled apple tree? It looked like the very tree he used to climb to get a spray of apple blossoms for his mother. There were no leaves left on it, but high in the top there was a small red apple or two that no one had spied. There was a bench under the tree and the walk curved to it and away to a fountain a little farther on, a fountain whose bright spray caught the late afternoon sun and reflected it into many faceted jewels.

A girl was sitting on the bench, droopingly, as if she were tired and discouraged. It was good to have a bit of green in the midst of the whirl, a quiet place where the traffic could not come, for tired people to rest in. But better still if the meadow were there the way it used to be!

Across the road beyond the little park and the other road there were tall beautiful buildings, but they did not look natural. He was almost sorry he had come out here to stay. It did not seem as if it was his home town at all. It hadn't ever occurred to him that the town would grow out into the country this way in just ten years!

His eyes wandered back again to the fountain where little brown birds were drenching themselves and shaking fluffy wet feathers, splashing like children in the marble basin and sitting chirping on the marble rim to dry.

The girl on the bench was not far from them but she did not seem to be watching the birds. She had put her head down now on her arm across the back of the bench, as if she were too tired to watch birds or enjoy bits of parks.

Then suddenly as he gazed the girl slumped in a little crumpled heap and slid off the bench, as if she no longer had the power to help herself. So slowly, almost unobtrusively the slender figure slipped down from the bench it almost seemed like an empty garment sliding from a chair where it had been carelessly thrown. Could it be that her spirit had fled?

Startled he looked at the still form lying there on the ground, one arm thrown up and back the way it had slipped when she fell, the white face turned upward. Was he seeing aright? Or was this some illusion?

He passed his hand over his eyes hastily and looked again. Something must be wrong with his vision. It could not be that a thing like that had happened before his eyes in broad daylight with traffic passing either way continually.

But there she lay, still as death, her hat tipped away from her face. And now he saw there were bushes all about which might have obstructed the vision of those on the road. He could see because he was looking down from above. She was lying there as she had fallen on the ground beside the bench, and no one seemed to be doing anything about it. He was perhaps the only one who knew, and she might be dying if she were not dead already!

Greg sprang toward his door and started down the stairs thankful that he was only three stories up, forgetting that an elevator could travel faster than his feet.

2

THE doorman was startled as Greg burst hatless into the street.

"A woman fallen off the bench over there!" Greg called breathlessly as the doorman rushed alongside. "I saw her fall. Better call a doctor!"

"Better call the police!" advised the doorman cannily. "You better wait till the police comes! You might get mixed up in some murder or something." The doorman put a detaining hand on Greg's arm, holding him back from an oncoming automobile.

"And let her die meantime?" shouted Greg, shaking off the detaining hand and dashing madly in amongst traffic.

The doorman looked uncertainly after him, then turned back to send a gaping bellboy to telephone for an ambulance.

Meantime a crowd had suddenly gathered and were staring. The clerk of the hotel came out and looked across to the park.

Greg had reached the side of the girl now and was kneeling, looking at her keenly, stooping to listen for her heart.

On the way down the stairs he had thought of possibilities. He hailed from a land where stray bullets were not uncommon, and of course that was the first thing he thought of. Someone had shot the girl, or someone shooting at birds had sent a wild bullet into the air.

But there was no sign of a wound, no blood on the ground, or trickling down the white face. Just a pinched tired look that went to his heart, just long dark lashes lying over deathly white thin cheeks.

Greg gave one wild look around and gathered her up into his arms.

"Better leave her lay, Buddie," advised a bystander with his hands in his pockets and his pipe between his teeth. "Always better ta leave 'em lay till the p'lice gets here, Buddie. You don't get no thanks for meddling."

Greg flashed him a look from his steady gray eyes.

"Get me a taxi!" he ordered. "She's not dead! Only fainted!"

"Ya can't tell, Buddie! She might pass out on ya!" said the bystander.

"Where is the nearest hospital?" demanded Greg, ignoring the man with the advice.

A boy dashed out into the road and stopped a taxi. A shabby man hurried to the fountain and filled his hat full of water from the basin. A woman walking through the park produced a bottle of smelling salts.

Greg wet his handkerchief in the hat and wiped the girl's forehead and lips. He let the woman hold the bottle of smelling salts under her nostrils, and they were rewarded by a long slow trembling breath from the girl, and then a lifting of the fringes of the eyelids just for a fleeting instant that showed great dark troubled eyes. The fringes fell almost instantly, but the crowd had seen that she was alive, and a murmur of sympathy went through them like the sighing of the wind.

But Greg saw the taxi draw up at the curb and he swept them all aside and carried his burden over. He got in with her in his arms.

"The nearest hospital, quick!" he ordered, and they whirled away leaving the gaping crowd to discuss the incident.

Greg sat holding the girl in his arms, looking down at the white face against his shoulder, the long curling lashes, the dishevelled brown hair. Her hat had fallen off and one of the bystanders had laid it in her arms, a little soft black felt with a tiny bright feather stuck cockily through the brim, a brave attempt to be like the world. But the rest of her attire was undeniably shabby. Little stubbed out shoes, worn down at the heel, but bravely polished. Shabby gloves carefully mended. He felt a sudden mistiness in his eyes, a sudden estimate of the preciousness of his burden. Perhaps she was very dear to somebody. There must be people who loved her, many perhaps, but for the time being she was *his* to protect, until someone else should claim her. He perhaps was all that stood between her and death!

He drew his breath in sharply. If she *was* living yet!

He looked down with fear. How white her lips were! Perhaps that look she had given had been her last one on earth! Oh, would they never reach the hospital? How light and frail her body seemed! There was something pitiful in the droop of her lips. Something that made him think with a pang of his mother in her last days. Was this death? He held her lightly and felt the wonder of her delicate face against his shoulder.

There! They were stopping! Yes, this was a hospital building. A white-clad doctor appeared! A nurse! They tried to take her from him but he bore her swiftly up the steps.

"Hurry!" he said. "She may not be gone yet!"

"The emergency ward is full!" he heard a nurse's voice say sharply. "That fire! They kept bringing them in! Two have died already, but the beds are full."

"Take her to a private room!" he commanded.

"A *private?*" another nurse said. "Who is she? We can't put her in a private room unless we know she can pay."

"*I* will pay. Get her somewhere quick!" said Greg.

Magic Money! How it oiled the wheels and hastened matters. No, they were not hard-hearted. They were used to emergencies. But there had been so many that night. And the head nurse was off on her vacation. It was only a substitute who was trying to be conscientious.

She was on a bed at last with a doctor and nurse working over her. Finally the doctor straightened up and looked around.

"Who brought her here? What happened?"

"I did!" said Greg. "I don't know what happened."

"Is she your wife?" the doctor asked, looking at him keenly.

Greg looked at him with startled eyes.

"Oh, no. I never saw her before. She was sitting on a bench in the park across from my hotel. I happened to be looking out the window and saw her fall, that was all."

"H'm!" said the doctor touching her pulse again. "A clear case of starvation I guess. That's all!"

"Starvation!" said Greg aghast. "You don't mean it! Not in a city full of people!"

"Oh, *yeah?*" said the doctor brusquely. "You don't pick food off trees in parks. Does she look like a girl who would go to your back door and beg?"

He turned to the nurse and gave low-voiced directions, and Greg stood looking down at the pathetic little white face on the pillow. Starving! How could that come about?

They were pressing a spoonful of something between the white lips now, and the girl on the bed drew a slow quivering breath again and opened her eyes for an instant.

"That's it, Sister," said the doctor cheerfully. "You're going to feel better now in a minute."

He watched the patient closely.

"A cup of that broth as soon as you can get it, Nurse," he said in a low tone, keeping his finger on the pulse. Then to Greg who was standing anxiously by.

"Yes, sir, you find 'em like this every day. Proud as Lucifer, lost their job, nowhere to turn. All the worse for them if they happen to be good."

Greg looked at the delicate high-born features of the girl and understood what the doctor meant. He looked at her slender patrician well-cared-for hands and read a tragedy. How had a girl like this one come so near to starvation?

When the broth was brought the patient swallowed obediently but did not open her eyes again. Greg watched from the doorway with misgiving in his heart. Was this little shadow of a girl going to slip away from them out of life after all, without giving a clue as to her identity? Was there perhaps a mother or some other loved one who was waiting anxiously for her home coming? Gregory Sterling without a person in the world to care for him lingered anxiously pondering on such a tragedy for the friends of this girl. Was there nothing he could do?

"Will this nurse stay by her all night?" he asked the doctor while the nurse was feeding her the soup.

"Oh, she'll be in and out all night," said the doctor. "You know she has this whole hall to look out for."

"I'd like her to have someone with her all night," said Greg. "I'd feel better that way. I feel sort of responsible because I found her, at least till her folks get here."

"Of course you could have a special nurse if you're willing to pay for it," said the doctor thoughtfully, "but it isn't necessary. She'll probably pull through all right."

"I'd like to have a special nurse," said Greg decidedly.

"Well, of course it's always safer in a case like this," said the doctor. "You can't always be sure about the condition of the heart."

So presently a pleasant-faced capable young woman appeared and took charge. Greg motioned her out in the hall and talked to her in low tones.

"This girl was sitting on a park bench when I first saw her from my hotel window," he told her, "and while I was watching she fell off the bench. I brought her here and I'm arranging for her to have this room as long as she needs it till she is able to go away. But she doesn't know me and I don't know her. Maybe she might not like it to have me meddling in her affairs, but you don't need to say anything about it, do you? Just let on the hospital put her in here, can't you? I don't want to put her under any obligation."

"I see," said the nurse. "We'll fix that up all right. It's awfully fine of you to do all this for a stranger, and you can count on me."

He looked at her wistfully.

"If there is anything else I could do I'd be glad," he said. "It seems a pity we don't know where to find her friends. I don't suppose she'll be able to tell us anything tonight!"

"No," said the nurse, thoughtfully. "Maybe not even tomorrow. It might be best just to let her alone and let her rest. You can't always tell about these cases."

"I wonder," said Greg almost shyly, "if I should leave you my telephone number would you call me in case you found out, or there was anything at all that I could do to help? In the night or any time! There's a telephone in my room. It wouldn't bother me a bit."

"Sure, I'll let you know if there is any change or anything you can do. But I guess you needn't worry. The doctor seemed to think her heart was pretty good. And I'll be right here all night."

"That's good!" he said and gave her a relieved smile.

So Greg went down and arranged for the private room, paying a week in advance.

"If she doesn't need it that long you can put some other little stranger in there after she is gone," he said happily, and swung off down the street to his hotel, thinking about the little white-faced girl lying in the hospital bed.

It seemed a strange homecoming, almost the first thing to find this girl sitting over there just where he and his mother

15

had picked violets. And now it seemed as though he could not do anything for himself until he knew the fate of this poor little stranger.

He went into the dining room and ate a good dinner, surprised to find that it was well on toward eight o'clock. Why, it had been still daylight when he took that girl to the hospital!

While he ate he was thinking about the hospital. He remembered various bronze tablets he had seen about on the walls as he waited for his receipt to be signed at the office.

Why wouldn't it be a nice thing for him to endow one of those rooms so it could be used for strangers? He could put up a tablet on the door with his mother's name, a memorial to her. Call it the Mary Sterling Memorial Room for Strangers. He would enjoy doing that with some of his new money. It would somehow give his mother a part in it. And she would have liked that. She was always doing beautiful things for lonely people. Perhaps he could get that very room the little girl was in tonight! That would be nice. The girl who had been sitting alone in the very spot where his mother used to pick violets would be the first one to lie in the room endowed to her memory. He would do it! The first thing tomorrow morning he would go over to the hospital and arrange it! He would get the bronze tablet made and put on the door right away. Then if the girl was worried about his paying for her room there wouldn't be any trouble. It would just be a free room for strangers.

The idea made him quite happy, and after he had finished his dinner he went out and walked beside the fountain in the little park, strolling past the bench where the girl had sat, even sitting down upon it a moment to wonder why she had sat there, and what had happened that had brought her into such a sorrowful situation.

As he got up his foot struck against something in the grass, something soft and yielding that slid across the pavement as he hit it.

He stooped and picked it up wonderingly. It was a flat purse with a strap across the back, one of the kind that most girls carried. It had a look of thinness about it that betokened nothing inside. He took it over and stood beneath the arc light studying it and turning it over thoughtfully. Could that belong to the girl he had picked up, and could she possibly have dropped it as she fell?

16

He went back and laid it down again just where he had found it, figuring out just how it might have fallen from her grasp. Then he took it back to the light once more and opened it. Perhaps it might give some clue to her family.

But it proved to be absolutely empty save for a thin letter addressed to Miss Margaret McLaren, 1456 Rodman Street, that city. There wasn't even a penny in the little middle purse that obviously was meant for change. His heart went out with pity toward the poor child, for he felt absolutely certain that this pocketbook belonged to the girl he had picked up in the park.

He studied the envelope carefully. Where would Rodman Street be? Wasn't there such a street down behind the schoolhouse when he was a boy? He could go and see. Perhaps it was her home. Perhaps her father and mother were waiting anxiously. It was late. He looked at his watch, almost eleven o'clock. Yet if they were worried they would be only too glad to be disturbed.

He looked at the letter again uncertainly. It was postmarked Vermont but the town was so blurred it was unreadable. Ought he perhaps to know what was in that letter? Well, not yet anyway. If he could find her people nothing else was his affair.

So he started out to find Rodman street and at last discovered the address on one of a row of old brownstone front houses.

There were lights in the second story, and a dim light coming from the transom over the front door but it was a long time before anybody came, and then the door was opened but a few inches over a sturdy door chain.

"Who's there?" asked a sharp elderly voice.

"Does Miss Margaret McLaren live here?" asked Greg.

"No. She certainly doesn't. Not any more!" said the sharp voice, "I told her this morning that she needn't come back tonight whining around for me to let her in. She can't step her foot inside this house again, not till she pays me the three weeks rent she owes me. And if it's her suitcase you've come for you can't have it till the room rent's paid. I told her that, too, this morning. I can't live on air, and I've waited for my money just as long as I can wait. I've got another party for her room and if she doesn't pay up they'll move in in the morning."

17

Greg was still for a minute considering.

"I didn't come for her suitcase," he said, "I was just trying to look up some of her friends, but it doesn't sound as if you were one. I had thought it might interest you to know that she had an accident this afternoon and she's in the hospital unconscious now. She won't need your room tonight, and perhaps not for a good many nights. I don't know that she ever will."

There was silence behind the chained door for an instant and then the sharp voice struck in again.

"Accident! Humph! Well they needn't try to bring her here. I don't intend to take care of any sick people. I got enough to do to look after my roomers. I'm sick and old. All I've got ta say is she deserves what she gets. Anybody that ud give up a perfectly good position just because she couldn't stomach the man that employs her deserves to get down and out. These aren't any times to be so squeamish about jobs. She had no business to leave her perfectly good place. He paid her, didn't he? What I wantta know is what she did with all her money? She didn't buy cloes, goodness knows. In fact I think she's pawned most of hers, for she's been going around that shabby. I was ashamed ta have her as a roomer. I ben up in her closet an' there ain't scarcely a thing worth holding for my rent. What d'you come here for anyway? Because you aren't likely to get it."

"No, so I see," said Greg indignantly. "Well, suppose I happened to come to pay her rent?"

The woman brought her face closer to the opening.

"Who are you anyway?" she hissed. "I never saw you with her. Why should you pay her rent?"

"I'm only a friend, and you never did see me with her, but I might pay her rent just to save her having to listen to you when she is able to come back again. How much is her rent anyway?"

"It's fifteen dollars!" said the woman belligerently, "and I won't come down a cent for cash either!"

"Is that all?" said Greg, amusedly. "Well, I'll pay if you'll make out a receipt in full to date."

"She'll have to pay in advance if she wants to keep the room," added the woman.

"Well, that's entirely up to her," laughed Greg. "I hope she doesn't want the room again. I certainly shall use my influence against it. I wouldn't enjoy staying under such an unfriendly roof myself."

18

"I'm not unfriendly," said the woman, "but we have to look out for ourselves. We have to live!"

"Do we?" said Greg. "Well, I don't know about that. Sometimes one can die you know. Your little friend almost died tonight. However, bring on your receipt and here's your money. Are you going to let me come in while you sign it or do I stay in the street?"

"I suppose you can come in," said the woman grudgingly. "If you're really going to pay." She eyed the roll of bills in Greg's hand greedily.

She sat down at an old rickety table in the hall, wrote the receipt painstakingly and handed it over. Greg folded it carefully and put it in his pocket, meanwhile glancing up the dismal staircase.

"Where is this room I'm paying for?" asked Greg. "Third story back?"

"Yes," admitted the woman, "and cheap at that. My neighbor next door gets seven and a half for hers."

As he walked out the door and down the street Greg was thinking of his clean little shack on the hillside with the whispering pines all around. Somehow there was something terribly desolate and dreary in this rooming house. And was this the place where the little white-faced girl had lived? For how long, he wondered?

But then, of course, the pocketbook might not have belonged to her. Or even if it had the letter might not have been hers. He couldn't tell a thing until he found out if Margaret was really her name. He had been a fool of course to pay for that room till he found out. Likely he was a fool anyway. But it was his money, wasn't it? He had a right to spend it as he liked.

He found himself recalling the landlady's words about the girl giving up her job because she didn't like her employer. How much was there to that? Had any rotten bounder dared to be unpleasant to a girl like that?

HE walked around by the hospital again, as if just to see the building would satisfy that vague anxiety that was in him.

Here he was the first night in his home town all mixed up in a strange girl's troubles, all anxious for her life. That little white face against his shoulder! He wanted her to get well. Poor kid! She must have been up against it somehow. He wished he knew more about it. Maybe he'd better read that letter after all, just glance at it. There might be an address. Maybe her folks ought to be notified if she was off here in a great city alone.

So when he reached his room in the hotel he took the letter out of his pocket, half reverently, and opened it.

It was only a torn half sheet of cheap note paper, and just a few lines written on it at that, no name signed either.

"Dear Child," [it read]

"Sam Fletcher is going down to the village so I write a line to let you know the money came safely. Your Grandfather says, 'Bless the child' and tell her not to send any more now. We'll make out. Get yourself a good warm winter coat. His knee is a little better now we think. Don't overwork.

Lovingly, Grandmother.

P.S. Is that man you work for all right? It kind of worries me what you say about him. Maybe you better try for another job."

Well, there wasn't any help here. No date except the blurred postmark, and no name of the town or people. Obviously he couldn't let that grandfather and grandmother know. He couldn't go all over the State of Vermont asking for Margaret McLaren's grandparents.

He put the letter slowly back into the envelope feeling

guilty that he had read it at all, even though he had a good motive in doing so. Now he had laid bare some more of her troubles. Poor kid! She certainly was up against it. And to have a heartless old bird of a landlady like that, with all the rest! No sympathy nor help to be had from her! He shut his lips grimly as he thought of her. Probably he ought not to have paid that bill till he knew more about it, but there was a kind of satisfaction at the memory of the greedy astonishment in the old woman's face as she took the bills in her hand. He really had got fifteen dollars' worth of pleasure out of the look on her hard, old, selfish face. But poor devil, she probably was hard up too! What a lot of people seemed to be hard up and to take it so hard! Why he had been hard up all his life, and now that he had plenty he didn't quite know what to do with it. Was he going to find a way of happiness with it? Or was he only going to waste it all and then have to go back to work again? Well, if he did, work no longer had a terror for him. He knew how to go without. Though he never had been hungry. That poor little white-faced girl had been hungry! *Starved*, the doctor said. How terrible! Would she ever come out of it all and would there be a way for him to do something for her? Perhaps she was going to make a terrible row about this hospital room. You couldn't tell. Well, he would get that fixed the first thing in the morning, so that the room was a genuine free one. He wished he knew how she was.

Early in the morning his telephone rang causing him to waken sharply to sudden anxiety.

"Is this Mr. Sterling? Well, this is Miss Gowen, the nurse. I just wanted to tell you that our patient rested nicely all night, took her medicine and nourishment like a lamb and is still sleeping. The doctor came in in the night and says she is doing well. He says she may sleep right on through the day, you can't tell. She seems thoroughly exhausted. Will you be over today? Well, I'll be here. No, I don't need to sleep. I rested well during the night, only up with her a couple of times for feedings. I'll get another nice nap sometime today while she is sleeping. You needn't worry."

Greg felt like a child with a holiday after he had hung up. Why was he so glad about an utter stranger? Well, he was. It was something to have somebody to care about, even a stranger about whom he knew nothing. He had saved her life perhaps. Didn't that give him some right to be glad?

21

He ate his breakfast joyously, planning what he would do.

He had intended going out to see the old landmarks that morning, his old home, the schoolhouse, the church where his mother and he used to go regularly on Sunday, the house where Alice used to live, all the places with which he had been familiar. But that could wait. He wanted to get this business of the hospital fixed up first.

He found there were formalities. He couldn't just transform a hospital room into any kind of a free place he wished at will. There were officials and there was a Board. But fortunately the Board had a meeting that morning, and he was informed that he could present his proposition at eleven o'clock.

The Board was gracious to this opulent stranger who was willing to pay cash for a room that very often stood idle because it was only available to wealthy people. When the arrangements were completed Greg went to see about having the bronze tablet made for the door, and it was late in the afternoon before he got back to the hospital.

He found the nurse just coming out of the room.

"I've been trying to telephone you," she said. "She woke up a few minutes ago and insisted on getting right up and going away. I told her that would be impossible until the doctor came, that we had no right to let her go away until she had been dismissed. Then she said she absolutely must. That she had to go somewhere and apply for a job. She seemed awfully upset that she hadn't got there by eight o'clock. I've had a time keeping her quieted down. I thought perhaps if you could come in and jolly her along a little it might help."

"I'll come!" said Greg with a light in his eyes. "You're sure she won't mind?"

"Well, I'm not sure of anything," laughed the nurse, "but I know something's got to be done. She's worrying a lot, I can see that, and it isn't doing her any good. I asked her if she hadn't some friends I could send for but she said no, they were all far away and she didn't want them worried. But I did find out her name. It's Margaret McLaren. I told her we had to have it for the records."

Greg drew a breath of relief. Then the purse *was* hers, and he had paid *her* debt and not some other girl's. That was good.

"All right, I'll see what I can do," he said, "but hadn't you better ask her if she is willing to see me?"

"Well, not exactly," said the nurse, "she might take it into her head to refuse and that wouldn't be well. I'll just take it for granted. That's better. We simply must stop her worrying!"

With which last whispered word the nurse swung the door open and said in a clear, cheery tone:

"Miss McLaren, I'm bringing a visitor to see you. This is Mr. Sterling who picked you up yesterday and brought you here. He's been anxious to know how you are, and I knew you would want to thank him."

The girl on the bed turned quick troubled eyes toward the young man, and a little color sprang into her white cheeks.

Greg went toward the bed with his cheerful grin in evidence. He wasn't thinking about himself or he would have been shy, for he wasn't used to girls. But this one had come very close to his heart and he was most anxious to help her.

"But say!" he exclaimed eagerly. "You're looking better already, aren't you? I certainly am glad. I thought you had passed out!"

The girl managed a wan smile.

"It was very good of you to care for me," she said. "I'm sorry I had to make so much trouble for everybody. You see, I hadn't been eating much yesterday. I was worried, and I just sat down there a little while to rest. I had no idea I would collapse like that. I suppose I'm rather run down. I've been working hard—"

"Yes," said Greg sympathetically, "I can see you would. And it's perhaps a good thing you did collapse just when you did. I'm certainly glad I was on hand to see you fall. You see you had picked out a place to sit where you were not very visible from the road, and if I hadn't happened to be up in my room looking out the window I wouldn't have seen you either. It was getting dusk too, and nobody might have found you until it was too late. Not so many people walk through that park. I'm just glad I had the chance to help in time. Say, I certainly am glad you're looking so much better."

He was rattling on like an eager boy, just because he didn't know what was the right thing to say. He was not a young man given to many words.

"But say," he suddenly caught himself and looked at the nurse, "am I talking too much? Are you sure I don't tire you, Miss McLaren? I wouldn't want you to have a set-back from my coming in."

"Oh, no," said the invalid quickly, "I'm glad you came.

Perhaps you can fix things up for me right away so I can leave. Since you brought me here you ought to know how to cut some of the red tape that seems to hinder my leaving."

"Why, sure!" he said reassuringly, "I'll see what can be done, but I don't believe anybody will be willing you should leave right away. You see you really need a few days' rest after such an experience. You don't want to go until you are strong enough you know."

"But I must!" said the girl firmly. "It's absolutely imperative that I go out and see about a job at once. I was to have met a man early this morning, and it is really necessary that I keep my appointment."

"Well," said Greg thoughtfully, "how would it be if I go and explain to him that you were taken ill?"

"No!" said the girl quickly. "He doesn't know me. He would simply take somebody else. And I *must* get this position!"

"But my dear friend," said Greg earnestly, "don't you know that it is Saturday afternoon?" He glanced at his watch. "By the time you could get there almost any office would be likely to be closed, if it didn't close at noon. You can just as well lie here and rest till Monday at the earliest and get strength to carry you on through the week. You know you wouldn't be in very good shape just now to take any job, not till you get a little stronger."

"Oh, but I *must!*" said the girl with a gray look of determination in her face. "I've got to get some position at once! There will be *some* places open yet."

Her voice trailed off into a desperate little wail, and his heart ached for her.

"Look here, little friend," he said earnestly, "we really couldn't let you go out and hunt a job today. And what could you do over Sunday anyway? You see here you will be cared for and have the right food and be made to rest—"

"Oh, but please," interrupted the girl earnestly, "you don't understand. I cannot *afford* to stay here. Even in the ward I couldn't afford to stay. I just haven't a *cent!* And this is a private room, with a special nurse. I don't know how it ever came about that I was put here, but it will be a long long time before I am able to pay for this one day here, and I simply cannot stay longer. I'm just as grateful as I can be for what you've done. But I ought to have been put in a ward, if I had to be here at all."

24

"Well, now there you are mistaken, Miss McLaren." Greg spoke gladly, confidently. "This isn't a regular private room and it won't cost you a cent. This room is a Memorial Room to my mother. I've been arranging it all with the officials of the hospital, and I'm just so glad to be able to tell you that it is for cases just like yours, where some stranger comes in and needs quiet and care for a little while. This room is yours for as long as the doctor says you should stay, without paying a single cent. It is just as free as the ward, freer, because in the ward I am told you pay if you can, but here you don't pay anyway. And the nurse goes along with it. Isn't that right, Miss Gowen?"

"It certainly is," said the nurse brightly, not knowing whether Greg was just cheerfully lying or had some foundation to go on, but she determined to play up to whatever he said. She liked Greg.

Margaret McLaren lay there looking from one to the other of them, and then suddenly her great eyes filled with tears.

"Oh," she said with a quiver of her lips, "I never heard of having rooms like this for nothing, but it's heavenly wonderful!" Her lips trembled. "I hope, someday there may be a way that I can do something for somebody like this. But now listen, please,—wonderful as all this is, and much as I would love to stay here and just rest—" the white lids quivered shut for just an instant over the big dark eyes, "I just can't! I've *got* to get back to work. There are reasons why—" she paused.

"You needn't try to explain," he said pityingly, "you have a right to keep your reasons to yourself,"—he felt a sudden pang of guilt that he had read that letter from the grandmother —"but listen to this. How about trusting your friends to look after a job? I really think I'm much more fit to do that than you are."

"You are kind," she said gently, "but—you aren't really even an acquaintance you know. I mean—of course you've been wonderfully friendly, but you are really a stranger. You don't know a thing about me."

"You'd be surprised," grinned Greg suddenly, "how much I know. One can't spend nearly twenty-four hours thinking about a person and trying to find her friends without turning up quite a good deal about her."

The girl's eyes flew open wide.

"You were trying to find my friends? But I haven't any friends about here."

"So I discovered," said Greg. "But you see I was thinking there might be a mother somewhere worrying and I thought I ought to do my best to find her."

The girl's face softened.

"No," she said with a hint of tears in her voice, "my mother and father died when I was a child. I have a grandfather and grandmother but they are away off in Vermont."

"Yes," said Greg. "I found that out too. I don't know as I should but I did. I was going to ask your pardon for that before we get through. But you see I kept thinking maybe you had somebody who would worry about you."

"Why how could you possibly find that out?" said the girl in wonder.

"Well," said Greg, giving her one of his pleasant boyish grins, "you see it was this way. After I got back to my hotel I walked over to that bench where you were sitting when you fell. You see I just got back to this town yesterday after ten years out west, and it happens that park used to be a meadow when I was here before, where I used to go with my mother sometimes to pick violets. So when I went back I sat down awhile and got to thinking about you, wondering who you were and if somebody was worrying about you, and then my foot touched something in the grass and I picked it up and it was a pocketbook. I wondered if it could be yours and I went over to a light and looked at it. There wasn't anything in it but a handkerchief and a letter."

The girl suddenly sat up in bed, a kind of fright in her eyes.

"Oh, you didn't telegraph to Grandmother, did you?"

"I couldn't," said Greg. "There wasn't any name signed but Grandmother, and there wasn't any address. Even the postmark was blurred so all I could get was Vermont."

"Oh! I'm so thankful!" said the girl dropping back on her pillows. "I wouldn't have Grandmother know for anything. She couldn't have come to me. She couldn't have done a thing! She is there all alone with Grandfather and he is sick! They haven't any money either. They lost everything they had in a bank failure this spring. And they would have been so frightened and so unhappy about me. I'm just glad you couldn't do anything about it."

Greg looked at the girl admiringly. There was a sparkle of

tears along her lashes. He thought how pretty she was now she was rested.

"So am I," grinned Greg, "if you feel that way about it."

The nurse came quietly and brought her a glass of orange juice.

"Am I staying too long?" asked Greg, springing to his feet and looking apprehensively at the nurse.

"No, you're being good for her," said the nurse. "It was just time she had this, that's all. She's going to be fine in a day or so now."

"But really," said the girl as she drained the glass and handed it back to the nurse, "I've just got to look up a job tonight and be ready to go to work Monday morning. I'm sorry to disappoint you two, you've been so good. But it's an absolute necessity."

"Yes?" said Greg, dropping back into his chair again. "I was coming to that job. Tell me about it. Did you really have something definite in mind or are you all up a tree yet?"

The color flamed into the girl's face.

"I had an advertisement that sounded hopeful," she said after an instant's hesitation, lifting truthful eyes to his face. "I wasn't sure about it of course. But I had no trouble in getting my first job last fall. But the head of the firm died and the business went into the hands of a receiver. Then this last job I had to leave. The man was—well,—just impossible! He was very offensive. I couldn't stand it. I had to leave without my pay which made things very hard. And—I wouldn't feel like going back for a reference."

"Of course not," said Greg firmly. "We'll manage without that I think. Now, suppose you tell me what kind of work you do."

"I'm a good stenographer," said the girl earnestly. "I can take dictation rapidly and accurately and I have a record speed on the typewriter. I understand filing, I can write a good hand, and I've done some bookkeeping. I'm willing to do almost anything."

"That ought to be a fairly comprehensive line I should say," said Greg gravely. "Now, Miss McLaren, suppose you just put this thing out of your mind and rest quietly here. I'll guarantee to get you a good job by Monday, or as soon after as the doctor thinks it's safe for you to go back to work, and in the meantime

27

this room and this nurse is yours free, and there's to be a bronze tablet to that effect put on the door early in the week."

"Oh, but I couldn't let you take any more trouble for me," protested the girl anxiously. "I really couldn't."

"Well, that's too bad!" said Greg smiling contagiously, "but I'm afraid you'll just have to this time. I really couldn't surrender my rights. I brought you here and I feel I have some little right to say what you'll do. I'm going to guarantee to put you in shape to work, and put you into a good paying job before I hand you over to yourself again. How's that? By the way, what salary do you usually get?"

"Oh, I'll take anything, *anything*, at first. I must, of course."

"No," said Greg, "you won't. You've got to have a good salary. You can't live on 'anything.' Would you mind telling me what you ought to get?"

The girl named a ridiculously small sum.

"That's what I got last, and of course Welfare and Insurance had to come out of that."

"That's outrageous!" said Greg drawing his brows together. "I had no idea anybody would have the face to pay such small wages."

"Jobs are very scarce," said the girl, looking deeply troubled. "I'm afraid you'll find out. All wages are very low indeed!"

"Well, the job that I'll get for you will have better wages than that!" said Greg with confidence. "Now, you go to sleep again and get really rested. I'll be seeing you again tomorrow if the nurse doesn't think I stayed too long today, and Monday I'll have some good news for you. Now don't you worry. I've killed a bear, and a rattlesnake and fought wild steers. There's just one more thing in that line I'd like to do and that is beat up that last fellow you worked for, and I will yet if he ever gets in my way. But meantime I'll land a job for you the first of next week. Now don't you fret another worry. Good night."

He took her slim little hand in his briefly, shyly, and then left, with a wave of the hand to the nurse, and a smile like sunshine.

The girl lay still looking after him, a wavering smile about her own lips, a questioning relief in her eyes.

"He—sounds very—sure!" she said doubtfully, and gave a tiny sigh. "It would be wonderful—if—he could."

"He will!" said the nurse breezily. "He's wonderful! He does

28

things. He's that way. They say he looked like a young giant when he brought you in, and he wouldn't let the attendants touch you. He just carried you himself in his arms in the elevator, and he wouldn't let them put you in the ward."

Margaret McLaren lay still for some minutes looking off into space, trying to picture herself being brought into a hospital room that way, her pale cheeks growing rosy, her eyes dreamy. Then she sighed again.

"I wonder if it's right to let him help me that way," she said in a troubled voice. "He's just a stranger and I never can repay him."

"I don't see that you've anything to do about it," said the nurse crisply. "He'd do it anyway whether you let him or not. Besides it will do him good to help somebody. It always does men good to help others. He'll probably get a kick out of hunting you a job, and for heaven's sake why should you quarrel with help when it comes your way? There's little enough of it going begging these days. And you never can tell about paying back—you might and then some!"

"But he's a stranger," urged the girl. "I don't know what my grandmother would think of my letting him help me this way."

"Well, we're all strangers more or less, no matter how well we know each other, and for heaven's sake, what's your grandmother got to do with it? She isn't here to be bothered, is she? And where would *you* have been if it hadn't been for this young man? Lying dead in the morgue as likely as not, and nobody knowing where to look for your relatives! By the way it's high time you let me have the address of that grandmother, if anything should happen to you. It isn't right for us not to know. Now, there's a pencil and paper. You write down the address, and then you turn over and go to sleep. You've a half hour before your tray comes up and you need every minute to rest in. If you're going to work next week you've got to conserve your energy. Now be a good girl and go right to sleep."

4

ON the way back to the hotel Greg passed a florist's shop and gave an order for roses to be sent to the hospital. He spent some time deciding between pink and yellow, and at last bought Ward rosebuds, dozens of them, with the deep apricot glow of sunset in their foldings and a rare wonderful fragrance. They would be sent up that night and be there to brighten Sunday morning when she awoke. He did not put his name with them. It was enough that she should just have them. He thought uneasily that perhaps she would not want roses from a stranger. She had tried distinctly to make him feel that he was a stranger. Well, if she objected he would just tell her that he liked to do it for his mother's sake, that his mother would have enjoyed sending them to her, if she were alive.

He thought a great deal about the girl that evening, remembered the sweep of her eyelashes, the proud little way she had of lifting her chin, the pleasant tones of her voice. It made a warm glow about his heart to have somebody to think about. After all these years of thinking in terms of cattle and soil it was nice to feel there was somebody in whom he might be interested, at least for a little while. Maybe if he found a job for her she would be willing to be friendly when she got to know him better. She seemed like the kind of a girl his mother would have liked.

Then he set himself to seriously consider how he would go about locating that job for her. It seemed as serious as the fortune he had promised himself that he would make when he went west. The fortune had come true; though not at all by his endeavors.

But the more that he considered the more he realized that it was not going to be an easy matter to locate a job for a strange girl in a strange city with nothing, absolutely nothing, to go on.

While he was waiting for his dinner order to arrive he took out his notebook and wrote down the names of people whom he remembered who used to be friends of his mother and who were in business. He thought of going to some of them, but he began to realize that it was going to be awkward, perhaps embarrassing both for him and the girl. How for instance was he to explain the girl, and why he was after a job for her? It was ten years since he had met any of these business men he was thinking of. They might not even recognize him. They had little to remember to particularly recommend him either. He had been just a willful, wild boy when he went away. They probably had all disapproved of him for not following their advice. No, it would be better to go to strangers for help.

He bought an evening paper and set himself to study the want advertisements, but was struck with the scarcity of them. Moreover the paper was full of talk of the unemployed. It appeared that employment was a problem, and that there was such a thing as a depression enveloping the land.

It hadn't reached to his wilderness home. It was *always* depression there. It was something he had expected and it didn't bother him. It was only astonishing that it had been lifted so suddenly and so fully in his case. Well, didn't that perhaps mean that there was an obligation upon him, now that he had money, to help others into something that would solve their problems? Instead of just taking his money as something that would make him independent for life, something that he was to absorb in his own selfish plans and pursuits, why oughtn't he to make that money work for others, in part at least? Perhaps that was why he had such an indifference toward trying to seek amusement for himself. Perhaps he was meant to enter into a scheme that would help others, and only through others could he really get the whole pleasure that his money was meant to give. Perhaps there was a business somewhere that he could buy, or set up, that would employ a lot of despairing ones. Almost every column of the paper had some story of a suicide, or death, or desperation of someone who was depressed because of business conditions. That was a terrible state of things. Why, there must be other people beside himself who had a little money. Why didn't they think out a way to make that money work for others as well as themselves? Not just give it away, for then soon it would be gone, but keep it going in a continual circuit to make profit both for its owner and for those who were employed through it? Well, there must be a way. He would have to think it out.

He wished he had a few good wise friends to talk this matter over with. He had come back into a world that seemed to be sick and sad and confused. He couldn't remember that things had been this way when he went away. But he had been only a kid and perhaps didn't understand. Still the papers spoke as if this was something comparatively new, this depression. Of course there had been more or less talk about it for the last year or two in the very few papers that had come his way but he had not taken in the real purport of it. Living off that way alone gave one a selfish point of view.

There was just one man, as he thought it over, who might have some sane solution of this problem. It was a man he had met on his journey eastward. He had known him only for a day, but his whole attitude of life had made a deep impression upon him. His name was Rhoderick Steele, and he had come to know him in a somewhat dramatic fashion.

It was the second evening of Greg's trip, and he was returning from the diner. As he reached his own section he saw coming toward him an elderly man whom he recognized as the inmate of the drawing room section whose door was just beyond his own seat. The man's face was ghastly, a blue look about his lips, and suddenly he put one hand to his heart as if he were in distress, reeled and fell headlong in the aisle.

Greg was on his knees beside him instantly, lifting him in his arms, fanning him with his newspaper.

The porter came rushing from the other end of the car, people rose from their seats and offered help. Someone brought ice water. A flask of brandy was produced. A doctor appeared from another car. The porter brought a pillow and slipped it under the sick man's head and Greg lowered him gently upon it.

Greg stood beside the man while the doctor worked over him watching the gray shadows gather over the haggard face, purple and gray under the eyes. He noticed the deathly pallor, the whiteness of the old lips. He knew this man was very near the end. He had the same look that old Luke had when he died. Strange, in spite of this man's distinguished garments he looked like old Luke. It came to Greg then that Death was no discriminator. He leveled all alike. This man was not immune because of his money and fine garments. The ashen look sat as desperately upon his well-groomed features as upon Luke's stubbly old face.

Then the sick man had opened his eyes, as a quiver of pain shot across his face, and his look went around the group, frightened eyes searching for something, for hope, for someone to help. He read his doom in the doctor's grave face. There was a convulsive twitch of his lips and his eyes started on their quest again, coming to rest on Greg's face.

"Get me a clergyman—! Quick!" implored the dying man.

Greg gave a swift glance around at the faces of the men in the car. None of them looked like clergymen.

"I will!" he said and started away.

"Preacher right back in the private cah, sah! Second cah back!" murmured the porter as he hurried past with the glass of water and spoon the doctor had demanded.

Greg followed the motion of the porter's head toward the end of the train, going with long strides. He burst into the luxurious quiet of the private car shocking its well trained attendants.

"Is there a preacher here? A dying man wants him quick!"

The attendants barred his way and eyed this strangely garbed young westerner coldly, but a young man rose from a chair by the window in the room just beyond and appeared at once.

"Coming!" he said instantly.

Greg gave him a quick appraising look and turned, satisfied. He wasn't much older than himself, and he did not wear clerical garb, but there was a light in his blue eyes and a purpose in his kind firm lips and chin that were entirely satisfactory. They did not stop for words.

The young minister knelt in the aisle with sympathetic eyes on the dying man.

"What can I do for you, Brother?" he asked, and the man turned his anguished eyes toward him.

"I'm dying—and I'm a Sinner!—A very—GREAT—SINNER—!" The last word came with another horrible grimace of pain.

"But you have a very great Saviour!" said the minister in a confident voice.

"But—He's not—*my Saviour!*" gasped the man.

"Oh, yes, He is, if you're willing to accept Him. He loved you enough to die for you."

"But—my SINS!" cried the man.

"He took your sins on Himself. He's paid the penalty for them. Do you believe, Brother? Will you accept the Lord Jesus Christ as your Saviour?"

"I do! I will," said the hoarse waning voice solemnly, his eyes fixed eagerly on the face of the young clergyman.

"Then He accepts you for His own. His Word says so: 'For God so loved the world, that He gave His only begotten Son, that *whosoever* believeth in Him should not perish, but have everlasting life.' Just rest down on that like a pillow, Brother, and you'll find it mighty sweet. Shall we pray?"

The sick man nodded and the younger man bent his head and prayed, bringing the dying soul close to the throne of God and committing him to the care of his Saviour. It was such a prayer as any soul might be glad to have uttered beside his dying bed. The other passengers in the car listened reverently, more than one wiping a furtive tear.

Gregory Sterling had stood at one side with his head bowed. He had taken in every word of the message and his heart was more stirred than it had ever been before. His mother had been a Christian, and had read him many Bible stories and taught him to pray, but since her death he had scarcely thought of God except bitterly, that He should have taken away his mother and home and left him to battle alone in the world. Now however God was suddenly put in a new light. It had never seemed before that God cared anything about human beings unless it might be to torment them. He studied the earnest face of the young preacher, watched the light of faith playing over his expressive features, took note of the strength in his face, the sweetness of expression that yet was not weakness, and drank in every word. At the prayer he bowed his own head and thought to himself wistfully, "I would like to know God as well as that. If God is a God like that He would be worth knowing and trusting."

When the prayer was finished the sick man drew a deep sigh and with a voice that was suddenly quite clear and strong so that all who were near him could hear even above the sound of the moving train:

"Thank you, sir! Now I can die trusting in your Saviour!"

"And yours," added the young minister.

A light broke over the dying face.

"And mine!"

Then the voice died down to a whisper.

"I'd like—to do something—for you—! But I guess—there —isn't time! I'll ask Him—" the voice flickered lower, "when I get—" the voice refused to finish and the man lifted a weak hand with an upward motion, "up—there!" The lips formed the words, and the dying eyes looked up. Then suddenly another attack came and in a breath the man was gone.

Kind hands carried the dead man into the little drawing room where but a short hour before he had sat in apparent health. They laid him on the bed which the porter had quickly prepared. The doctor had asked the patient his name and address while Greg was gone for the minister. Telegrams were sent to his relatives and the undertaker at the next station. Presently the car settled back into its normal life again, demanding berths to be made up, while some sought to change their reservations to another car, and the world whirled on without the pompous gentleman who had been one of their number a little while ago. Yet it could not be that they would ever forget that death scene and the words that had been spoken there. It somehow put a new dignity into life, a new hope into death.

But the minister had touched Greg on the shoulder.

"Friend," he said with a warm smile in his eyes, "suppose you and I sit in there with him till somebody comes to take charge. Wouldn't it be rather decent, don't you think? If he were our father we'd be pleased to have someone do that, wouldn't we?"

Greg assented and they went in and sat down on the long couch opposite the sheeted figure, but somehow Greg had a feeling that it was not Death but God who was presiding over that little room.

They talked together and Greg began to see that here was a rare man that had come to him. Whether he ever saw this man again after they reached their destination, or not he would always feel that here was someone to whose soul his soul was knit. When their vigil was ended a couple of hours later at a stop along the way, and an undertaker took charge for the family of the dead man, the handclasp of both promised a real friendship between the two.

"Come back to my car in the morning and have breakfast with me," smiled the minister.

Greg had looked down at himself, and then at his new friend and became suddenly conscious of his attire.

"I'm not fit to go in a private car," he said decidedly. "I've been in the wilderness for ten years and I'm out of date."

"What difference does that make, Friend? I'm the only

passenger aboard that car and it isn't my car either. It's just loaned to me. An old classmate of mine in college owns it. He's out in California, about to sail for the Orient, and his car was being sent home. When he found I was coming this way he offered it to me. That's the story. Come and share my temporary luxury. He said I might bring as many of my friends as I chose."

So Greg promised to come, and went back to his section to bed. But tired as he was he had to lie awake and think over the happenings of the evening, living over the deathbed scene, seeing again the flash of assurance in the eyes of his new friend as he pointed out those clear directions for salvation.

In the morning Greg discovered a barber on the train and came forth from his hands much improved. He was beginning to get wise to the ways of the civilized world once more and very self-conscious about his own discrepancies.

However, he wore his faded khaki with an ease acquired from long habit of not having to think about public opinion, and when he came forth from the hands of the high class tonsorial artist more than one passenger looked after him with an approving eye. He certainly was, a good-looking young giant, and he did not seem to be in the least aware of it, which made him all the more attractive.

He spent the most of the next two days in the private car or sitting on its observation platform in pleasant converse with his new friend. They talked of many things. Of the west and the south and the east. Of world affairs in Europe and over here, of the significance of situations political, commercial and spiritual, and through it all a book figured impressively. Not the tiny testament that Rhoderick Steele had used when he pointed the dying man to Jesus Christ, but one slightly larger, worn and limp and full of finely written notes on the margins. The Bible! Gregory Sterling was amazed to find how interesting the Bible became under the magic reading of this new-found friend.

Greg had not been without literature in his exile. His school days and his early home life had filled him with a love of reading. Little by little he had acquired a small library. A volume or two that he loved when he was a child, "Robinson Crusoe," "Lorna Doone," and "John Halifax, Gentleman." He had bought them through a mail-order catalogue. Then he had added a little history and biography, some essays and poetry.

Longfellow and Tennyson and a volume of Browning because the advertisement had quoted two lines of a poem he liked about a star, one of his own stars. A few scattering volumes of Scott and Dickens, Macaulay's "Essays," Oliver Wendell Holmes' "Autocrat of the Breakfast Table." It wasn't a bad collection, but of course not up to date. Modern literature had not yet arrived when Greg, fresh from high school, had taken his far journey. So he had gathered what attracted him from advertisements and from his memory of familiar titles. Not much, but they gave him a background and a bond of intellectual sympathy with Rhoderick Steele who had read every one of his books and loved them. They made him feel at home at once.

For Greg had read his small collection over and over many times in his long lonely life, rainy days and winter evenings, and knew his books almost by heart. He had left them in the cabin on their rough board shelf. "For some poor devil who doesn't know what to do with himself sometimes!" he had told himself, reflecting that he was now able to replace them all and add new treasures to his store.

But now as they grew more intimate, Rhoderick Steele began to open up the treasures of the Bible to him and he listened with amazement as prophecy was brought forth and its fulfillment pointed out both in the past, and in present day happenings.

Greg wasn't up on current events. He took a newspaper once a week, but the news was stale when it reached him, and seemed unreal to him out there on the hillside. But now he began to hear what was happening out in the world to which he was speeding and he felt like a child listening to a fairy tale.

Once when they sat on the observation platform together speeding away from a gorgeous sunset with deepening shadows on either side of the way, and majestic scenery melting into the obscurity of twilight, Rhoderick Steele began to talk of his childhood home in an old Virginia farmhouse amid cotton plantations, and lovely hazy blue mountains. He told of his father, a man of God, and the firm foundation of the Gospel that had been laid in his young life; of the family worship where he and his brothers and sisters knelt and heard themselves prayed for daily. He spoke of his own early turning to God, of his struggle to earn enough for the education he

37

must have if he went into the ministry, and of the wonderful way he had been led through his youthful years.

Then shyly, hesitatingly, Greg was led to tell of himself. Of his own lonely thoughts and feelings. Of the fierce fight to get a foothold, and how he had just sold his holdings for a price far beyond his wildest dreams.

They held sweet counsel that last evening of their journey together, and lingered talking far into the night. The private car was to be switched to a southern train in the morning, and they were loth to part.

When at last they said good night, Steele gave him a Bible like his own.

"When I bought it I thought I might find someone who would enjoy it. Now I'm so glad to have something I love to give you. I've written a bit of a note on the fly leaf. Read it when we're gone on our way. And don't forget you're to let me know when you get located. I want to keep in touch with you, and when I get a home of my own as I'm hoping to soon I want you to come and visit me. It won't be grand like this car,"—he looked around on his borrowed splendor with his pleasant smile,—"but it'll be home, and you'll be greatly welcome."

Greg left him finally, his heart warmed and comforted. Here was one who would be a friend always. It was great to know there was such a man in the world. He went to sleep planning that when he got a place of his own he would have this man often to see him. Maybe he could give some money to help along whatever he was interested in. He remembered the light in his eyes. He laid his hand on the soft yielding roughness of the beautiful little Bible that lay by his side. He resolved to look into it, to study it, and if possible to find the mysterious secret it seemed to have imparted to this prince of a man who was his friend.

That had been only a few short days ago that he had parted from this man whom he had come so to admire and love, yet he seemed almost like a dream now. He had kept his word and sent him his address that first night he had located at Whittall House after he came back from the hospital, but of course had heard nothing from him as yet.

Greg got up and paced back and forth through his hotel room and began to go over the whole experience in his mind again. How he wished that Rhoderick Steele would drop in for a few minutes this very evening. He would like to put his problems before him. A man like that would have insight and could help.

He thought of the Bible. He hadn't read in it much yet. Perhaps it too would help to solve problems, only he felt so very inexperienced and helpless when he read, even with the help of the enlightening footnotes in the margin to which his new friend had introduced him. When things settled down he must study that Bible and get to know it better. His friend had told him it would be a lamp unto his feet and a light unto his path.

By and by when he got this little girl started in some position where she was safe perhaps he would run down to Virginia and see his friend, or get him up here for a few days. He would talk over what a man should do in these days to help get the world straightened out again. This man would know, he was sure he would know.

He went to bed eventually but he did not sleep much. He was trying to see just how he was going to keep his promise to Margaret McLaren. Some kind of a position must be forthcoming by Monday morning and he had to thrash it out before he went to see her on the morrow.

5

MEANWHILE in an altogether up-to-date apartment not many blocks away from the Whittall House where Greg tossed the night through and worked out his problems, a girl whose name had once been Alice Blair wakened late that Sunday morning, and lay luxuriously reading the society column in the morning paper while she toyed with grapefruit, and ate delicate bits of Melba toast, and drank strong coffee.

Idly she ran her eye down the columns, the débutantes of the coming season, the luncheons and teas, the theatre dinners, the dances of the younger set, eagerly lapping up all the news of the cream of that ultra higher social set to which she had never as yet obtained an entrance.

There was news of the great hospital drive to which the smart set of the city was lending its gilded influence. Alice cared nothing for that except that there were occasional openings in such activities where an outsider might slip in and render a service that would be recognized and give *entree* later to more sacred circles. Then suddenly as her practised eye ran down the column a name stood out that made her catch her breath and read more carefully.

It was just the last paragraph of the column about the drive and the opening luncheon at which all the great were to appear. It said:

> "The committee is announcing a gift just received, the endowment of a perpetual free room for strangers who need special quiet and rest and should not be placed in the ward. The endowment is in memory of Mrs. Mary Montgomery Sterling and given by her son, Mr. Gregory Sterling who has recently returned to his native city and expects to make his home in this vicinity."

Alice Blair read the paragraph over several times with narrowing vision, considering just what this might mean. If Greg had returned and was doing things in this high-handed way in memory of his mother he must have prospered. He must have made some money!

Alice half closed her eyes and looked off into space through their yellow fringes, at least as much space as there was between her rose taffeta shrouded couch with its billows of pillows, mounted on its silver dais, and the queer construction she called a dressing table flanked by great pointed slabs of mirrors set in the wall.

Alice considered her former friend. He had been big and fairly nice looking, only far too much devoted to his prudish mother. But that mother was gone now. She wouldn't be a drawback any longer.

So Greg had returned!

But he hadn't come to hunt her up, though almost any of his old friends could have given him her history. Alice smiled shrewdly. Well, he might be worth looking up. She had no doubt but she could call him to her side again if she found it worth while. And one couldn't have too many admirers.

So Alice arose, put on her warpaint, got out her feathers, and took to the warpath.

She drove a high-powered cream colored roadster and wore

40

a stunning crimson dress. She drove about the city in various haunts new and old, she made descent upon various hotels and inquired sweetly if there was a Mrs. Hemingway-Smith staying there. Not that she knew a Mrs. Hemingway-Smith but that made no difference to Alice. She had made up the name on her way in.

The clerk of course would shake his head and hand over the registry book saying, "Those are our arrivals today." And Alice would run through the list for several days back and finding no name that interested her she would sigh and say that she must have been mistaken about the date, and hurry out to her cream colored car, and pass on to another. At the next hotel she would have a different friend to inquire for, and always manage to run through several days' records in the registry.

Alice was not easily balked. She had a gift of continuance. But it was not until mid-afternoon of Monday that she found the name Gregory Sterling in the same old familiar scrawl she knew so well, registered at the Whittall House. She had a bunch of letters tied with blue ribbon in her desk, done in that same scrawl, a little more unformed perhaps, but still the same characteristic turn to the letters.

It gave her quite a thrill to see his name once more.

A whimsical smile played around her thin red lips. He might be very well worth looking up. She had been told that he had taken it hard when she ran away to marry Murky Powers.

Well, she would go cautiously. She didn't want to get entangled with him again if he was an undesirable, but—well, there would be ways of finding out.

Greg slept late on Sunday morning, and then, without waiting for breakfast, because it was almost eleven o'clock, he went down the broad avenue, and presently found the street where was located the old brick church that his mother used to attend. It somehow seemed to him that the old church, and the old back pew under the balcony, where they used to sit so long ago, was the fitting place to come that first Sunday morning in his home town. He wanted to do the thing that would have pleased his mother, and this he knew was what she would have wanted.

But he scarcely saw a familiar face as he sat there under his balcony and cast a keen glance about. He found himself looking among the boys and girls for his friends, and then remembered that ten years had passed since he was a boy.

41

They would be older. But he could not identify any of his former companions.

There were one or two elders, grown more feeble. There up near the front was the old grouch who wouldn't lend him the twenty dollars to start his newsstand. There he was with the same old projecting under jaw, the same old beetling brows grown a trifle whiter perhaps, the same old look as if he never smiled. A rich old miser in a seedy coat. Greg wondered what he would say if he could know what his present bank account amounted to.

There was a little woman who always used to smile and speak to his mother after church. She was wearing spectacles now and looked frail and thin. The church somehow made him sad, but he sat there dutifully for his mother's sake and bowed his head when they prayed.

The minister did not have a message like the man he had met on the train, but he did say that God was Love, and that He wanted us to do good to one another, and that seemed somehow along the line of Greg's thoughts. He put a five dollar bill in the collection plate, and noticed that the plate held mostly nickels, and very few bills. Then he wondered if his five dollars would do any real practical good to anybody there. Somehow the church seemed so musty and dead, and the message so sleepy. The music wasn't very inspiring either, but he sat there with his eyes closed and remembered how he used to slip his hand inside his mother's hand during prayer, oh, so very many years ago when he was just a little kid first beginning to go to church, and the tears came into his eyes.

Then his thoughts wandered off into what he might do to help Margaret McLaren and he failed to find out whether the message came alive or not, for here in the house of God his plans seemed to mature and ripen, and he suddenly knew what he was going to do. Not fully, just a hazy sketch, but enough to make his problem of the next day clear, a step at a time.

And that afternoon he went to the hospital to see her.

The nurse had fixed her up in a sweet little blue bedjacket of her own, trimmed with scallops and lace on the edge. The sleeves were wide and fell away from the soft line of the slim young arm, and the neck line was fluffy with frills of lace. Her hair was all soft and curly about her face, in brown waves and little rings over her forehead, and Greg stood a moment admiring her, his eyes lighting with pleasure. She was just as pretty as he had thought she was in his dreams all night, and he was strangely happy to see her. The coolness of her slim hand in his was something precious, a privilege that made him shy. And she smiled at him like an old friend.

She wasn't angry about the roses then.

The roses were there on the little bedside stand beside her and one was tucked in the throat of the little jacket just where she could smell it.

"Of course you sent the roses," she challenged him, "and you know you shouldn't have done it, but I couldn't help being glad, you know, that they were here. I couldn't help enjoying them. And I thank you very, very much for being so kind to me."

He smiled down upon her with a glad light in his eyes.

"I thought my mother would like you to have them if she were here," he said with a quaint formality, though she saw his eyes were pleased that she liked them. "The flowers just go with the room you know. You don't need to feel uncomfortable about them. But I'm glad you enjoy them. And now, how are you?"

"I'm fine!" she said, her eyes shining. "I'm all eager to get up and go to work. And unless you have already found something for me you'd better let me release you from your promise. For I know it's not going to be an easy thing to find a job for another person, especially a stranger."

"I protest," he said with a grin. "You're not a stranger. You may have been once, but we're really acquainted now, aren't we?"

"Well, you've been very kind," she said, "but I'm afraid any man who hired me to work for him wouldn't exactly think you knew me well enough to recommend me."

"Well," he said gravely, "joking aside. I promised you a job tomorrow sometime, and I mean to keep my promise. All I ask of you is to lie still till the doctor comes on his rounds,—when is that, Nurse, about eleven o'clock?—Well, I'll be in about twelve, and if the doctor says you are able we'll go into the matter and get it all fixed up. Now, shall we just let it go at that, and will you be good and not think about it till tomorrow? You know yesterday it was too late to do anything about it, and I naturally couldn't see anybody on Sunday."

"I know," she said looking troubled, "and that is why it

43

seems as if I'd better go out too, because you know I just might happen to land something and go right to work. And you can't of course be sure that you'll find anything."

"I beg your pardon," said Greg gravely, "I have a job for you now. You could go to work tomorrow morning only that there are a few little details I'd like to settle first. But if you must get active tomorrow I'll promise you it can be done."

She gave him a keen glance.

"Really?"

"Yes, really. I'm going to give you a job myself. You see I've only been in this town a few days and I haven't got everything doped out the way I want it yet. That's one reason why I didn't want you to be in such a hurry. But if you must go to work at once, all right, we'll get right on the job and get you an office."

Distress came into the girl's eyes.

"Oh, please, I couldn't think of letting you do that. You're just getting up a job for me to be kind to me."

"No, I'm not," said Greg earnestly, "but if I had been would that be a crime? However, you can put your mind at rest about that. I've fully decided to go into business, and I hope it's going to be something that will be a real help in the world today. I feel that it's just a godsend that you happened in my path. If you hadn't I should have had to go out and hunt somebody very soon, and try out this one and that, and I might have got the wrong one."

"But you don't know but I'm the wrong one," laughed Margaret suddenly. "Perhaps I'll be an awful failure."

"No," said Greg quickly, "I'm sure you won't. I feel you'll understand and be a great help."

"Well, thank you," said Margaret thoughtfully, "but suppose we fix it this way. Suppose I go out and get me a temporary job. There are usually chances to get a job for a few days at something special, like waiting on the table in a restaurant. And then when you are ready to go to work you can send for me."

"No," said Greg decidedly, "I'd rather you would begin now. I can be ready by tomorrow afternoon with my plans. That is if you are willing to do what you said, anything that is needed. You can help me a lot in choosing a place, and then, well, there'll be some selecting and purchasing and there'll be a few letters to write almost immediately. It will certainly be a help to have you start right off. You may not be kept very busy

44

every day, not just at first, but it will be worth a great deal to me just to have you there to advise with me about the purchases I'm making. Right at the start that'll be a good deal of your work, to select things, furnishings for the office, and help me get started."

She gave him a puzzled look.

"But what's your business?"

He looked at her sheepishly and grinned, a nice frank grin.

"You'll laugh at me," he said, "but right now I don't honestly know which of several things I'm thinking about I'll really do. And I guess I'll need your help about that too perhaps. But if you really think you're ready to go to work tomorrow, and you don't mind being a sort of a jack-of-all-trades for a few weeks till I get going, why I'll come for you tomorrow about eleven o'clock and we'll go and try to find a location. This town has changed a lot since I went away ten years ago, and I don't know whether my ideas about location will be out of date or not, but it doesn't really matter at present. All I want is a quiet street where I can get a fairly comfortable office. It doesn't have to be especially fashionable, just respectable."

The nurse looked up with interest while he talked, and he could see that the girl was studying him.

"How about you?" he asked. "Are you anxious to go back to that human dreadnaught on Rodman Street? You know I had an interesting interview with her, and I don't especially care for her type." He grinned.

"You went to Rodman Street?" said the girl with wide eyes of astonishment.

"Sure! I covered every clue I could find. I thought the old bird might be grieving her life out on your account, but I found her only interested in your financial standing."

"Oh!" said Margaret, crimson to the roots of her hair. "She was awful! You see I had been expecting to pay her the day I had to leave my job without my wages, and she flew into a rage when she found I had left and couldn't pay her."

"I know," said Greg dryly, "she gave me all her views on that subject. When she got through I had a very high opinion of you indeed."

"She wouldn't allow me to touch any of my things," said the girl. "I shan't be able to get my suitcase until I've paid her."

"Yes, you can get it any time now," said Greg amusedly. "I fairly took her off her pins paying your account. I let on I was a

45

friend and had come to pay it for you. I told her you had had an accident and were in the hospital. I thought maybe she would calm down then and show a little sympathy, but her only concern seemed to be lest you would expect to come back to her to be nursed, so I thought best to give her the money and stop her rank old mouth. I hope I didn't let her put anything over on me. Was it fifteen dollars?"

"Yes," said Margaret, shamedly, "but to think you had to do all that for me! I never saw anyone so kind."

"Oh, that was just human. That wasn't kind. I couldn't let the old bird get away with that line. And I made her give me a receipt too. It's in your purse. But you won't have any trouble getting your things now. I meant to tell you that yesterday but forgot it."

"Well, I don't know how to thank you enough."

"Don't try," said Greg. "This is purely a business proposition. I'm working this out entirely for my own interests. You see, I thought if we could rent an office, maybe in some nice old lady's house, get her downstairs parlor you know, and then perhaps you could get an upstairs room and board right there, then rainy days you wouldn't have to go out at all unless you wanted to. I thought if we looked around we could find some place like that where it would be pleasant for you to live, and I wouldn't be around in the way at all when I came to the office. There ought to be such places with a door into the front hall, so the rest of the house would be sort of separate and the business wouldn't interfere with the house much."

"I know the very place," said the nurse eagerly. "There's a dear old lady on Twenty-third Street. She owns her house. She's lived there ever since she was married. It's not far from the business section, not a fashionable residential section any more, and she can't seem to rent her rooms. But it's a real nice old brownstone front house with big pleasant rooms. She's in great distress about it, afraid she may have to let her house go, and she loves it because of old associations. She'd love to have a boarder. She cooks the daintiest little meals sometimes and invites me over when I'm off duty. She'd mother you, Miss McLaren, and you wouldn't need to feel so alone. She's quiet and respectable, and not the sort to be obtrusive. I'm sure you'd like her. And I know she has a great big front room, in fact there are double parlors that would make a nice office or double office."

46

"That sounds all right!" said Greg eagerly. "Does it to you, Miss McLaren? How about you, Miss Gowen? Could you get off duty tomorrow morning and go with us? I think it would be a good thing for Miss McLaren to be introduced. I'll bring a taxi and come for you at eleven-thirty, then. There'll be a few things I'll have to attend to before that."

They talked a little longer about plans, the nurse telling more of the old lady who had the rooms, and the girl listening in relief and wonder to the way life was being worked out for her. Then Greg took his leave, a quiet gravity upon him as he said good night.

"It seems wonderful!" said the girl again after he was gone. "Do you really think it is all right? It seems too perfect to be true."

"Of course," said the nurse. "He's all right. He's a real man, you can see that. And anyway, how many rotten employers have you seen since you landed in this city? You had to take your job where you found it, didn't you? Well, you've run away from one. You can always leave again if things are not satisfactory you know. But I just know they are going to be all right!"

So Margaret ate everything on her supper tray happily, and went to sleep with a smile on her lips.

Late that night the head nurse got back from her week-end vacation, which hadn't on the whole been particularly satisfying, and went on duty early the next morning with a sour look upon her face.

And the very first thing she did was to walk down the hall to the room where Margaret McLaren was eating her nice breakfast and fling the door wide open.

"What's all this?" she cried in a tone of authority. "I thought I gave orders that this room should be thoroughly cleaned ready for a patient at eight-thirty this morning. Miss Martin, are you on duty here this morning? What does this mean? This room was to have had a thorough cleaning."

"It was cleaned, Miss Grandon."

"And you put another patient in here? Who is she? What right has she here? Who gave the order? Is she paying the full price? How long has she been here? This room was reserved for Mr. Mountcalm. Nobody had a *right* to put anyone in here."

"Why, I think it was an emergency case," explained a

47

passing nurse who was an undergraduate and very much afraid of her superior. "I don't know who gave the order, but the doctor said it was all right."

Miss Grandon marched into the room and confronted Margaret who was listening to the altercation wide-eyed.

"How much are you paying in this room?" she demanded severely. "This is one of our most expensive rooms for private patients. Were you told of that? Are you paying full price?"

"Oh, no," explained Margaret sweetly, "I'm not paying anything. I told them I ought to be put in the ward, but they explained to me that this was a memorial room for strangers, and then I felt better about it. It was wonderful to have had such care—!"

"Memorial room for strangers?" snorted Miss Grandon. "Nothing of the sort! We haven't a room in the institution like that! Who told you that extraordinary story?"

"Why, the gentleman who brought me here, and the nurse. My nurse is Miss Gowen. She is down at her breakfast now but she will be back any minute and explain it to you."

"Gentleman!" sniffed Miss Grandon. "So there's a man in it, is there? I might have known it! Well, young lady, your young man has been putting a fine story over on you. This room is one of our most expensive private rooms and never has been nor never will be a memorial to anybody. For *strangers!* The very idea! Well, I suppose one can know what kind of a girl *you* are then, letting a *man* bring you to the hospital. Wasn't he any relation to you?"

"Oh, no," said Margaret, her eyes flashing now, and her cheeks suddenly glowing, "he was just a stranger who picked me up—"

"Oh, he picked you up on the street! Yes, I know that kind of man. And you *let* him, of course! You didn't object to a stranger bringing you here to the hospital."

Margaret's face had grown very white now and she answered quietly:

"I was unconscious. I had fallen. I didn't know what was going on!"

"Oh, well that's a nice excuse and it may be true and it may not. However, you're not unconscious now, are you? You're able to get up, aren't you? If you aren't I'll have you moved over to the ward. But if you're able to walk you better get your clothes on and get out of this building before the people down

48

in the office find out what is going on. As for your nurse I suppose she was bribed. You can't trust one of them. Has that man been here to see you?"

"Yes," said Margaret looking her steadily in the eye, "twice, and he's not at all the kind of man you think he is."

"Yes, I suppose you would say that. But you're probably not so innocent as you try to appear. Just let me tell you, young lady, decent men don't bring strange girls to the hospital and then come trailing after them and telling them lies. That man has some ulterior motive of course, and if you really haven't suspected it and aren't as bad as he is, just let me warn you now that you had better get out and away from here where he can't ever find you again if you want to save your reputation! I should think you could see that for yourself, a man that would tell you lies like that about an expensive hospital room! If he dares to come back here again I'll see that he's arrested. Now, get out as quick as you can! I'll give you five minutes to dress. Miss Brady, send for the scrub woman at once, and tell Anna to have the linen all changed and take down the window draperies. There will have to be fresh draperies. Mr. Mountcalm is very particular, and he always pays extra."

Trembling so that she could scarcely stand, Margaret crept from her bed and found her clothes where the nurse had so carefully put them. Her knees were all but collapsing under her, and her fingers were shaking so that she could scarcely fasten her garments, but she got herself dressed in an incredibly short space of time, put on her little hat with the brave feather, took up her flat pocketbook and got herself down the great marble hall, which she was thankful to find for the moment deserted. Got herself slowly, step by step down the interminable flights of marble stairs and walked out of the door and down the street.

She had hoped that her dear nurse would come before she left, but for some incredible reason she did not appear, and after a little Margaret began to reflect that it was just as well. Likely she was in the game. Perhaps she had been bribed as that awful head nurse had suggested. It didn't seem possible, but probably it was true. Oh, this world was a mess! And she was going from bad to worse. To think of her being in such a position! To have been talked to in that awful way! When she had thought that everything was so wonderful and heavenly!

How she wanted to sink down on the wide marble steps and sob out her heart and then die. Just *die!*

But instead she must get out and away quickly before that young man returned. She never wanted to see him again. To think that he could have told such awful lies! And what for? She shuddered! What awful purpose had he been going to bring about this morning? And the nurse was in that too. She had been going along! She must get away quickly where they never could find her again!

Fear, wild panic, lent strength to her feet, her frightened feet, and she was able to get around the corner and into another street, and another, until breathless she arrived in a part of the city she did not know. She saw a railroad station, went in, sat down in an obscure corner of the ladies' waiting room, and tried to think what she should do next.

6

It was beginning to grow dark in the old farmhouse and Grandmother folded up her knitting and sat back in her patchwork-cushioned rocking chair.

Grandfather got himself with difficult ease into a standing posture and looked anxiously toward his sweet old wife.

"I think I'm feeling better, Mother, I think I'll go out and try a hand at milking tonight. Old Sukey has been bawling for fifteen minutes and it's getting pretty late. It'll be dark in a few minutes now."

"Oh, Father, don't! Please! You know Sam said he'd be sure to be here, even if he was late. It's terribly raw tonight, and you'll just get all that pain back in your leg again."

"No, Mother, I won't. I think it will do me good!" declared Father. "Besides I'm not going outdoors. I'll just go through the woodshed into the barn and open the door for Sukey from the inside. Now, Mother, you mustn't interfere. I've been docile as long as I thought it was necessary. But now I really feel I must get back to work again. It doesn't do to baby one's self too much. I'm not an invalid yet you know."

"No, but you're trying hard to be. I wish you would wait. Perhaps Sam is coming up the hill now."

Mother got up and trotted anxiously to the window.

"Father, it's snowing! It really is!" she said in alarm.

"Well, that's all the more reason Sukey should get in out of it, and the snow isn't going to reach me inside the barn. For pity's sake, be reasonable, Rebecca!"

Father went to the closet and took down his old coat and cap from the peg. He wound a woolen scarf twice about his neck with elaborate care to show Mother how well protected he was.

"Put your galoshes on, Father! Yes, you know the ground is damp and it will strike in all the more because you've been sitting by the fire all these days and are tender. You don't want that pain back in your leg you know, after all the liniment I've rubbed into it."

"All right, I'll put them on," consented the old man, "but I'm not going out on the ground."

"The barn floor is like ice, John, you know it is."

"All right, Mother. I've got them on. Better get that hot mash ready for the hens and I can feed them after I bring the milk in. You're not fit to go out yourself tonight, Mother. I heard you sneezing in the bedroom just now. I'm afraid this business of having a fire only in the kitchen isn't going to be very economical after all."

"Now, Father, you hush. I was just sneezing because I spilled some pepper when I was redding up the cupboard shelf. Hurry up and get done, if you will go out, for it's getting dark and growing colder every minute. I'm glad we've got plenty of wood in the woodshed. And look around for Emily. She ought to be coming in pretty soon. She's probably out in the barn hunting mice. She didn't have a very big dinner today, no meat in the house."

Grandmother hurried around and set the table for two, trying to make it look cheery when Grandfather came in. She put the kettle on, cut two slices of bread for toast, and got out the teapot. On second thought she got out two eggs from the bowl in the pantry. Father needed to be nourished. He was sort of run down. She cut two pieces of gingerbread and fixed two china dishes of applesauce. Then she went and stood at the window looking down the hill toward the road to watch for Sam Fletcher. How late he was! Perhaps the mail was late and he had waited for it. Oh, she hoped he had! There ought to be a letter tonight. It was almost a week since Margaret had written. She was always so faithful. Could the child be sick?

Emily was meowing at the door now. She was licking her lips as if she had had a feast of some kind. She came in as soon as the door was open and went over and sat down near the stove, licking her white mitts carefully, scrupulously. There was no light in the room except what came through the front grate of the old cook stove, and the dusk was coming down fast now, but the brightness from the stove made a rosy spot on Emily's white vest, and the white star in her forehead. Emily had been out foraging, browsing around the barn for the last two hours. She had found her prey and was well filled. Presently she curled down with her two clean paws tucked neatly under her chin and began to purr contentedly, turning an occasional furtive eye toward her uneasy mistress at the window.

There was no sign of Sam Fletcher yet so the old lady turned away and got out the pan for the mash, pouring hot water on the bran and mixing it with bits of food she had saved up and a few grains of corn for a relish. Then she put an old woolen shawl over her head, crossed it on her breast, tied it behind at her waist, and went out through the back kitchen to the woodshed, and so to the door of the chicken house, taking the warm mash with her.

She passed the stall where the old horse used to be hitched, with her eyes down. The old horse had been sold two months ago, but the old lady still felt a pang when she passed his stall. It had hurt to sell Old Gray! And the cow would likely have to go next! Father couldn't keep on milking all winter and Sam Fletcher might not be able to come up every night when winter set in. But how they were going to get along without the milk was a puzzle. Of course there was canned milk, but they had never had to use it. Well, they would have to get used to it.

She sighed deeply as she opened the rickety little gate that separated the hen's end of the barn from the rest. It was hard to see things going slowly down hill, little by little, and Father's strength failing. Father who had always been such a tower of strength, such a rock of defence.

The hens clucked around her feet as she came within their separating palings and held out her pan, dropping little portions at their feet. The greedy red rooster came sputtering to get more than his share, and there was a great flutter of feathers and clucking and contending. She put the pan down at last and let them peck it clean. They played a little tune with their hard bills against the metal pan, a pleasant little domestic sound that almost seemed like old times when the yard was full of fowls and there was plenty of corn with which to feed them.

The old lady closed the gate carefully behind her and went over to where the cow stood in a stall of her own. The old man was almost done milking and she stood beside him till he finished and rose with his brimming pail.

"You're tired, Father. Let me carry it in!"

"No, I'm not tired. You run on in. You'll get more cold. That thin shawl! It's nothing to carry in a little milk. Run quick. I'll feed Sukey now and then we'll have supper."

The old lady hurried in and lit the lamp. It was quite dark in the house now save for the glow from the kitchen stove. Emily was rumbling away contentedly, sound asleep by the hearth.

The old lady made the tea, put the bread on a long fork holding it to the blaze of the front grate. She put the eggs into the boiling water. It was a nice supper, but why didn't Sam Fletcher come and bring a letter from Margaret?

The old man washed his hands, put away his galoshes, coat and cap, and washed his hands carefully by the kitchen sink. The old lady slipped to the window again and cast a glance down the hill.

"Now don't you worry about Sam Fletcher, Mother. Like as not he stayed in town to see his cousin awhile. And anyhow it isn't likely there was a letter so soon again."

"Now, Father, you know we should have had one last night," chided Mother coming back to the stove and bringing the brown earthenware teapot to the table. The toast sent forth a cheerful fragrance and Emily stirred in her sleep and untucked her white feet, crossing them over in the opposite way, dreaming doubtless of her pleasant mice, and others she would catch tomorrow.

They sat down to the table and bowed their heads.

"Our Father, we thank Thee that thou hast given us abundance for our needs, and we thank Thee for the things Thou didst not send, because we know there must have been some good reason for withholding. Make us truly thankful for all that we have, and bless and keep our dear child Margaret."

The Amen was scarcely spoken before there came a knock at the door, and a sound of feet being wiped on the old piece of burlap on the doorstep.

Sam Fletcher's face was round and rosy and he let in a cold draft of air as he responded to the bid to come in. Emily twitched her ears unpleasantly one at a time as the air blew upon her, and opened one eye uneasily.

"Brought you the evening paper. Sorry I didn't find any letters. I reckon there'll be one tamorra," he said in his loud cheerful voice. "Gonta be a storm tonight I guess. See ya milked the cow. Now, that's too bad. You shouldn't ha done it —" Sam's eye was on the pail of milk that stood on a table by the sink. "I tried ta get here sooner, but I hadta wait ta get my harness mended. I had a bad break. I reckoned Sukey'd wait all right!"

The old man smiled with a twinkle in his eye.

"Well, you see, Sam, I stole a march on you. I've just been waiting my chance to get back on the job again, and this was a good excuse. I thought you wouldn't mind for once, and I really think it did me good."

"Yep!" said Sam looking at him with admiring eyes, "I'll bet it did. You certainly are a game one, sick as you've been, milkin' a cow at your age! Well, got plenty of wood? It's gonta be a cold night. The wind's turned."

"Yes, plenty of wood, thanks to your kindness," said the old man with a courtly bow of his white head and a kindly smile. "Won't you sit down and enjoy our frugal meal with us?"

"No, I guess I better be gettin' on. Hetty'll be watchin' for me, an' she'll be keepin' supper hot. Well, if there's nothing else I can do for ya I'll beat it. But don'tcha ferget, ef ya want anything in the night just ya ring the big old dinner bell. I'll hear it. I'm a light sleeper. Well, s'long. I'll be goin'." And Sam Fletcher slammed the door shut behind him with another gust of wind that stirred Emily's whiskers and caused her to twitch her ears again.

Mother poured out the tea into two cups and made a little stir putting more toast before the coals with her back turned toward the table. Once she sniffed, just a tiny sniff, and the old man looked up suspiciously.

"Now, Mother, you have been catching more cold!" he charged.

The old lady turned quickly brushing a tear away from her eye.

"No!" she said sharply, "it was just the draught from the door made me feel like sneezing!"

Her husband eyed her keenly.

"Now, Mother, you're not crying! You're not feeling bad about Margaret not writing again, so soon after sending us that long letter?"

"No," said the old lady quickly, turning her face away to watch the toast and blinking back the tears. "No, of course I'm not crying. But it does seem strange we didn't get a letter. It's almost a week, Father!"

"Well, that's nothing, Rebecca. She's probably got some extra work the way she did the last time she didn't write for three days. Don't you remember? She'll write in a few days and tell us all about it."

"A *few days!*" said the old lady's dismayed voice. "Now, Father, you don't think we won't get any letter *tomorrow!*"

"Well, it might be possible you know. We mustn't despair when things happen like that. Our Father is watching over her down there in the city just as much as over us here."

There was a silence while the two took small bites of toast, put salt on the soft boiled eggs, and dipped the tips of the two thin old silver spoons in the tea. Then the old lady spoke again.

"Sometimes, Father, I think we shouldn't have mortgaged the farm to send her to college!"

"Why, I don't see that college did her any harm," said the old man with persistent cheerfulness. "It was a Christian college, which is much to be thankful for in this age of the world, and she came home loving us just as much as when she went away. She didn't get her head turned. She loved the old farm too. If I mistake not she's going to feel it some when she knows we had to part with Old Gray."

"She will of course!" said the old lady. "Sometimes, Father, I wish we'd just kept her here. Why did she need college? She had schooling enough, and she was happy here, and so safe. Sometimes I think how she used to dance in and out and sing all day long. I look down to the lake sparkling through the trees on bright days and think I see her coming up the hill in her red sweater and cap, her skates over her shoulder. Don't you remember how she used to flash over the silver of the ice just like a red bird? And how she would whistle and call to us as she was coming up the hill?"

"Yes, but, Mother, remember how worried you used to be when she went swimming in the lake, and how you'd turn away from the window and catch your breath when you saw her dive, and watch for the flash of the sun on her white arms and face. What a little fish she was to be sure, and what antics she cut up in the water. And remember, too, Mother, how you worried when she first got her canoe. You thought she was going to drown every day. God took care of her then, and don't you think He will care for her in the city?"

"Oh, but, Father, the city is so full of sin and wickedness! There are bad men in the city, and Margaret is beautiful, Father!"

"Yes, I know! But our Heavenly Father knows that too."

"But He gave her to us to take care of, and we shouldn't have let her go off alone that way."

"There wasn't anything else we could do, was there? I was sick, and we had no money, and Elias Horner was set on foreclosing the mortgage if we couldn't pay the interest. If we had to give up the old farm where would we go? Since the bank failed and took everything what else could we do but let her go when she got a good chance to earn a salary? It really was a godsend we thought, when Mr. Pearly wrote he could give her a job."

"Yes, but Mr. Pearly died, and this other man—Father, I'm awfully worried about that man. He's trying to be familiar with her. I know from what she said he must be. It isn't like her to feel that way about any *good* man. You know she said she wouldn't ask him any favors, and she was trying to find a better place."

"Now look here, Mother. It isn't like you to fret and worry. For years you've always trusted to our Lord, and He's always protected us all. Margaret is a good girl, and she is the Lord's own. She will be protected."

"Oh, I know," said the old lady wiping away her tears and trying to put on a cheerful expression, "I know, and I do trust. But sometimes I get to thinking, what if Elias Horner does do as he threatens, and forecloses the mortgage, what would become of us all? And Margaret? Suppose she got sick with no home to come to, and no money to buy food?"

"Now, Mother! Mother!" cheered the old man. "Have you

forgotten that verse, 'I have been young and am now old, yet have I never seen the righteous forsaken nor his seed begging bread'?"

"But, Father, perhaps He doesn't count us 'righteous.' I've been very rebellious in my heart all this winter. It's just awful to me to have Margaret away off down there alone."

"Dear heart," said the old man with a loving look in his eyes, "He knows. But that doesn't make any difference about the righteousness you know. It would if it were our righteousness, but it isn't. It's His righteousness that He in His wonderful mercy put upon us, because He has bought us with His blood."

"Oh, I try to remember that, Father!"

"It's true!" said the old man with a ringing tone. "Praise His name it doesn't depend on me to be righteous enough for His care. He knows what's before us, Rebecca, and His grace is sufficient!"

Suddenly the old lady put her head down and tried to stifle a little helpless sob.

"It doesn't seem as if there was any way out, Father."

"There is always a way *up!*" said the old man reverently.

"Oh, Father! You mean—!"

"I mean that He has *ways!*"

The old lady was still for some minutes thinking it out.

"Yes," she said, "if He would just take us both! I have often prayed that He would take us both at the same time. It wouldn't be hard to die if we were going together."

"We mustn't limit Him to our ways, dear heart. He has a plan for every life. And He's going to do the very best for us each, *His* very best, not ours, and some day we're going to be glad that He had His way and didn't always give us ours. We in our blindness can't always tell what we're going to enjoy the most."

"I've always rather dreaded dying, Father! Not that I'm afraid. I know it's going to be all right, Father. I believe Him. But I can't help dreading it. For you, and for me too."

"Well," said the old man with a glory light spreading over his sweet old face, "it might just be in His plan for us that we aren't going to die. You know His coming for His own may be *very* near at hand. I've been thinking a lot about it lately. Wouldn't it be nice if that should happen? It might be tonight, or tomorrow."

"Oh, Father! Wouldn't that be wonderful! But Margaret! If she were only here with us I could just look forward to it with such joy!"

"Why worry about Margaret? She is the Lord's own. She would be caught up too in the air to meet Him with us. He isn't coming for just the church in Vermont. He's taking them all you know."

"But—maybe it would be some time before we could find her," said the old lady fearsomely. "It would all be so new and strange up there."

"Oh, no," said the old man with a ring of joy to his voice. "She'd be right close to the Lord Jesus, and we'd only have to look at Him to find her close by His side."

Something of the glory and the peace from the old man's face began to be reflected in his old wife's eyes now and she looked up with a smile.

"You always do make it easier for me, Father. I don't know what I would do without you. It's always been your faith that's been the strongest."

And then suddenly while they lingered around the humble little tea table there came a sound of steps crunching outside on the icy pathway, and a preemptory knock at the door.

The old lady started and half rose from the table, apprehension darting into her eyes, her lips trembling a little, so that she put up a frail hand to steady them, and settled back into her seat again.

The old man arose from his chair with an attempt at alertness in spite of his recent rheumatic trouble, and stepping to the door opened it, holding a lamp from the tea table high that it might shine into the caller's face.

"Oh," he said with a gentle dignity that would show no dismay at the identity of the visitor, "it's you, Mr. Horner. Won't you come inside? It's a stormy night. You must have had a hard climb up the hill. It's not a nice night for traveling."

The man came in, shaking the icy particles from his shaggy coat, flinging the sleet from the brim of his old felt hat.

"No, it's not a nice night," he said in a gruff voice, "but one can't always wait fer June weather. Had a little business up this way, and I thought I'd just stop and serve you notice too. Kill two birds with one stone you know!"

His hard furtive eyes glittered toward the gentle old lady like a snake's eyes.

"Yes?" said the old man with a sudden catch in his voice as if warning himself that he must be ready for anything. Then:

"Come in, sir!" That "sir" somehow placed a distance between the householder and his visitor, and perhaps the other man felt it, for he flung himself inside and sat down in a chair by the door as if he had a right. His eyes traveled quickly about the comfortable kitchen, taking in the depth of the windows in the thick stone wall, the heavy ancient beams of oak that crossed the whitewashed ceiling. His glance was an appraising glance. The old lady recognized it and her lips grew white with fear.

"I just thought I'd step in and remind you that the interest on the mortgage that I hold on this house and farm comes due the twenty-ninth day of next month, four days after Thanksgiving."

"Yes," said the old man, "I am expecting to meet my obligations at that time." He said it with a quiet confidence, but the old lady looked at him wide-eyed and caught her breath softly. The fright quite evident in her eyes, did not escape the sharp eyes of the visitor.

"Are ye getting ready ta pay the principal as well as the interest?" asked the caller eyeing him sharply from his shaggy grizzled brows. "Because that's really what I called ta tell ya. I'm askin' ya to pay the whole amount. The mortgage was for three years, ya remember, and the three years is up this November!"

The old man met the frowning adversary with a clear keen glance.

"Yes," he said, "I know. I've been thinking some of asking you to renew the mortgage for another couple of years. I'm not just sure yet."

"Well, that's what I came fer. I came to say that I'm callin' in my money an' I'm not renewin'. I need the money and I'm foreclosin' ef ya can't pay!"

The two old people sat there stunned for a minute, the little old lady wide-eyed with sorrow, a slow tear stealing down the cheek that was turned away from the caller.

The old man still kept a calm sweet look on his face. He took it like a blow that had been long expected.

"Do—I understand—that you—are wanting to take over the farm yourself? Or—were you expecting to sell?" He asked after a minute, quite coolly.

"Well, both," said Horner sliding his underjaw out in an ugly way he had when he knew he ought to be ashamed of himself. He knew he was putting these two dear old people through a cruel torture. It was the house where the old lady was born. Four generations had been born in that house. It was dear to them both.

"Ya see," went on Horner tilting back in his chair against the wall and setting his big muddy boots on the lower round, "I got a man what wants ta go in with me. We cal'clate ta make this a popular summer resort. That there lake needs ta be commercialized, he says. Bath houses around it in summer, canoes ta hire, a hot dog stand, and in winter a skating place, an' skiing off on the hills. Build a little movie the*ayt*er down at the foot of the hill, an' campers' shacks around. It's a wonder you ain't never thought of developin' yer property. So, ya see I mean business. Ef you can't fork over my money in November I gotta foreclose. Just thought I'd let ya know."

"Yes," said the old man, gently, still with that courtly dignity. "Thank you. It is always best to understand things thoroughly."

"Wal," said Horner, half embarrassedly, "that's about all. That's what I come fer. So, ef you ain't got the money yerself ya better get busy running around among yer rich friends."

He laughed a hateful little gaffaw and stood putting on his rough knitted mittens with their leather palms, smoothing them back on his wrists comfortably. The old lady thought she never would forget that dreadful motion, and the sneer in Horner's eyes as he gave another possessive glance around their snug kitchen, just as if he owned it already.

"Well," said the old man, "that might be an idea. I'll think about it. I have one very wealthy friend indeed. I think I'll consult with him. I'm sure if he thinks it wise he'll see that I am able to pay the whole."

The old lady gave another little gasp and looked at her husband standing there with the glow of the lamp on his white hair as he lighted the visitor out into the storm again. How handsome he looked. How gallant! How dared he brave that cold hard man?

Horner gave a quick suspicious glance back at the old man as he answered. Was it possible he did really have a rich friend? But no! Impossible! The whole country round knew the Lorimers, knew their history for a century back. Margaret

McLaren, their granddaughter was down in the city trying to eke out a scanty living for them all. Through the postmistress' sister who was a connection of the Horners he knew the size of the money orders that came. He felt sure they were not even going to be able to pay the interest. He had been biding his time and waiting.

So he flung back a hateful laugh and said:

"Well, get busy then," and climbed into his rackety old machine and sent it chugging down the mountain.

The old lady waited until her husband had closed and locked the door, set down the lamp upon the supper table, and started to wind the clock. Waited until the sound of the chugging flivver down the mountain had died away in the distance before she spoke. Then she said:

"Father! You were wonderful! I feel as if Satan had just gone away from here!"

"'Since God be for us, who can be against us?'" softly quoted the old man. "In God have I put my trust: I will not be afraid what man can do unto me."

The old lady was still for a minute and then she lifted troubled eyes:

"But, Father, I never heard you tell anything that wasn't *true* before. Father, you—you *told* a *lie!* What made you do it?"

The old man came around and looked down at her sweet trembling face.

"What did I say that wasn't true, Rebecca?" he asked, smiling down at her.

"You said we had a very rich friend and you were going to consult with him."

"And so we have," said the old man, "and so I will. Dear heart, isn't our Father rich? Doesn't it say 'the silver and the gold is His, and the cattle upon a thousand hills?' Come, Rebecca, let us go and consult Him right away. It shall be just as He says."

He reached down and took her two fine little frail hands and lifting her up led her to the old patchwork-cushioned chair. There they knelt as they had done many times before, his arm about her, her two hands held close in his own warm brave one.

"Father, we've come to ask you what you want done. If you want the old place to go for an amusement park to make Elias

61

Horner rich it's all right, but Father, if you're willing to let us keep it the rest of our journey, then you'll have to send some miracle to save it for us."

And while they knelt there, telling all their anxieties and laying their burdens upon the Almighty, the old plotter drove down the dark mountain road smiling to himself as he thought over the interview. Rich friends indeed. The Lorimers hadn't a friend who had a cent to loan! The farm and the mountain and the rare old house and the gem of a lake were as good as his already. He could go on now and make his plans. There wasn't a thing Lorimer could do!

And the Lorimers, hand in hand, knelt and prayed till they could look up with shining faces and say "Thy will be done!"

7

JUST about the time that Margaret was vanishing around the first corner from the hospital Miss Gowen arrived at the door of the room where a half hour before she had left her patient quietly eating her breakfast.

She had paused for an instant in the hall to speak to another special nurse who was on a case at the other end of the corridor, then gone swiftly on, a light in her eyes, a pleasant smile on her lips, for she had a box of violets for her patient and she guessed from whom they came. She liked the two young things for whom she was working just now, and she was anticipating the excursion of the morning. Hospital life at best had so many sad happenings that it was enlivening to come on a morning when one could go out and get a little breath of the outside air and forget for a little while that there was so much sorrow and pain in the world.

And it was especially interesting this morning to think that she could bring pleasure to the little old lady who wanted so much to rent her treasured rooms and so keep her beloved home for a while longer.

So she went with springy strides to the door, swinging her wrist up to consult her watch and see how much time there was in which to prepare her patient for the trip.

But what was this? The door, standing wide open, and the scrub woman down on her knees just sloshing the first application of soapy water onto the floor. Why! How outrageous! What could this mean? This room was just cleaned before the patient came in and it couldn't need cleansing now. Besides it was beyond precedent to go at a room this way with the patient still in bed!

She gave a quick glance toward the bed which was a trifle out of the range of vision from the doorway, and behold there was no patient lying in it! The bed was stripped of its linen entirely. Another glance showed a stepladder by the far window and a man standing on it taking down the curtains! Had she made a mistake and turned the wrong way in the corridor? She looked back to the desk that stood at the junction of the two halls. No, she was in the right wing of the building. Well, she must have come to the wrong floor. That was it. This wouldn't do! She must snap out of this. A nurse ought to have her faculties about her all the time, no matter if she wasn't on a critical case. It was a bad habit to fall into.

She wheeled about and started back to the elevator, but just then the door of the room across the hall swung open and there she saw the little woman with the broken leg lying in her bed as usual, and her own special nurse just coming out the door. Why, this *was* the right floor! What could it mean?

She whirled about again and spoke to the scrub woman. "What on earth are you doing in that room, Maggie, and where's my patient?" she demanded.

"This is what I was ordered to do, Nurse, and do it quick, she said!" replied the woman, slapping her sudsy cloth down recklessly on the floor and rubbing away.

"But I don't understand," said the nurse. "I haven't been down to breakfast but half an hour, and I left my patient in the bed eating her breakfast. What have they done with her? What happened? Who ordered this?"

"I'm sure I don't know," replied the woman stolidly. "This was orders from the head nurse and they was pretty snappy. There wasn't no patient in the bed when I come. I just got here and hadta leave my breakfast half unet ta come. The bed was just like you see it when I come. I'm doin' what I was ordered ta do."

Miss Gowen, now thoroughly bewildered, hurried down the hall to the desk.

"Where is the head nurse?" she asked of the nurse who sat there answering the telephone. "Is she back yet?"

"She's back with bells!" said the young nurse with a dark look. "Stole in on us all as usual and found everything all wrong! She says she's going to report me to the board for neglect of duty, and I was only down getting medicine the doctor had ordered. She's down in the other corridor now raising a rumpus. I wouldn't advise you to get in her neighborhood even if you are a special. She's no respecter of persons this morning. She must have had a disappointing week-end."

Miss Gowen set her lips and hurried down the other corridor and presently located the head nurse. She had perhaps forgotten some of the reverence due a head nurse as she approached her.

"What have you done with my special patient, Miss Grandon?" she demanded excitedly.

The head nurse swung around upon her, offended dignity in her manner.

"Oh, it's *you*, is it, Miss Gowen? Well I wondered when you'd turn up. Just what have you been trying to put over on the hospital authorities I should like to know? Letting a charity case into our most expensive private room that had been under special orders for one of our best paying patients?"

Miss Gowen's pleasant eyes flashed fire.

"I had nothing to do with letting my patient into the room," she said, "she was there when I came on the case. I understood that she was placed there by orders from the office. I have nothing to do with that, but I do have to do with looking after my patient. I was paid to see that she was specially cared for and had no excitement nor anything to exhaust her. Will you kindly tell me what you have done with her? I will go to her at once and you can settle the other question with the people who put her there. Where is she?"

"I'm sure I don't know," was the cold reply. "I told her that I would give her five minutes to dress and get out of the hospital if she was able to go. If she wasn't I said I would have her moved to the ward where she belonged. She seemed to think she could go, so I hope she has gone. I suppose perhaps I ought to have held her for arrest or something, but I really hadn't time to bother with her. But how you all let a girl of that stamp get away with a thing like that is beyond my comprehension. You'll probably have plenty of chance to explain to the office. The idea, a girl like that in that room!"

"What do you mean, a girl like that?" asked Margaret's nurse now thoroughly roused. "She was a lovely girl. I never saw a lovelier."

"You being the judge!" sneered Miss Grandon. "Well, we'll see whether the board of directors agree with you when it comes to a showdown. However, in case you haven't been informed of the facts, she told me with her own lips that she was a charity patient and ought to be in the ward, that she had told you so, and she owned up that a strange man had brought her here, a man she never knew before, just a pick-up on the street, and that he was paying for her. Perhaps she *thought* he was, I don't know, but in this age of the world strange men who scrape acquaintance with a girl on the street and then bring her to a respectable hospital and visit her here, aren't to be trusted."

"Did you dare to tell her that?"

"Dare?" said Miss Grandon with a lifting of her eyebrows. "Dare? Yes, I dared. Just please remember who you are talking to! Certainly I told her that. And some other things. I told her plenty! This isn't a reform school and we don't keep our most expensive private rooms for young women who run around with strange young men who pretend they are paying for it, and tell lies about memorial rooms."

"But it is a memorial room," said Miss Gowen breathlessly, "the bronze tablet is expected to arrive today!"

"Oh, so he put something over on you too, did he? It seems to me you are old enough to have a little sense and judgment after all these years of nursing. I begin to see why they never made you a head nurse!"

Miss Gowen grew white with anger, and her eyes grew dark with indignation for an instant. Then she turned and strode away down the hall to the stairs and disappeared, while Miss Grandon watched her with a supercilious smile, and then remarked to a young interne who had been near enough to hear the altercation:

"Ah! I thought that would finish her! Did you ever happen to hear why she never went back to St. Luke's after that case of the man who took the wrong medicine? Well, I guess if the facts were looked into we'd be surprised. I have heard whispers, but I wouldn't like to say."

But Miss Gowen had already forgotten the sneering insinuations, the stinging tones of the woman who had been her enemy for several years back because of the preference of a rich patient. She flew down the stairs, not waiting for the elevator and hurriedly located the young nurse who had been in Miss Grandon's place during her absence. When found this nurse had a look like a scared rabbit, but admitted that Miss Grandon had been furious with her, and she denied any knowledge of the vanished patient.

Miss Gowen inquired wildly of every nurse and attendant who had been about during the last half hour but none of them had seen Margaret McLaren, except a man down in the front office who thought he had seen a young woman come down the stairs a few minutes ago and slip hurriedly out of the street door.

The nurse went out in the street, up and down, wildly, in her uniform, the cold wind blowing her hair untidily about her face but there was no sign of her patient.

She dashed back into the hospital and interviewed all the nurses on her hall, but no one had seen Margaret leave, and all she gained was a glowing account from a couple of nurses who happened to overhear the conversation between Miss Grandon and the patient.

At last, filled with chagrin and embarrassment, Miss Gowen took her way to the telephone booth and tried to call up Greg.

Now Greg had arisen early, for he realized that he had many things to set in order if he was to be honestly a business man before he took on a secretary in earnest. He had spent much time in his room formulating plans for he felt keenly that this girl would be suspicious of him if his mind appeared to be in chaos regarding his business. Indeed he had spent much of the night thinking things out, tossing on his hotel bed and sighing for the quiet of his wilderness shack. How could any man think in a noisy place like this? Thundering of trains, clang of trolley cars, whirr of motors, bang, bang, bang, of fire engines, whistle of sirens. He didn't remember that home used to be so noisy. And then he recalled that he hadn't been near his old home yet. Well, that could wait till he got this girl settled. Then, later, he would go and look up little old Maple Street and the white cottage where he and his mother used to live. If it was for sale perhaps he would buy it and go and live there. Probably it would be quiet down around Maple Street. It used to be. But now he had much to do. He felt that the first and most important thing was to get that tired sad little girl located in a comfortable room, and somehow provide her salary in advance so that she would be relieved from financial worry. He could see that was the thing that was troubling her above all else. Perhaps it was almost time to send some money to those old people who had written her that pitiful little letter he had read.

So he had taken out pencil and notebook and set down in order exactly what he had decided to do and what he meant to say to the girl about her salary. That was the most difficult matter he would have to deal with, for he foresaw that the girl would not be willing to be befriended. Whatever he did must be perfectly legitimate and reasonable. After much deliberation he decided to find out the normal salary for high class work of various kinds and pay her a salary that would be a sort of an average of them all. He would need help in so many different ways. Buying a house, furnishing it. Surely people paid big salaries for such work. He had read about that in a stray magazine that dealt with farm and garden and country houses and their decorations. It had called the workers in that line interior decorators. He would find out what interior decorators usually received. He was sure the girl, from her whole dainty appearance, had good taste and would be worthy of a good salary for that. Whatever he offered must be reasonable or he felt instinctively she would take alarm and have none of him.

He ate a hasty breakfast and betook himself to the big department stores where he sought out heads of departments and asked a lot of questions, setting down facts in his notebook that he might be able to show her what was the normal price for certain service. Therefore it happened that when the little French telephone instrument in his hotel room rippled out ring after ring, it fell upon silent unresponsive air, and word came back to the hospital booth, "They do not answer. Shall I keep on ringing?"

Miss Gowen had Mr. Sterling paged through the lobby, halls, dining room and writing rooms, but they said he could not be found. She was fairly frantic and ran back to her own hall, routing out the head nurse again, demanding more information about the disappearance of her patient.

The head nurse was coldly sarcastic, calmly triumphant, and

when Greg finally arrived on the scene and went up to the room as had been arranged, leaving his taxi waiting outside, he found an agitated Miss Gowen, his box of violets still in her hand, confronting an icy superior outside the door of the room. There were tears on Miss Gowen's cheeks, angry tears, baffled tears, and a look of frantic despair in her eyes.

"There he is now!" he heard her say, and the head nurse turned to look haughtily at the man who had dared to invade her sacred precincts and disarrange her order of things.

"She's *gone!*" said Miss Gowen to Greg, suddenly smothering her agitated face in her handkerchief.

"Gone?" said Greg, the look in his face that used to come there when he discovered an enemy had been among the cattle. "Gone?"

"Yes, gone!" said Miss Gowen catching her breath in a kind of a sob. "I suppose you'll blame me, but I never dreamed any such thing could happen. They drove her out while I was at breakfast. They told her this wasn't a memorial room and you had lied to her. They said awful things to her and told her to get up and get out if she was able. They said you weren't an honorable man and that she was not decent if she let you come here to see her—!"

Miss Gowen was excited of course. She knew that the head nurse was standing right there beside her with the power of her position, able to smash her own reputation to smithereens, and yet she poured forth the tale hot from her angry heart. This man should know the truth whatever happened.

"Who did that, Miss Gowen?" asked Greg, his voice coldly steady, his gray eyes alert, his firm jaw set in a way that made him a formidable foe. "Who dared to tell her that?" Greg's voice somehow resembled the blue of steel in a gun pointed straight at a vital part.

Then up spoke the head nurse with her most important airs.

"I did!" she said coldly. "I am the head nurse. It was my business to see that there were no interlopers. I discovered that someone had put over a gigatic fraud on the hospital, and I made it very plain to the girl who had presumed to accept a private room, that she was not wanted there. I offered to have her moved to the ward where she belonged if she was unable to leave the building, but she declined most ungraciously. I gave her to understand that respectable girls did not let strange men offer to pay large sums to keep them in luxury—"

Greg's eyes were fixed upon Miss Grandon now, and there seemed to be points of light in them that made them burn like fires. Miss Gowen watched him startled. She wondered if the head nurse realized how angry he was. Suddenly he put up his hand and interrupted the hard cold explanation.

"I see!" he said in the stern tone a much older man might have used. "You need not say anything more now. We'll deal with that afterwards. The point is where is Miss McLaren now? Don't let's waste any more time!"

Three nurses and an interne had gathered up the hall listening. The doors of two rooms had been opened and heads poked out to see what the trouble was, and across the hall the special nurse came out and joined the group further up the hall.

Just at that point a doctor arrived on the scene, the doctor who had taken the case when Margaret McLaren had been brought in, and behind him walked a white clad man from the office below with a workman in his wake, who carried a large bronze plate.

"This is the room," said the white clad attendant to the workman, pointing toward the open door of the room where Margaret had been such a short time before. "The plate is to be on the door," he said.

"Yes," said the workman putting down his kit of tools and looking questioningly toward the group gathered right in his path. "I measured it for the door panel. I guess you'll havta ask these folks ta move."

"What's all this?" asked the head nurse sharply, swinging around upon the workman.

"Just a bit of work to be done here, Miss Grandon," explained the attendant. "It won't take long. Only a matter of a few screws. There won't be any noise connected with it."

"But I don't understand!" said the head nurse sharply. "What work could be necessary? I haven't ordered anyone up here to work."

The doctor stepped forward pleasantly, yet with an air of authority, to explain.

"This room has been made a special memorial room, Miss Grandon," he said. "This man has the bronze plate for the door."

"Bronze plate!" said Miss Grandon, the color rising suddenly in her face. "Memorial room! What do you mean! There must surely have been some mistake. They wouldn't take this room. This is the room that several of our wealthy patients always choose. And when could this possibly have been done? I was only away from Friday till Sunday night. You certainly have made some mistake. It seems one can't take any time off in this institution without everything getting upset."

"This was done Saturday morning at that special meeting that was called to arrange for the extra nurses in the baby ward. It was the donation of Mr. Sterling, a native and former resident of our city. Let me introduce him to you, Miss Grandon, Mr. Sterling. And now, Mr. Sterling, how is your patient? I understand I am to have the pleasant duty of dismissing her from our care. I've just been studying her report card and it couldn't be more satisfactory."

Miss Grandon's face was a study in sudden crimson and Greg acknowledged the introduction only by another stern steady look. Then he turned to the doctor.

"I'm sorry," he said gravely, "there seems to have been some very unkind work going on here and our patient has been driven away. I'll leave you, Doctor, to find out who is at fault, while I go out and try to find the patient. When I find her, *if* I find her, I will bring her back to you. I am sorry to discover that the hospital where I had chosen to put my mother's memorial should have allowed anything like this. I don't think I shall be likely to want to put any more money into the institution where a patient was treated in so cruel and discourteous a way. But I have no time to lose. I am very anxious about Miss McLaren, and if all I hear is true I'm afraid she will take pains that we shall never find her again. Are you coming to help me, Miss Gowen?"

The doctor looked from one to another in perplexity, but Greg walked quickly away to the elevator with the nurse, and the groups about dissolved hastily, so that Miss Grandon was left to face the doctor's accusing questioning eyes alone.

8

THE taxi was chugging away at the door and Greg put the nurse in it. She had come just as she was except to stop long enough at her room to snatch her cloak.

Greg had given the order to the driver to go around the streets that were nearby to the hospital, and as they drove he looked down at the nurse and found her weeping softly.

"Look here, now," he protested, "you mustn't feel that way. It certainly wasn't your fault."

"Oh, I can't help feeling it was," she said, brushing away the tears. "She was such a sweet little thing and it must have been awful for her to be talked to that way. I know Miss Grandon. She has the sharpest tongue in the hospital, though she's a good nurse of course, and an excellent disciplinarian. The nurses are all afraid to transgress."

"I should think they would be," said Greg grimly. "But let's forget that now. Let's find Miss McLaren first. We can make it up to her. Come, help me think. Where do you think she would go first?"

"Oh, I don't know," said Miss Gowen, "I've been trying to think, but my mind gets all bewildered."

"Do you think she would go to her old boarding place and try to get her things first?" asked Greg thoughtfully, though he was watching the street both sides as they passed, and not a single passerby missed his searching gaze.

"No, I don't believe she would," said Nurse Gowen. "I think she would hunt a job the very first thing. Of course it was early when she went out. It couldn't have been more than half past eight. I think it was just a little before that because I wasn't gone from the room half an hour. Oh, if I had only done what I planned to do and gone to my breakfast early before she was awake! But I waited to fix her up and she had her breakfast while I was gone. She seemed so eager to get her hair combed and begin to get ready to go."

"There!" said Greg soothingly, "don't blame yourself. Let's

71

think hard. How would she go about getting a job as early as half past eight? Most places aren't open that early are they?"

"Well, not many. Of course restaurants and places like that. But there are employment offices. Only she wouldn't have money to pay her fee. But of course there are some that take the fee out of the first week's wages, or get the employer to pay it."

"Then let's go to the agencies in this region. She couldn't have walked far. She was too weak."

So they got a directory, conferred with the taxi driver, and visited every agency in the neighborhood, but found no trace of Margaret, though they asked at every one if she had registered there.

They bought all the newspapers and studied the advertisements, Greg noticing with a pang how few there were that a girl like the one for whom he was searching could hope to get. They followed clue after clue, but all to no purpose.

"Well, perhaps we'd better try her old boarding place now," said Greg at last.

"I don't think she'll go back there till she has a job," said the nurse again. "She's very proud, and she told me how disagreeable that old landlady was. But of course it wouldn't hurt to try."

So they drove to Rodman Street and interviewed the human dreadnaught again.

"Miss McLaren was to have left the hospital today," said Greg politely, "I am wondering if she has returned here yet or has gone to some friend's house? I have a message for her."

"No, she ain't here," said the old woman, looking him sharply over, and then taking in the white-capped nurse in the taxi. "Has she got a job yet? I don't want her back unless she has a job. I can't stand waiting fer my money. I'm poor. I lost all my money when our bank busted."

"Miss McLaren has a job," said Greg firmly, "but I don't think she intends to return here to stay. I heard her speaking as if she would have to board where it would be more convenient to her work."

"H'm!" said the old woman sourly, "I suppose you put her up to that! You with your prying into what room she had!"

"I think Miss McLaren will probably come or send for her things very soon," said Greg ignoring her insinuation and speaking with far more confidence than he felt.

"Well, she better come soon or I'll havta charge her storage for 'em. Ef you see her you tell her I can't have my house cluttered up with folkses things ef they ain't goin' ta be a payin' proposition. When people leave things more than two weeks I always send 'em ta the second-hand and get what I can out of 'em."

"In that case I'll just get you to sign a receipt for Miss McLaren's goods right now, and I personally shall hold you responsible for everything she had. She is a friend of mine and I intend to see that she is protected. She is not very strong yet and it may be several days or even a week or two before she feels she can come back and get to work again. In the meantime her baggage is hers and you are responsible for it."

Then he raised his voice a little and called:

"Miss Gowen, will you kindly come and witness the signing of this receipt?"

The landlady was a trifle awed by the nurse in her white linen cap and heavy dark blue cape lined with crimson, and she submitted finally to signing her name to the paper that Greg wrote out and read to her, binding her to hand over Margaret's things when called for.

They drove away into the sunshine of the day that was to have been so very pleasant for them all, filled with trouble and perplexity.

"Have you any other suggestions?" asked Greg looking at her with the expression of a little boy who had lost his best treasure and didn't know where to hunt next. "Did you tell her the address of the place where we were going this morning to look at rooms?"

"Why, yes, I did!" said Nurse Gowen, hope springing in to her eyes again. "I told her all about it. She asked what part of the city it was in and I gave her the name of the woman and told her what rooms she had. I could see she thought it would be almost heaven to get into a place like that. I don't wonder, either, after seeing this creature she's been boarding with, and that noisy dirty Rodman Street. She's not used to noise and dirt, you can see that."

"No, she's not," agreed Greg, thinking what a sensible woman this nurse was. "She's lived in a good home. Well, shall we try your friend?"

So they drove to the house where Nurse Gowen's friend lived and saw the pleasant double parlors that might be had for an office, and went upstairs to the big back bed-sitting room with a bath adjoining, that might be had for his secretary, and Greg said he would take them on the spot. He said it might be several days before he could bring his things and before his secretary came to board, but he would like to secure the rooms for they just suited him, and he proceeded to pay a month's rent in advance. The board was to begin the day his secretary arrived, and he furthermore left word that his secretary's name was Miss Margaret McLaren, and if she should happen to arrive sooner than he expected to look at the rooms she was to be told that she must call him up at his hotel immediately, and he left his telephone number.

It is queer what a difference it makes to be doing something at a trying time. They came out actually cheered because they had secured those nice rooms, but then they went on hunting. Scouring every street within walking distance of the hospital.

"She couldn't really have gone any farther than this without money," said Nurse Gowen. "Even this is farther than she could have walked I am sure. Of course one can go a long way on nerve under the stress of anger and fear, but she really wasn't a bit strong. I had her up in a chair yesterday and she felt topply and dizzy."

A quick look of anxiety passed over Greg's face.

"I know," he said, "that's what I've been thinking. But, you see she did have money. Didn't she tell you?"

"No," said the nurse looking up surprised. "Why no, from what she told me she must have spent her last cent."

"But I put some bills in her pocketbook when I brought it back. Didn't she get her pocketbook? It had the receipt for her room rent in it. You remember I told her it was there. And I had put twenty-five dollars inside the envelope that had the letter. I thought she would find it when she went to go away and perhaps it would be nice for her to have a little to start on. Don't you think she found it?"

The nurse shook her head.

"She didn't say a word about it. I don't think she even looked at her pocketbook, though I think she must have taken it with her for it was gone. There wasn't a rag nor a shred left that belonged to her. I went in and looked around very carefully before they had done anything to the wardrobe or bureau. I'm sure she must have taken it with her for it lay right on the top of her clothes in the bureau drawer when I left. My

74

but it's a comfort to know you put money in it! That was awfully kind of you! I never heard of anything kinder. And she will find it, surely, sooner or later she'll open that pocketbook, at least to get out her handkerchief, and she'll find it and she won't be absolutely penniless!"

Greg looked troubled.

"Well, I'm glad I put it there," he said with a sigh, "but she doesn't think there is any money there and she may not open that for days. Not unless she remembers about the receipt for her baggage. But say, here I'm keeping you all this time without any lunch. Why, I declare, it's after two o'clock. We're going right away to get something to eat!" and he ordered the driver to take them to a restaurant and come for them again in half an hour.

For three long weary days Greg carried on the search, combing the city carefully, taking every lead he could think of and following it out, only to find in every case nothing. He spent hours going from one small place of business to another inquiring if a Miss McLaren was working there, but found nothing, and his heart sank more and more over the ghastly thought that perhaps he should never find her again. Perhaps he would always have to go on through life wondering where she was, if she had fallen off some lonely bench in a far park again, starving, sick, and no one to pick her up. Her white face looked up at him as when he had first seen her, from every shadow in the darkness when he laid his weary head upon the pillow, and the thought of her smile that last time he had seen her haunted him during the days and drove him from one possibility to another.

He had gone back to the hospital that first afternoon and had an interview with the powers that be. He had said things to the head nurse and her overlords that had brought down her pride and sharpness and caused the hospital officials to make great apology. Here it appeared was one who could have given even greater benefits than he had already covenanted to their institution! They were mortified that the gift which had indeed been generous should have been so unfortunately received. The head nurse was in real trouble. She went about with a furtive fear on her countenance, red rims to her cold eyes, dark hollows under them. Apologies had been demanded of her by the Board of Directors, but the rich young donor would receive no apologies himself. He said that when the insulted patient was found—if she ever was found, and his heart quailed at the thought,—it would be time for apologies, and he wanted them made to her, not to himself.

So the days dragged by in fruitless search, each morning dawning with new hope and fear. Greg began to lose his fresh color of the wilderness and took on a haggard grayness about the eyes.

The people of the hospital did all in their power to help. It was through their influence that the courtesy of other hospitals was extended to him and he went about in the wards searching the faces in the narrow white beds, and becoming suddenly conscious of the awful suffering in the world.

It was the third day of the search that he thought of the morgue and forced himself to go to that grewsome house of death, looking into strange unknown dreadful faces, relieved that he did not find them familiar. But still the whereabouts of Margaret McLaren remained a mystery.

Going back to the hotel one night about a week after the disappearance of the girl who had come into his life so unexpectedly, and gone out with such seeming finality, he sat down disheartened and began to examine himself.

Probably he was foolish in the extreme to act this way about an utter stranger. He had done his best for her while she stayed, and would have done far more. Surely he was not to blame if she came to further disaster. It was wholly her fault, running away like that. She knew he was coming at eleven o'clock. She should have waited, at least until she sent him word, at least until her nurse returned. She should have trusted him.

And yet why should she? He was an utterly unknown quantity to her, and the insinuations of that head nurse were enough to send any self-respecting girl into hiding. It was easy to see that she had been carefully brought up, and would shrink from having people question her relationship with a strange young man. And when you came to think about it of course it was utterly out of the ordinary.

Sometimes at night his heart had told him he was a fool to put so much time and thought on her. She might be anything but what he thought her. Yet he knew that was not so. She must be sweet and good and true, and very likely was horrified that she had listened to him for a moment. She probably now thought him a false-hearted adventurer.

76

That thought stabbed him like a knife. He could not bear the idea of her going on through life always thinking of him in that way. But more than that he knew he could not bear the thought of her going on somewhere suffering all alone, toiling for a pittance, weary, sick, sad, and no one to help her. Always, especially at night, he saw her face as it had been that first night he found her, white, upturned against his shoulder, felt her frail weight in his arms. He had had her then, a sweet responsibility to care for, and he had been somehow so clumsy as to lose her. He was a fool of course, but he knew he never could be satisfied until he had done his utmost to find her and put her where she was safe. Then perhaps he could go on about his business. He must of course. Only he hadn't any real business. Well, perhaps tomorrow, if he found no trace of her, he would give it up. Of course he might put the matter in the hands of the police, but he shrank from that. She would not like it, and he had no possible claim upon her. She would resent it he was sure.

So he went to bed to toss another night through in fitful slumber and wish he knew what to do that he had not already done.

But tomorrow brought no further light and another Sunday dawned.

A new idea had come to him through the night. Perhaps if she were still alive and well enough, and still in this part of the world, she might go to church. He would go to church and look for her. He would go to a great many churches.

So he started early, and made the rounds of all the churches in that part of the city, and he was amazed to find how many there were. He would slip into a back seat and carefully search the audience, then not finding her would slip out again and go on to another.

Now and again he would see a familiar face, grown older since he went away, but he had a strange reluctance to make himself known to anyone. He hadn't time, and he had lost interest.

Before the day was over he had covered a good deal of denominational ground, but had not found the object of his search, and he was heart weary and dog tired. Late in the afternoon it had occurred to him that it was a cold day and Margaret had no warm coat. The little jacket to her suit that she had been wearing was wholly inadequate for the weather of today. Besides it had been shabby. Perhaps she would not feel that she was well enough dressed to attend church, and he was only wasting time. He recalled the pitiful sentence in her grandmother's letter bidding her save her money to get a warm coat. No, of course she would not be likely to go to church. He recalled the caustic remarks of her former land-lady about her pawning her clothes. Probably her old coat had been pawned. But perhaps she would go and redeem them now, if she found the money he had put in her purse.

He got up the next morning with an ache in his heart. He had resolved to give it up. Perhaps he would find her again unexpectedly the way she had come to his notice the first time. At any rate it was foolish to spend his time this way in a useless search. She was nothing to him, and the sooner he made himself realize it the better. He would go this morning and look up his old home and try to turn his thoughts in another direction.

As he started out into the chill wind of a surly November day he found himself longing with a sick thrill for the freedom and hard work of his western life. How ridiculous! Here he had had nearly two weeks of the home town and he hadn't even approached to doing the things he had planned to do when he came! It was high time he stopped this and got something new to think about. There would be no point in losing his mind, or getting dyspepsia, when he had money enough to do anything he pleased. He would just stop being philanthropic and think of himself. He was lonesome and he must get himself some friends. He wished he could see Rhoderick Steele, the man he had met on the train. He had a feeling that an hour with him would be like a breath from his western mountain and give him new life and strength, blowing away the morbidness from his mind.

So he turned his footsteps toward Maple Street and the little white cottage of his boyhood, the house he had loved in those dear dead days when he was a boy with a home and a mother who cared for him.

Eventually, in spite of changes, he found the little white cottage where he used to live, but it was no longer white, nor pleasant in any way. A boiler factory had come to the section behind Maple Street, that used to be a wide field where the boys of the neighborhood played baseball in summer eve-nings, and the consequent noise and dirt had changed the whole neighborhood. A railroad siding ran behind the house cutting off a part of the yard where his mother used to have her garden.

The little white cottage was grimy and run down. The steps were broken, a window light was replaced by a piece of cardboard, one shutter hung by a single hinge, the roof showed rotted shingles, the whole place needed paint.

A swarm of clamoring dirty children fought fiercely in the muddy front yard that used to be so trim and tidy with its speck of a lawn that he had always kept in order, and its border of bright flowers that his mother tended so carefully.

The narrow board walk that led from the gate to the front door, the side door, and around to the back door, had so many missing boards that one wondered why its framework was allowed to remain and rot. There wasn't any gate, and many of the palings of the fence were gone. Later he discovered the gate down in the back yard in full view of the street, helping to house a pig under a rude roof of clumsy construction, and a bevy of hens swarmed around the house contending for a late bug they had found in the rotten wood of the walk.

He stood in dismay and surveyed the surroundings. The neighboring houses were just as badly run down. How could all that have happened in ten years! Did neighborhoods always change like that? How ghastly, how terrible it seemed! He wished he had not come. Why, he had long harbored intentions to buy that house and live in it, to make it as nearly as possible as it had been when his mother was living. He had even thought that perhaps there would be a way of tracing her furniture that had been sold after her death to pay her funeral expenses. He had spent time on his journey thinking about that, writing down a list of the things he could remember. Her old walnut bedroom set that her father had given her when she was married, just a year before his death. How many times she had told him the tale of her surprise and delight when he showed it to her. It had marble tops. He had thought every feature of it out. He had tried to remember the name of the auctioneer who had sold the things.

Then there had been the round dining room table, the chairs and the sideboard, golden oak his mother called it. And there was an old sofa that he used to go to sleep on nights when he had finished his lessons. It had been because of that sofa that he had bought the old humpy couch for his shack. And there had been the parlor table with the big glass lamp that had lambs and a shepherd painted on the shade. How dear it had all been. Why, he could remember his mother in the evening when the lamp was lighted and she sat in the corner in her haircloth covered mahogany rocker, singing softly, "The Lord is my Shepherd." The memory of the soft quaver in her voice in those last months when she was ill brought the tears to his eyes now as he stood in the wind and looked at the wreck that house had become. There were green shades at the windows, and a woman with untidy hair and an unclean, yelling baby in her arms, opened the front door, paused to spank a two-year-old screaming on the top step, and then went in and slammed the door. His one brief glimpse of the inside of the house had showed a cluttered floor, and a drunken man sprawled at full length on a wooden settee across the room, sound asleep. So his home had become that! It seemed somehow to strike at all that was holy and dear in the past. It filled him with a disgust for life. To think that a little white sanctuary such as his mother had made and kept could become a place of horror like this. No wonder the man drank, the woman was untidy, the children fought and the baby screamed! Was life all like this? Had it always been so? Was it so everywhere? If so why had he come back? What was the use? Better loneliness and the desert.

Just to cheer himself he walked about the streets. Alice Blair had lived on a wider street with three-story twin brick houses. He had always had an ambition to grow up and buy his mother a brick house some day. It had seemed grand to his youthful ideas. Yet when he walked the three or four blocks to Alice's old street, and paused before the door where he had so often waited to say good bye and hand Alice her armful of school books that he had carried home for her, somehow the house had shrunken to squalor. This street even more than his own home street was swarming with dirty yelling children. The houses were grimy and ill kept. A vacant one here and there had every pane of glass broken, the targets of the neighborhood. And the house where Alice used to live had become a shop! A dirty grimy little cigar shop, where cheap sensational news sheets hung in the window beside chewing gum and pipes and a few loaves of bread! There were discouraged-looking bananas too, and a small measure of specked apples. A mere travesty of a store. He gazed aghast at what had once seemed to him a fine home. He gave a quick furtive look up and down the length of the street, which appeared to be pretty much all alike, and beat a hasty retreat. There was a feeling at the pit of his stomach that made him want to lie down. A single line of an old hymn that his mother used to sing sometimes around the house at work came to him, utterly out of its setting:

"Change and decay in all around I see!"

He did not know what came next. He did not want to know. He was filled with sorrow at having come home and found no home. Life was a great delusion. Why should one live?

He walked on over toward the old schoolhouse, but here too the boiler factory, and an iron foundry had encroached upon what had been a pleasant memory, and a crowded population had swarmed into the happy wide areas and changed them almost beyond recognition. Still, he kept on. The school building was there, evidently still being used as a schoolhouse. There were a lot of little gamins playing in the cinder court outside. He walked past them, up the old steps, into the long musty halls smelling of chalk, stale lunches, and little unwashed humanity. Even the school had degenerated!

Still he forced himself to go upstairs to the senior room where last he had sat over by the window, with Alice at her desk across the room, smiling, signaling, flipping notes across!

He looked sadly about and was comforted that at least here there was no change. The desk a little more marred and scratched perhaps, but still in the same place. He sat down in his old seat and realized that it was hard to get his long legs under the desk. He tried to think of himself as he used to be, to feel that the rest of the class would presently march in and take their places, and that Alice would give him a golden glance and go on to her place. But the empty spaces gave back a solitary look and sound to his eagerness. He wanted to put his head down on the desk and cry!

He got up and walked quickly down the stairs and out the door. He got himself out of that street and vicinity. He went up where the banker used to live, near the great stone church which his mother and he used to attend. The church was there, yes, with a dim and distant dignity. There was a new name on the bulletin board under the word "Pastor." Another new name for the janitor. Nobody anywhere around that he knew! Only ten years and everything changed! It seemed incredible. There must be some familiar faces somewhere.

He walked on past the stone mansion where the bank president used to live and behold, a great board announcing: "THIS PROPERTY FOR SALE. Apply to Hamilton Real Estate Trust Company."

He asked a workman who was resetting the curbstone. "Don't the Hamiltons live here any more?"

It was a foolish question. One could see at a glance that no one lived there now.

The man looked at him curiously and shook his head.

"Not sence the bank shut down, and that's ben most two year now. Folks say they went to Europe somewheres cause they could live cheaper there."

Greg gave a startled look at the ornate old mansion that used to represent to him all that was grand in the way of a residence and walked on thoughtfully.

Away to the upper end of the town he walked where the sunset used to stretch out beyond wide sunny meadows filled with violets and daisies and buttercups girdling the home town with rest and peace.

But the sunset was hidden now behind giant apartment houses, tier upon tier of brick colonnades, windows and windows! How the town had grown! And beyond those more new mansions, greater and more pretentious than any that the town had boasted before he went away.

And then a great rolling expanse of green, even late in the fall though it was, and far in the centre a low rambling building, neither mansion nor dwelling. He did not quite know how to rank it till he came to the stone-arched gateway bearing the inscription "Meadow Springs Gold Club." Golf! He looked at the words startled. He knew what it was of course, he'd read about it. A silly way for the idle rich to spend their time! People who did not know how to do real things! That was the impression he had.

He stood a moment looking out across the wide spaces in the dusk that was fast coming down. Little groups of people, men and women idling back to the wide low building that was beginning to brighten out with twinkling lights. Groups differentiating into other groups, climbing into cars that shot down the driveway, some of them walking down together with

82

long free strides, men arrayed in curious garb, sweaters and knee breeches. Fancy stockings. Gray-haired men tricked out! Oh there was no doubt the world had been making changes in itself since he went to the wilderness. Somehow he didn't seem to be linked up with this new world as he found it in the home town. There was no place that his interest caught on. He had money now to play the game as others played it, but it didn't seem worth while.

Oh, eventually he would go out and get him some friends he supposed, but somehow just now he didn't have the relish for them. He had a heart hunger that he had half expected to be satisfied by someone, something in the home town, and it hadn't been! Well, he was a fool of course. But he must soon get an interest in something!

So he strode back to the Whittall House. He wondered what was the matter with him? Was it all himself? Was he unadaptable? Had he stayed too long in the wilds to conform to the world and get any enjoyment out of life?

Then he unlocked the door of his room and heard his telephone ringing wildly.

With a quick beating of his heart he strode to the instrument and picked it up.

"Is that you, Greg?" came a strangely familiar voice thrilling over the wire. "This is Alice!"

9

GREG found himself breathless. Was something really coming to him at last out of his past? Alice! That was Alice's voice! For an instant his mind reeled back into his boyhood and the old familiar drawl of the sweetly indolent voice played upon his senses and drew him with an irresistible power.

"Yes?" he managed to respond, trying to find his way out of the bewilderment that her call had wrought. Then she spoke again.

"Is that really you at last, Greg, after all these years of silence? I never thought you'd cut me cold like that. Don't you know me, dolling? This is Alice. Have you forgotten your old sweetheart, Allie Blair?"

"Alice *Blair!*" For an instant the wild thought went through his brain, perhaps it had been a mistake. Perhaps she never ran away and married Murky Powers! Perhaps the report had been false.

"Alice Blair!" he repeated dazedly, eagerly, again.

"Oh, you've come alive at last have you, dolling? Well, you've taken your time to it. Here I've simply been languishing at home for days expecting you to come to call on me, and at last I've been driven to put my pride in my pocket and call you up. I positively couldn't stand it to wait any longer. Why haven't you come, Greg? You haven't forgotten me, have you, dolling?"

As a matter of fact Alice Blair had not been languishing at home during the days that had elapsed between her reading of the news item about the memorial room and this telephone call. She had been exceedingly busy trying to find her former admirer. And Alice was resourceful. She had scoured the town among his old friends and had called up various hotels and investigated other stopping places. An old friend who was well enough off to give a memorial room to a hospital must surely be worth looking up. Although she reflected that it would be like Greg to have scraped together enough for a memorial for his mother, and left nothing for himself to live on. That had always been the trouble with Greg to her mind, he thought too much of his mother. She had been always having to combat ideas and standards that his mother had given him.

But when she found that he was staying at so distinguished a place as the Whittall House she was all the more eager to find him and secure his attentions once more. If he could afford to stay at the Whittall House he must have *some* money at least, and Alice loved money and the things that money would buy.

So Alice had called up several times that day while Greg was out, until she finally found him. And now her voice lilted into pathos with a hint of the old time lure as she asked pathetically whether he had forgotten her.

Greg found himself stirred by various emotions as he struggled to answer her. He was trying to think out quickly what might have happened in those ten years of his absence. Murky Powers wasn't dead. He was sure of that. He had seen his name on the sporting page of the paper just the other day.

His mother's fears, and an innate caution were battling with his delight that she had called him, his longing to find some friend.

"Why,—I—thought you were *married!*" he blundered out bluntly at last.

A silvery laugh trilled over the wire and rippled in his ear, making pleasant little shivers down his back. It was as if suddenly all his disillusionment had rolled away and Alice Blair was just a little golden girl again that his mother didn't quite understand yet, but would some day.

"Married!" she lilted. "Oh, that's precious, Greg. Are you really as innocent as that yet? Now don't tell me you've been kept a babe in arms! *Married!* What's that got to do with it? Of course I'm married. Twice married for the matter of that. I divorced Murky, that prince of brutes before a year was up, and I'm just back from Reno now getting rid of his successor. Safe and sane and disillusioned. But that's neither here nor there. Once sweethearts is always sweethearts, isn't that so, Greggie dolling? Or am I mistaken? Is it?"

Greg found himself bewildered by her chirruping. He hesitated an instant and she went on, her tone graver now with a hint of tears behind it.

"But seriously, Greg, aren't you coming to see me right away? I need you. I really do. I've been through terribly hard experiences and I need a *real friend*. As soon as I heard you were in town I rejoiced, for I knew you were just what I needed."

"But I don't see how you knew I was here," murmured Greg, still bewildered. "I didn't let anybody know I had come."

"Oh, I heard," triumphed the silvery voice. "Those things get around quickly in the Home Town you know. And I was *hurt*. Really I was, Greg dear. I supposed of course you would hunt me up at once the minute you landed. And I was *terribly hurt*, hour after hour, not even *hearing* from you."

"I didn't know you lived here." Greg's voice sounded blunt again. He felt strangely embarrassed at the way this grown up Alice was taking things for granted, calling him darling and telling of her divorces. "Last I heard of you, you were living in New York."

"Oh, but that's ages ago. I went to Paris for two years, and then Florida for the winter. Took a trip to the little old Panama

Canal incidentally. Oh, I've been around a bit. But now I'm home at last. For a while at least. Mother's still living here you know. She took a house on the West side. What's that? No, I'm not with Mother. Her ways are not my ways, never were, you remember." A careless little laugh rippled over to him. "No, I couldn't be bothered living where I'm watched every move I make. I have an apartment in The Claridge. It's really quite swell. And that brings me to the point. I want you to come over and take dinner with me, just us two you know. Come about seven and we can have a real talk. You better dress because there'll be others dropping in later in the evening, and we'll likely get around to a night club or two before morning. We always do, so come prepared. Now, you won't fail me, will you, Greggie dolling! It's so nice to have you back!"

Greg turned from hanging up the receiver and looked about his room. It was the same strange room but somehow it looked less lonesome. There was somebody in town who cared. He was going out to dinner! He was going to see Alice again! His heart was warm and eager.

Then he gave himself to the matter of garments. This would be the time for the clothes he had got in Chicago. He recalled the careful directions his brief casual questions had elicited. He hadn't been at all sure that he would ever need evening clothes in the new life that was before him, but at least he had prepared himself for an emergency, and here it was.

But whoever would have thought he would be going to take dinner with Alice of all people? Alice who had been so utterly removed from him all these years by that marriage with Murky Powers! And now to find out she no longer belonged to him! It filled him with elation. And yet—he had always felt that divorces were dreadful things. His mother had left him fine high standards of clean living. He had never favored divorces. Still—there must be cases where it was justifiable. He recalled the adjectives Alice had used to describe Murky, "prince of brutes" and his blood boiled. Anybody who could ill-treat a little delicate golden girl like Alice must be a brute. He had never liked Murky. It had been terrible to him when Alice ran away with him. Poor little golden Alice!

Of course his mother had said, "There, *you see*, Gregory!" but he had always thought his mother just didn't understand

Alice. She hadn't a very pleasant environment at home, according to her own story. Poor Alice!

The disturbing thought came that she had married again after one sharp experience, and was again divorced. He knew how his mother would have felt about that too. He winced himself as he thought about it. Well, at least he would see her and after he had talked with her he would be better able to understand.

He was full of anticipation as he prepared for the evening, even whistling a wild bar or two of a nondescript song. Ten years in the wilderness had not tended to increase his repertoire.

It was odd how the wilderness had given him poise however. When he stood at last in the ornate vestibule of Alice's apartment waiting to be let in, his manner was cool, repressed, self-contained. The casual observer would never have dreamed that this was the first time he had ever appeared in evening clothes before except in the store where they were purchased. They sat upon his finely knit figure as well cut clothes should do, and did not flaunt themselves as alien garments. Greg Sterling was as well turned out as though he had been living on Fifth Avenue all his life.

Only in his deep gray eyes was there a light of eagerness that a discerner of character might read how greatly he was moved. But his outward calm was perfect as the door was opened by a trim maid in uniform.

Greg entered the strangest looking room he had ever seen. There were hangings of black velvet and silver cloth, and a lot of queer, triangular mirrors in unexpected places. There were flowers everywhere, rare hothouse flowers. It suddenly occurred to Greg that he ought to have sent her flowers.

His mind flashed back to High School Commencement time and how he had taken over another fellow's early morning milk route for several weeks to get extra money to get flowers to send up to Alice when she read her essay at Commencement. A dozen little pink roses! And now he could get her as many dozens as he pleased, and he hadn't remembered to get them!

It occurred to him to wonder who had sent her these roses. Great yellow ones with a glow of crimson in their hearts, dozens of them in a copper bowl reflected in a slab of mirror on a low table. Crimson roses in a tall crystal vase with stems almost a yard long and a perfume that was rare and beguiling.

White roses in a strange black jar with silver edges. Pink roses in an alabaster urn. Did Alice buy these roses for herself? Was she rich enough now to revel in luxuries of this sort, or did other men send them to her? The uneasy question shot like a pang through his heart, and then he saw her coming and forgot everything else.

She was wearing a frail evening frock of palest petal-pink satin, whose lovely revealing lines brought out every charm and grace and enhanced the beauty of her exquisite neck and arms, the contour of her slender back. Her face was like a lovely flower, and her pale gold hair was drawn back smooth and close about her small symmetrical head and gathered into a knot in her neck, leaving her pretty little ears uncovered, and giving her an innocent childlike air which the vivid dash of carmine on her small petulant lips only half belied. If it had not been for the sweet pitiful shadows under her great appealing blue eyes she would not have looked a day older than when he saw her last.

A necklace glittered on the whiteness of her neck, there were jewels flashing from her small white hands and arms, and there were long slender earrings dripping down from the little ears, that twinkled as she stirred.

A moment she stood poised at the upper end of the long room, letting him get the full effect of her entrance, fairly taking his breath away with her loveliness, appraising him with a delighted glance. Then, with all the gush of the Alice of old, only with perhaps a new touch of artificiality, she cried out joyfully:

"Oh, you *dolling!* Aren't you perfectly *stunning!*"

Then she rushed forward and before he had any idea what was coming she had seized his face in both her slim smooth hands and kissed him smartly on his mouth.

He started back from her. There was something in that contact he did not like, or was not prepared for. It was too soon, he told himself. She seemed a stranger. He had just been looking at her as if she were some supernatural being, and now to have her rush upon him this way somehow cheapened her. Made her seem just a common stranger. He stiffened and met her onslaught almost stolidly.

"*Dolling!*" she reproached tenderly, holding him off and looking at him fondly. "Aren't you glad to see me?"

In his wilderness home he had accustomed himself to meet

all sorts of emergencies. He had trained his face to express no emotion before the unexpected, be it friend or foe, or only a trespassing creature. And he had ever been a lad of few words.

So, now, as he would have done in front of his shack in the wilderness had some strange wild creature approached him and begun to be familiar, he stood warily regarding her. He did not let her see his shrinking, nor guess how he disliked this sort of thing. He just stood and took it solemnly, as if he had withdrawn within himself. And strange to say this attitude on his part was merely more intriguing to her. She flung the sweetness of her personality against his indifference, determined to strike a spark of interest from those deep gray eyes whose lights she used to know so well, whose interest she had caught on the first glimpse, but whose light seemed suddenly to be no more lit just for her benefit.

She was clever. She did not press her point. She led him to a great deep velvet chair beside the table with the mirrored yellow roses.

"You're perfectly stunning there, you know," she declared, looking at him as though he were a picture she had just purchased, and then she suddenly stooped and kissed him again, this time on his forehead just where the crisp hair fell over the whiteness of the flesh.

He took that caress also as though it had been buck shot rattling off from his coat of armor as if it were not worth noticing. But something inside clicked. He knew he did not like that either. Not now anyway. Not so soon. Not until he had asked for it.

Was he perhaps old-fashioned? Did women give themselves freely now at their will before they knew that they were desired?

But Alice divined his mood. She sat down quietly, opposite him, sat so her lovely profile was turned toward him, just the sweet curve of her back with the folds of satin so like her soft skin showing gently against the velvet draperies of a great arched window of leaded glass. Sat with a sudden sweetness upon her and a quiver of her delicate chin, while she told in hushed sentences, with downcast eyes, of the sorrows that had been hers since last he saw her. Told it as one confides only to the dearest and nearest, a hint here, a frank word there, a dignified reserve at a climax where far more is implied than is told. A little well-trained tear or two stole out and down her soft cheek like dew on a rose petal and trembled there without doing much damage to her make-up.

Sterling sat and watched her, his heart warming to her. Ah! This was the real Alice! This was the Alice that he had always dreamed his mother would discover in his girl some day! And this dear sorrowing girl had kissed him twice when he came in! Why had he taken it so coolly? His senses stirred as he watched her now in her sweet gentleness. If she were to come and kiss him now he would receive her with open arms. He would like to go and sit over there beside her, put his arm about her, draw her head down on his shoulder and tell her how his heart ached for her. Brutes, those men had been who had married her and made her suffer so. Brutes indeed, and she was well rid of them! Little delicate lovely Alice Blair! To think that men would dare to marry her and put her through so much!

Dinner was announced while they were talking, and the subdued mood seemed to last. She seated him opposite to her with a quaint dignity and a gentle deference that put him within an atmosphere of intimacy. More and more as the meal went on and he looked into her eyes as she raised them meaningfully to his, he was thrilled with the fact that he was sitting here with Alice, dining with her, just as if they belonged together, as if they had always belonged together.

Once when the waitress had been sent from the room she passed him the dish of bonbons across the table, and their fingers touched and lingered. Ah! Had he perhaps come home, really home to something real at last?

He tried to put out of his mind that she was a twice divorced woman, and that it was against all his traditions to marry a woman under those conditions. There were condoning circumstances. There would be some way out for his conscience. His heart grew tender as he watched her.

But the quiet intimate dinner was over at last, and almost at once a caller was announced. An older man with baggy pouches under his eyes. He who answered to the name of "Mortie" greeted her with outstretched hands, and patted her cheek, called her "Blair, dear," and dared to kiss her fingers. Greg distrusted him from the moment he saw him, hated him, registered a vow to stick around and protect Alice from his attentions.

Then others began to drop in, blasé men who eyed Greg

90

indifferently, noisy girls in abnormal costumes, an artist or two and a musician who had already been drinking.

Alice introduced them in a group as "the gang" and called Greg "An old sweetheart of mine." They stared at him briefly, and all began clamoring for drinks.

Greg settled down sternly in a corner to watch this new development, took up a book of modern prints and looked them over without seeing them. When he looked up again Alice, his delicate lovely Alice, was sitting beside that obnoxious Mortie on the couch lighting a cigarette from his, then puffing away and exhaling from her delicate nostrils. He could see the vivid red of her lips, the flashing of her white teeth. Everybody was drinking and Alice was drinking too. The light gay trill of her laughter rose foolishly above the chatter. She seemed to have forgotten him. She wasn't the same woman who had sat through that lovely intimate dinner with him. His soul turned sick within him. What was the matter with everything? Was the matter perhaps with him? Had he stayed too long in the wilderness? He was the only one in the room who was not drinking. Alice noticed him at last and called across the room to him.

"Greg, dolling, aren't you having anything to drink? Oh, I forgot, you used to have principles, didn't you? But they weren't your own you know, they were just your mother's handed down. Where've you been in this age of the world that you haven't got over them before this? You'll have to, you know, now you're back in the world! Better begin tonight!"

Greg answered nothing and presently discovering that for a person who had been used to setting his bedtime by startime it was growing late, he arose and looked about him.

No one seemed to be paying the slightest attention to him. Why should he not go? Someone had turned on the victrola and they were beginning to dance. They were all as alien to him as if he had been a great rock out on his own desert.

But Alice perhaps divined his thought and waving her hand called:

"Come, folks, we're going out to find a nice place to spend the evening!" and she floated over to Greg and nestled up beside him.

"You're going to take me!" she confided to him with almost the sweet and gracious air she had worn at dinner, conferring her greatest favor upon him.

Something stirred within Greg again, the old attraction. He knew he didn't belong to this orgy. Yet he did not seem able to resist that look in Alice's eyes. After all, why blame her so? She had lived in Paris. She had lived with men who did these things. Perhaps she was not so much to blame after all. Surely a face so lovely, so tragic in some of its moods, must have great good in it. He hesitated.

And while he hesitated the man named Mortie came over to her with the white fur wrap her maid had brought.

"Come on then, Blair, dear!" he said possessively, holding out her wrap and folding it intimately about her shoulders.

Alice let him put the wrap about her but she lifted her azure eyes to Greg's face.

"You may put on my wrap, Mortie precious," she said languidly, "but I'm going with my old sweetheart, Gregory Sterling!" and she slipped a little jeweled hand inside Greg's arm. "Come on, folks," she called. "We're going out to find a night club."

10

MARGARET had sat in her obscure corner of the inner waiting room embattled by her thoughts for perhaps an hour before any sort of order came out of the chaos.

It was as if that awful head nurse had followed her here and were saying over and over all that she had said to her a little while before. All the contumely and scorn were heaped upon her head, the sharp words of rebuke went deep into her soul again, and she just sat there and took it like one caught under fire.

To think that she had allowed herself to be put into such a situation! Occupying one of the best private rooms at the expense of a stranger who had told her lies to keep her satisfied! And it would appear from what the head nurse had said that he hadn't even paid the expense, only pretended he was going to so that the nurses and the doctor would allow him to put her there! How terrible! How she had been deceived in that man! He had seemed so genuine, just as if God had sent him to her in her distress! Never again would she trust any human being whom she did not know. Her judgment was all at fault. What could possibly have been his object? She shuddered at the thought.

Well, it had not been her fault in the first place. She was unconscious when he picked her up. Her only crime had been in trusting their word when they told her the room was a memorial gift for just such strangers as herself.

That nice kind nurse, too! She must have been in the conspiracy, if it was a conspiracy. Or perhaps the young man had deceived her also. She had certainly been on his side.

But presently the shame and humiliation of having been ordered out of a hospital on the ground of non-respectability, cleared away, like smoke from a battleground after the shooting is over, and she began to see more clearly.

It wasn't her fault anyway. Sometime if she succeeded in business she might go back and pay every farthing she owed that hospital. Pretty soon when she got on her feet again and was earning money enough to buy some decent stationery she would write that head nurse a note and tell her so, or perhaps it would be better to write to the hospital and explain the whole thing. That was it, she could write and explain it all, and they would understand that she was a respectable girl and had not been to blame.

The idea seemed to ease the pain and humiliation of the whole affair and to give her back her ordinary common sense.

Now, she must put it utterly out of her mind. She obviously couldn't do anything about it just now. Her first need was to get a job and provide against the immediate future.

Nobody of course would pay her right away, and she would have to get along somehow till the end of the week, but how was she going to work unless she could eat? Could she get her new employer, provided there was such a person in existence, to pay her a little at the end of the day, just to tide her over a few days? She could live on very little. Some milk and crackers, a bowl of soup now and then, or an orange or banana. She had had large experience in finding out cheap meals that would last. As for a place to stay, she could spend one night at least here in this station. If she came in late in the evening no one would notice her. She could move in the middle of the night when she might be supposed to be going to a train, from the big outer room to this one. She could even perhaps get a chance to lie down on that big couch over in the opposite corner, for an hour or two, at least until the attendant asked her to move on. Yes, she could very well get comfortably through a night or two in this station. And there was another station in the other part of town. Perhaps she could change to that when it became noticeable that she was hanging around here.

Of course when she got a real job she would have to hunt a room, but it would have to be a very small cheap one, and she resolved that she would never go back to Rodman Street to stay again with that old virago. She wouldn't even go back for her things until she had the money to pay what she owed. For of course if that young man had been a liar, all that story about paying her room rent for her had been a lie also. What a fool she had been not to see that. As if anybody would be so silly as to pay back rent for an utter stranger who had no claim upon him! She certainly had been gullible. And how she had prided herself upon her ability to take care of herself in a big city! Well, she would be cautious enough hereafter! And she wouldn't go near Rodman Street for sometime yet, not till she felt safe. The young man knew that had been her home. If he wanted to annoy her further he might go there, and she might have difficulty in evading him. She could get along somehow without her things. She reflected that there were pitifully few of them left anyway. Most of the brave wardrobe with which she had come to the city was now represented by a few pawn tickets hidden away in a little box in her suitcase, and it would be a long time before she could hope to redeem them. But she would get along. She must. She could not fail! God wouldn't let that happen with those two dear old people up in Vermont utterly dependent upon her!

Then Necessity arose familiarly and stung her into action. She must not sit here another minute wasting precious time in useless thought. The day was slipping fast away and she must get a job.

So she clutched her thin pocketbook in her hands and started up, trying not to realize how weak she felt, how her knees shook under her, and her feet felt like lead when she walked. She simply must not give way to this feeling. She must get a job and go to work at once, and how could one work feeling like an invalid?

"Oh God, help me!" she breathed. Then she took a deep

breath, tried to set a pleasant assured expression upon her face, and went forward.

She didn't notice which way she was going. All ways were alike so they did not lead in the direction of the hospital from which she had fled. She tried to remember how fortunate it was that she had finished her breakfast, or at least nearly finished it, before that terrible head nurse had flung open the door and begun to rail at her. There had been one lovely last bite of toast and egg and one more swallow of coffee, she remembered, but she must not think of that or she would begin to get hungry before night, and night was the first time she dared hope to eat again. Even then it might be impossible.

So she shut her lips firmly, pleasantly, and started out.

She found herself headed into a street that she did not know, a street of small dirty shops, printers, stencilers, grimy wholesale places where they kept electric fixtures in little dark discouraged rooms, and where their windows seemed never to have been washed. That was an idea, how would it be to go into some of those places and ask them if they didn't want their windows washed? She could wash windows beautifully. Yet, she couldn't wash windows in the only decent clothes she had. One day would put them beyond hunting for a more lucrative job. Besides, she was too shaky for such strenuous work. She probably couldn't last out a day at it. That would be foolishness, unless there really was nothing else.

Then just across the street she saw a window where a man was leaning over putting a large white lettered card close to the glass. Even at that distance she could dimly make out the words "GIRL WANTED" and with wondering relief she turned and sped across the street. What marvelous luck to be the first to see it. No, not luck. God was surely being good to her! Yet, perhaps it was some kind of skilled work needed that she could not do!

She entered the shop with fear and trembling and looked about her fearsomely.

It was only a tiny shop and its shelves and counters and even the floor seemed to be cluttered with small pasteboard boxes. On the counter were several of these open, and beneath the wrappings she could see some kind of metal contrivance for household use.

There were two men in the shop, the younger one unloading more little boxes from a large packing box in the middle of the room and putting them on the shelves. The older one, a stooped elderly man with sharp eyes and an unpleasant mouth came forward and looked her over suspiciously.

"Can you write a good clear hand?" was the first question he asked her.

Margaret smiled with relief.

"Oh, yes!"

He shoved forward a pad and pencil.

"Show me!"

He pointed to an address and Margaret copied it, trying to keep her hand from shaking.

"O.K." said the man when she had finished. "Now I got a lotta circulars I want folded and addressed. I pay by the hundred." He named a pitifully small sum. "It's upta you how much ya make. I wantta get 'em out as quick as possible. Ef you don't work fast enough I gotta get somebody else ta help. There's all them! How fast ken ya work?"

He waved his hand toward a counter at the back where were stacked what seemed to Margaret like millions of printed sheets, and quantities of envelopes.

"Oh, I can work fast!" promised Margaret breathlessly.

"Want I should get a helper fer ya, or ken ya do 'em alone, an' make it snappy?"

"I should like to do them *all*," she answered quietly, "I'm sure I can do them very fast. I'm a rapid writer."

"Well, I'll try ya till noon on it, but ef ya don't get enough done I'll havta get a helper. Mike, take that card outta the winder, an' stick it up on the shelf awhile. We might want it again."

So Margaret hung her hat on a nail by the window in the dusty back end of the shop, and sat down under a green shaded lamp before a stack of envelopes. The pen wasn't very good, and the envelopes were cheap, the list was long and the surroundings were unspeakably dreary, but Margaret was exceedingly thankful. She had escaped from no telling what peril that threatened, and she had a job! It was barely enough to keep her, and it was obviously temporary, but she was glad.

By tens she laid the addressed envelopes in long lines about her on the desk, till they presently began to assemble into hundreds, and when the desk was full she stopped and folded circulars and filled them.

Now and then one man or the other would walk by her,

pause to watch her flying pen, scan thoughtfully the piles of finished envelopes that were growing on the counter beside the desk. There was no doubt but that this new girl they had hired could work rapidly.

But as it came toward noon the tense work was beginning to tell on her. She felt strength running from the tips of her fingers, she felt a deathly faintness stealing over her. The memory of her breakfast became very dim. This was the time that Nurse Gowen had brought her the glass of orange juice yesterday and the day before, but she must not think of that.

At noon she drank two full glasses of water, thankful that water was free, and went on with her work.

On through the afternoon she worked, a giddy faintness beginning to take hold of her. She felt shaky whenever she rose to gather up the finished work and stack it on the counter, but her hand, gripped in a nervous tension, held steadily on its way, though it ached unbearably whenever she released her hold on the pen for a moment. Could she make it? Could she keep on till night? She knew she was working on her nerve alone. She found herself praying in her heart.

"Oh, God, keep me from fainting again. Oh God, help me through!"

At half past five the men began to put up the shutters and put on their coats.

The old man came over to the desk and surveyed with satisfaction the great stack of finished work.

"You've worked good!" he said nodding his approval. "I guess you'll make the grade without a helper ef you can keep it up a day ur so longer. You better go home an' get yer dinner now."

Margaret looked up with a weary smile.

"Could you—," she began hesitantly, "*would* you be willing to let me have just a little money *tonight*?" she asked. "I have been out of work for several days."

The man eyed her keenly.

"Sure you'll come back tamorra? I wouldn't wantta break in a new hand. I gotta get these out right away."

"Oh, yes, I'll come back," said Margaret, wondering what he would think if she should be unable to come and somebody else would pick her up and take her to a hospital.

"Fifty cents do ya?"

"Oh, yes, thank you!" she said.

He flung a fifty cent piece down on the desk beside her half reluctantly. "It ain't my custom ta pay till the work's done," he said grudgingly, "but seein' you done pretty good I'll chance it. Now, tamorra I'll have the stamps here an' we'll mail these, see, an' then get another batch off in the afternoon mail. Ef you work as good the next two days as you done today, there's a dollar bonus in it fer ya, see?"

The color flooded into Margaret's pale cheeks. It was so humiliating to be groveling for a dollar bonus. To have a man suspecting that she might not return! But she tried to answer meekly, "Thank you," put on her brave little red-feathered hat and went out into the dark street, gripping her fifty cents in one hand and her thin pocketbook in the other. Somehow it never occurred to her to put her money into the pocketbook. She knew she must use some of it at once, or collapse, and she hurried down the dusky street, searching for a cheap restaurant.

A bowl of soup, a cup of coffee. It didn't cost so much! She looked wistfully at the change. If only she could find a cheap bed and have a good night's sleep, but she must have breakfast. There was barely enough left for a meagre breakfast and perhaps a sandwich to eat at noon. She mustn't indulge in a bed. The railroad station would do tonight.

So she dropped the few small coins into the inner pocket of her purse, never noticing now thick the pocket containing the letter from her grandmother had grown since last she saw it, and hurried away to the station.

She found a corner in the big outer waiting room, a bit sheltered from the glaring lights, and sat down, resting her head back and sleeping fitfully for a couple of hours. Then a wedding party breezed in hilariously and filled the station with clamor and merriment.

Margaret watched them a few minutes wearily, noted the happy look on the bride's face, the pride on the bridegroom's face, wondered how it would be to be riding away on a wedding trip, joyous, light-hearted and free, no worries about money, someone to care for you always, someone to love you and protect you!

She tried to banish the thought of Sterling and the look on his face when she had thanked him for the flowers, tried to realize that he was false, and had deceived her. But somehow sleep had banished those facts and brought back the vision of his kindness only, the heavenly plans he had suggested. She let her weary mind revel for a little in the thought of what it would have been if it had all been true. A lovely second floor room for herself, an office right downstairs in the house where she boarded! A man to work for such as Sterling had seemed to be, a chance to earn a good salary, and perhaps be able to get together enough to save the old farm for Grandfather and Grandmother! Ah, that would have been heaven below. If there only were men such as Sterling had almost succeeded in making her believe he was, what joy it would be to live!

Then suddenly she became aware of a burly policeman who kept walking back and forth, looking in her direction, and panic seized her. She knew it was against the law for vagrants to hang around a railroad station. She must not stay here too long.

She started up and looked at the big clock, noted that it was almost midnight. The wedding party had trailed off to the train shed. She could hear their gay voices laughing, she could hear them singing jolly scraps of songs, and laughing again. She could see the path of rice and rose leaves that lingered in their wake. She got up and followed out to the train shed, for now an offical was calling out a local train and she went as if in answer to the call.

Out in the train shed she mingled with the crowd for a little and then found her way back by another door, and entered the Ladies' Waiting Room.

There were not so many people in here and it was quieter. She sat for a long time behind a big post, anxious lest that policeman should trace her. Finally she went into the inner room and found a rocking chair unoccupied. That was a great rest, almost as good as lying down. The couch was occupied by a woman with a little baby in her arms, both sound asleep, but about two o'clock the porteress came and touched her on the shoulder, told her that her train was called, and she arose hastily and hurried away. Then Margaret with a furtive look around slipped into her place on the couch and stretched her weary limbs out straight. Ah, how good this was! She thought of the hospital bed she had left so hastily that morning, its clean sweet sheets, the roses on the little bedside stand, like the roses the bride had carried to her wedding train, and she drifted off into deep sleep. By and by it came about that the wedding procession was coming back, only strangely enough

99

she was the bride, and Sterling was the bridegroom, looking at her in that tender way he had looked when he told her he thought his mother would have liked him to send her the flowers, and her tired heart thrilled with the joy and peace of it, till suddenly the head nurse came with a broom and drove them all away, filling her with chagrin and humiliation, and she awoke suddenly to find the porteress tapping her on the shoulder. She looked up out of a haze of pain and loss and sleep not knowing where she was.

"There is a sick woman being brought in," said the porteress. "She was taken sick on the train. Would you mind getting up and letting them put her here? She is having a heart attack!"

Margaret arose quickly and found the early dawn was stealing in at the windows. The woman was brought in looking ghastly in the mingled light of night and morning. Margaret hurried into the wash room and dashed cold water in her face. She felt sick and sore from head to foot. Every muscle and nerve was crying out for rest and relief, but she remembered her job and took heart of hope.

She went out again and sat in one of the rocking chairs with her eyes closed till morning was fully come and it was time to go and hunt a cheap little excuse for a breakfast.

For three days and nights Margaret went on in this way, with only broken scraps of sleep here and there in some public place, working with superhuman energy in the daytime, driving herself in spite of weakness and pain and faintness, eating the least that any human being could get along with and live and work, and at the end of the third day she finished the last envelope, stamped the last stack of circulars, and looked up to see her employer standing before her with a few grimy bills in his hand.

"You done good!" he said. "Here's the rest of your money what you ain't had, and your bonus. We got no more use for you just now. Any time you come around and see that card in the winder you come in. You're sure of a job. But we ain't got no more use fer no helper till after the orders come in. Maybe we need some help then. You stick around oncet in a while. See?"

Margaret saw, and her heart sank. She had begun to hope that this was permanent at least until she could find something better. Still, she was glad to get a little money and there was always Hope stalking ahead of the way.

Wearily she put on her hat and went out. It had turned cold and she shivered in her little fall jacket that matched her suit. She turned the scanty collar up around her neck, and bent her head to the sharp wind that went through her like a knife. It was almost dark and she felt as if she just must have a real bed tonight. She must go somewhere and think it out. Perhaps that Traveler's Aid woman she had read about in the framed certificate on the wall of the station could help her to find a cheap respectable bed. She would try her. They had lodging houses for men where you could get a bed and coffee for a quarter. She had read about them. Did they have places for destitute women also? It seemed terrible for a daughter of a fine old New England family to have come to a place of need like this, but she just must save what she had and make it go as far as she could. There was no telling how long it would take to locate another job. But first she must go to the post office. There would surely be a letter from home. There hadn't been time to go and she had been too tired to make the extra effort since she came out of the hospital.

So Margaret went to the postoffice and found a letter from home. She cried all the way back to the station in the darkness of the street over the joy of just holding the envelope that she knew the precious old hand of her grandmother had touched.

She sat down in a rocking chair in the Ladies' Waiting Room and read her letter before she even stopped to get the food which she needed so much.

"My precious girl":   [said the letter]

"We are in great distress because we have not heard from you in five whole days. At least I am in distress. Your grandfather says he is not worried. He thinks you are very busy. He says we must trust you with God, and I do, only somehow I am so hungry for word from you. We do hope you are not sick or anything. And it is rather hard not knowing just where you are located. When you wrote and said you were thinking of moving to another boarding place and told us to send your letters to the General Delivery, I thought right away, what if you should get sick, and we wouldn't know where to come to you. But of

101

course you will let us know soon. I am just writing this to tell you how much we want to hear from you. So if you have written on your regular day and something happened that it went astray please write another line right off to let us know you are all right, and where you are staying, because it is dreadful to me not knowing your right address. Perhaps you better telegraph it, only that would cost so much more. No, if you are all right, just write a postal card. I'll wait. I know I'm a silly old fool worrying about you when we have such a wonderful God. But you're the only child we have left you know.

"And now I'll have to tell you some bad news. I didn't want to tell you, but your grandfather said you would be hurt if we didn't, and he says it's all right, anyway, that God knows what He is doing, and it will be all for the best.

"You see Elias Horner came in the other evening and told us he had to have his money. Not just the interest, but the *whole* mortgage money that we borrowed a few years ago. It comes due just after Thanksgiving and I guess there isn't any way out of it. Of course your grandfather has written to an old friend who used to know a lot about mortgages, to find out if there is any way we could get a new mortgage with someone else. But he isn't counting on it much. He's been going ahead planning just as if we'd lost the farm.

"We had figured that we could sell the furniture—you know a lot of it is real old and is said to be worth a good deal of money. And the farm implements ought to bring something. And then there is Sukey. Of course your grandfather really isn't strong enough to milk her himself any more, and he won't let me try. A man has offered thirty dollars for her. It doesn't seem much, but every little counts.

"We thought if we could get together a thousand dollars perhaps Elias Horner would accept that now and let the mortgage run another year or two.

"But if he won't, and if we lose it, why we thought perhaps we would just go down the mountain and find some place where they would board us for what we could do this winter. I'm still able to cook, and your grandfather can do clerical work. He writes a beautiful hand, and even

102

if we weren't able to sell our things for much we'd get along. So you're not to worry. He thinks his friend Elihu Martin will let him keep books in his hardware store. Of course he couldn't pay much because he hasn't much business in the winter. But they might let us have a room in return for what he could do, and then I could bake bread and cake and things and make out to get the little we need to eat.

"So we are quite cheerful about it now. And I'm just writing to suggest that perhaps if you would speak to some of the rich ladies that come into your office sometimes, perhaps you could get them interested in buying some of the old furniture. You know that old walnut chest is over two hundred years old and really ought to be worth something."

Margaret suddenly stopped reading, put her head down and sobbed softly into her two hands, thankful that there was so much noise in the station that no one could hear her.

Presently she summoned strength to brush away the tears and read the rest of her letter.

There was a paragraph of loving trust and resignation, and then down at the bottom in fine hasty writing a postscript.

"Your Grandfather just said that he feels there might be just a possibility that Elias might weaken and let us have a little longer time on paying the mortgage if we could be sure of having the whole of the interest in hand the day it is due. He thinks he can get together enough all but twenty-five dollars, and he is wondering if you would have any way of getting that other twenty-five by Thanksgiving? Perhaps your office will let you have a little in advance just for once? Let us know what you think.

"Your loving grandmother,
Rebecca Lorimer."

Eventually Margaret got control of herself, but not until she had decided to spend some of her precious money to send a telegram. She ought to have written before. It was dreadful to let them wait so long and be anxious, but she had been in such a frenzy to get those awful envelopes finished that she hadn't

103

had time. Besides there hadn't been any paper or envelope or stamp or pen or anything. Well, there wasn't now either, and if she bought all those necessities to a letter it would cost almost as much as a telegram, and then wouldn't reach home for two days, because one always had to allow for someone to go down the mountain to the village to bring up the mail.

So she walked steadily to the telegraph desk and wrote out her telegram. It had to be abrupt but they would understand.

"New job. Awfully busy. Depend on me money Thanksgiving. Lovingly.

Margaret."

She paid for the message and turned away somewhat relieved in mind. They would get it sometime tomorrow and it would set their fears at rest. But where was she to get the twenty-five dollars?

She counted over in her mind the few dollars she had just been paid, well knowing the least amount she could live upon, remembering that the sixty cents she had just paid for that telegram would have kept her almost two days, living as she had been doing, yet was glad she had sent it. But now she must get a real job somehow. And to that end she must have at least one good night's rest. So she went to the Traveler's Aid and asked questions, discovering a place where she could get a clean bed for thirty-five cents.

She stopped at a drug store on the way and got a cup of hot soup and a sandwich, realizing that when she had paid for her bed nearly two of her precious hard-earned dollars would be gone.

Her heart sank as she hurried down the street toward the sleeping quarters. She had relieved the minds of her dear family for the moment, and had fed and housed herself for the night, but she was in a desperate situation. Great walls seemed to be rising on every side about her and closing in to crush her to death. What was she to do? Twenty-five dollars! Twenty-five dollars! Where could she get it? She had had the effrontery to promise to send it in time and how was she to get it? She counted the days to Thanksgiving. There would be no way to get it but to ask her Grandfather's God! And how *could* God give it to her? There seemed no human means. Did God ever really nowadays use any other? There were no miracles now as in the Bible times. One had to depend on human means. How silly she had been to think that handsome young Sterling had been God's miracle to care for her and lead her to a job!

She sighed deeply as she entered the clean bare precincts of the charity dormitories. Twenty-five dollars! Twenty-five dollars!

She paused inside the warm entrance hall to slip her grandmother's letter into the little compartment with the other letter she knew was there, patted it tenderly, choked back a sob, strapped it in with the other, and went in to the desk to apply for a bed.

11

GREGORY STERLING looked down upon that little jeweled hand on his arm and something protective flared in his heart. He looked up at the flabby Mortie triumphantly. He was needed here to shelter Alice from these half-drunken people. Poor little Alice! She had never been half taught. He would get her away from them presently and bring her home and try to dissuade her from this sort of thing. He remembered their beautiful intimate dinner, and looked down at her again, her face turned in profile there against his shoulder. What did that remind him of?

There had been another face quite recently, turned thus against his shoulder, closer than this, white and sweet and fragile in its beauty. Margaret! Involuntarily he drew back just a fraction and looked at this beautiful painted face. Somehow it did not belong there. Somehow it gave him a start. What was it like? Those red lips, glaringly red under the bright light of the vestibule chandelier?

Ah! Those girls on the train. Those girls who had advised him to go and get his hair cut! Those fresh uncouth girls! How he disliked their memory. They had dogged his steps on the train, come through and tried to find him more than once.

The day he had his hair cut by the barber on the train they had spied him again. He had forgotten all about them and

105

taken a walk to the front end of the train. He had seen them too late to turn back. They were sprawled over their seats in various stages of afternoon naps, their kinked hair in disorder, their bright dresses creased and soiled with travel, their painted faces smeary, one red mouth wide open. He walked by them in disgust. When he returned from the front of the train they were just coming awake and recognized him. The one in red called out chummily to him as he went by, "Good old boy! Got 'em cut after all, didn't ya?" And the one in blue had added in a high falsetto, "It looks just *darling*, Buddie!" He remembered that now, and recalled how Alice had called him darling! Then it was a kind of nomenclature of the present day, a thing they had in common, Alice and these girls of the lower class.

He had been angry with himself for having put himself in their way again and strode on back to his place without a glance in reply. An hour later when the train stopped to change engines and make some slight repair, most of the passengers alighted to stretch tired limbs walking up and down the platform, or partake of the refreshments offered at the little wayside booth. He had gone out to walk with the rest and had suddenly found himself surrounded by these girls all clamoring at once.

"Be a good sport and stake us to a soda over there at the counter! We're parching for a drink!" shouted the red one.

"I want ginger ale!" cried the blue one.

"I'm simply dying for a chocolate ice-cream soda," said the third.

Greg had surveyed their eagerness with disgust, then moved by a kind of pitying contempt he marched over to the counter, tossed a bill to one of the busy waiters behind the counter saying,

"There, Buddie, give these girls what they want and keep the change!" and then turning strode away, back to the train.

The three had looked after him disappointed, a blankness coming over their eagerness.

"Gosh! Can you beat it?" he heard the red one call in dismay. "I can't get his number, can you?"

A half hour later when he was sitting quietly reading the paper he had purchased at the newsstand, he heard a bubble of laughter in chorus emerge from the front end of his car, and stealing a quick glance over his paper he caught a glimmer of

106

red and blue and green. Although he was a young man acquainted with emergencies, used to stalking wild animals, never swerving in critical times, he crouched low behind his paper as a screen and vanished from his seat, to the wash room, before they had even discovered his identity. They had been all too evidently hunting for him, to thank him perhaps, or compel further intimacy. He had heard them later bubbling noisily by, calling out fresh remarks to the passengers, making their conversation most public. He could hear fragments of their talk outside the heavy green curtains of the men's compartment.

"He mebbe got off at that station. He mebbe waited for another train."

"Aw, guess again. He's on board all rightie. He's jus' tryin' to give us the slip."

And then nothing daunted they had the audacity to stop the conductor who happened to be passing and question him. They stopped just outside the men's compartment to do it.

"Say, we're lookin' for a young fella in khaki, looks like a cowboy. We wanta thank him for something he did fer us. He didn't get off at that last station, did he?"

The conductor looked at them amusedly, a mask upon his face.

"I really couldn't say," he answered noncommittally.

"Aw, think a minute. You know who we mean," said the one in red, Greg knew her voice by this time. "Looks like a regular guy. Got a cartridge belt on, and boots. You've noticed him, you know you have. You couldn't help it. He looks diffrunt."

"I may have noticed him," said the conductor in a disinterested tone, "but I can't say what's become of him. I can't keep track of every passenger."

"Aw shucks!" said the girl in blue as they reluctantly gave up the search and drifted back to their own car.

A moment later the conductor parted the green curtains and stood in the doorway sending a swift glance about the little room and letting his eyes rest upon Sterling for one quizzical instant. But Greg did not lift his eyes from his paper, nor relax the studied frown on his face, and with a quickly suppressed smile the conductor passed on his way again.

Greg stayed in the men's compartment until time to retire and went to sleep at last behind his own curtains glad that they were due to arrive in Chicago the next morning.

So now as he stood there with Alice's jeweled hand upon his arm, he remembered it, and a sudden likeness in her face to those girls flashed upon him.

Of course it was ridiculous. Those had been cheap common girls without refinement, tawdrily dressed, crudely painted; and Alice was exquisite in every detail, the make-up so perfectly applied, and yet she reminded him of them, and a certain shock came to him with the recognition. Refined, educated, exquisitely garbed as Alice was she yet resembled somehow those girls, those dreadful girls! Or *was* she refined? He didn't know. He honestly didn't. His mother didn't use to think she was refined as a girl, but he had thought her wrong. If he had asked himself that question at the dinner table he would have unhesitatingly said she was, but since her friends had come into the picture there had been something about her that grated upon his finer senses, and now as he looked down at those red, red lips, that confident alluring face so near his shoulder, she looked like those other girls! So utterly unlike the girl he had taken to the hospital! The girl who had run away from him because a nurse had insinuated that he was not respectable. The girl who even now might be in some kind of peril and he not there to help!

Suddenly he felt as he had felt when those girls had asked him to treat them. Then as suddenly with all the ease and nonchalance with which he had flung that bill to the soda clerk and told him to treat them and keep the change, he lifted the lady's hand from his arm and held it out to Mortie.

"With all appreciation of the honor you would put upon me," he said to Alice, "I must forego the pleasure. This gentleman I believe has prior claim, and I have a duty in another direction. I will bid you good evening—Alice!"

Then with a slight inclination of his head toward the others of the party who had not noticed him until now, he went out the door and left them.

He heard a clamor of exclamation behind him, partly subdued by the opening and closing and reopening of the apartment door.

"Oh, *Alice!* Alice *darling!* You got it in the neck that time!" shouted one hilarious feminine voice. "You thought you had someone to pay your gambling debts, didn't you, darling? But you thought too soon!" And then a perfect avalanche of laughter gurgled after him and re-echoed down the corridor as

108

he stepped into the elevator and dropped to the level below out of sound of it.

Greg stepped gravely forth from the elevator and out into the night, the hot blood burning in his cheeks.

So that was Alice! His old sweetheart!

And he had almost been caught by her wiles!

If it had not been for her little bright painted lips so like those crude painted lips on the train, if it had not been for the memory of that other girl, so sweet and white and frail against his shoulder, he might have yielded. He recognized suddenly in himself a weakness toward the old Alice, toward what he had thought was her womanhood and beauty. A weakness that was pregnable to her wiles.

Yet now as he thought of her silly laugh, that had come after she had had a drink or two, of the way she let that cur of a Mortie hover about her with flattery, his heart was hot with anger and shame.

Was there in every man a tendency toward degradation? He had always been doubtful about the story of man's fall as his mother had taught him from the Bible. He had always felt that Adam was worse than most men, yielding in that easy way to temptation. He had always as a boy felt that if he had been in Adam's place, and had really seen and talked with God, that he never would have sinned. Adam was just a poor fish, that was all, and not a self-respecting man at all. He had looked upon him as a forefather of whom to be ashamed, and one with whom he had nothing in common. Now he suddenly began to suspect that there were possibilities of sin and weakness in himself, and that somehow, by some power beyond his own, he had been hedged about by thoughts and memories, or by his mother's prayers, or even by his mother herself as guardian angel, showing him his danger.

Alice! Lovely Alice, with her divorces, and her tearful confidences, her delicate fragile startling beauty! And then Alice with her wine glasses and her men friends and her drinking, smoking women friends! Alice with *gambling debts!*

So that was what she wanted of him!

Somehow she had learned that he had money? How could she? Well, sooner or later she would. But Alice was not for him.

His business for the present anyway, was to find that other

girl who had been flung across his path when he entered his home town, and now was gone, and was perhaps in peril.

So back to the hotel he went.

"A letter in your box, Mr. Sterling," said the night clerk as Greg passed toward the elevator.

Greg turned with eagerness. A letter? Who could be writing him a letter?

As he went up in the elevator he studied it. It bore a Virginia postmark. That would be from his friend Steele. What an experience after all these years of loneliness to have a letter! His heart warmed, although he owned to himself that he had hoped just a little that it might be some word from Margaret. But of course that would be absurd. She didn't know his address, wouldn't know where to hunt for him unless she went back to the nurse to get it. Of course it was conceivable that she might find the money, suspect that he had put it there, and come back or write back to thank him. But he didn't remember that she had been told where he stayed. Unless perhaps she had gone back for her things and her landlady had given her the word he left for her. But she was probably gone out of his life forever, he thought sadly, as he fitted his key into the lock and switched on his light. Then he settled down to read his letter.

"Dear Brother," [it read]

"You don't know how glad I was to get your card bearing your address, and to know that we really are to be lasting friends, for now I can find you, and write you, and perhaps come to see you, and hope to have you visit me sometime. I find I was a bit afraid you would forget the man who traveled with you on the way toward the east, and think of him as a mere passing acquaintance. And to tell you the truth that would have been a great disappointment, for I found my heart was knit close to yours and I did not want to lose you.

"But I am especially glad just now that I know where you are for it happens that I found a letter here when I got home asking me to come to your city and address a Bible Conference that is to be held there this very week. They are paying my expenses so that the journey is financially possible for me and I am as eager as a boy to know if you

110

are to be free and I may hope to see you some of the time
while I am there? I expect to arrive Tuesday morning at
eight o'clock and am enclosing the address of the Conference where mail will reach me. Perhaps you will let me
know what time of day you are at leisure? In any event I
shall call up your hotel as soon as I know where I am to be
placed, and find out when we can meet.

"I have been praying about you every day, and I do
long to see you again.

> "Your friend,
> Rhoderick Steele."

When Greg had read that letter through twice he sent a
telegram to Steele's train. He had learned that trick on his own
trip east, having witnessed the arrival of messages to travelers.

> "Greatly rejoiced at your coming. Please arrange to be
> my guest while you stay. I need you, and am at your
> service in any way. Have important matters to talk over
> with you. Will meet your train.

> > "Gregory Sterling."

That night Greg had the first full night's sleep since
Margaret disappeared.

The two young men were like two boys when they met the
next morning. Greg had never had a man friend since his High
School days and he was overjoyed to find this man just as
thrilling as he had remembered him. So many things and
people had been disappointing that he had found himself
looking forward to this meeting anxiously, but the anxiety fled
in the light of Rhoderick Steele's smile and strong warm
handclasp.

They went in a taxi to the hotel. Steele called up the
committee who had invited him, learned what were his
appointments, and then they went down to a late breakfast, for
Steele owned up he had only taken a cup of coffee on the train,
and Greg grinned and said he had wakened too late to eat
before he went to the station. So over a good breakfast the two
cemented their friendship again.

"And now," said Steele as they went back upstairs to the

room to talk for awhile before he had to go to his appointment, "what is the matter, and why did you need me, Brother?"

Greg met his smile with a warm rush of emotion. It was so good to have someone to talk over his problems with, someone who seemed to really care.

"Well, I've come to my home town to find the old house all run down, the neighborhood awful, the surroundings changed utterly; to find my old girl that I used to think I cared for, twice divorced and a *mess!* There isn't a thing as I hoped it would be, not a thing as it was. Even my enemies over whom I hoped to triumph are bankrupt or dead or moved away, or else so utterly down and out that I wouldn't have the heart to triumph. And the first night I landed here I had a wonderful girl flung in my path to care for, saw her from my window over there fall off a bench in the park and lie unconscious. I took her to the hospital, and found out ways I could help her, planned to get her a job and put her on her feet again, and then suddenly, through a stupid and very cruel woman who was head nurse, I was misrepresented and she disappeared. I can't find her anywhere, and I happen to know she is in dreadful need. I've got to the place where I don't know what to do, and I needed to talk it over with someone."

The eager eyes of the new friend were watching him sympathetically.

"Tell me all about it!" he said, and Greg began at the beginning and told, not omitting his own decision that he must have some legitimate business himself if he were to help the girl, and his own perplexity as to what would help most in this strange state of things that since his return to the world he had found existed everywhere.

The young minister held his peace all through the recital, though his eyes lighted wonderfully at the suggestion that Greg wanted to be of use in the present world depression in some way that would really help individuals.

But when Greg had finished his story, even through the account of the dinner with Alice Blair and what followed, Rhoderick Steele asked:

"Have you prayed about it, Brother?"

Greg looked up in surprise, an embarrassed color tinging his cheeks.

"Why no," he said looking down at the floor, and then lifting his eyes frankly to his new friend's face. "No, I hadn't thought of it. To tell the truth I'm not strong on prayer. I don't believe I've prayed much since my mother died."

"Let's pray about it, Brother," said Steele rising and putting a compelling hand on Greg's shoulder, and together they knelt while Steele prayed.

"Oh, God our Father, we thank Thee that we have such a great Father who knows the end from the beginning, and who loves us enough to hear our faintest cry. And now we come to Thee with a great burden. This matter of the little lost girl whom Thou hast placed upon this my brother's heart. It is a mystery and a perplexity to us, but we are glad to remember that it is neither a burden nor a mystery nor a perplexity to Thee! Thou hast made her. Thou lovest her. Thou didst die for her, and Thou knowest just where she is now and what she needs. We would lay our burden down at Thy feet and ask Thee to undertake in the matter for us. If she is in need supply it from Thy great store. If she is sick or frightened or troubled, wilt Thou be beside her in an especial way and comfort her. Most of all wilt Thou reveal Thyself to her so that these hard experiences through which she has been passing will be only a blessing to her and lead her nearer to Thee. And now, if Thou hast anything that my brother Gregory should do in the matter wilt Thou show him just what it is, and relieve his mind about the matter. Help him to trust it all with Thee. It is very plain to me that Thou art for some reason calling to him. Wilt Thou help him to understand that call, and see what it is Thou dost want? And this matter of the business he should enter into with the money Thou hast placed in his hands, wilt Thou open that up and make it also very clear to him. Help him to see it from Thy point of view and not the world's. Help him to understand that it is himself Thou needest, even more than his wealth. Let Thy Spirit draw his spirit to accept Thy Son as his personal Saviour, so that he may know he is saved, may understand that he is born again, and has a right to claim Thy resurrection power and life in whatever he shall try to do for Thee.

"And Lord, we would not forget to pray for that poor soul who has seemingly sold herself to the world. Let Thy Spirit go after her also and strive with her if so be that she too may see Jesus, accept His cleansing blood and be saved eternally. But grant dear Lord that she may have no power to harm my brother Gregory, nor to deceive him nor lure him into the ways of this world. Establish him upon a Rock, dear Lord, the Rock Christ Jesus, so that he cannot be moved though the powers of hell be turned against him.

"And now about this little lost girl, again, dear Lord. Help us to rest the matter entirely with Thee, and not be troubled, but if it be Thy will help Gregory to find her and be the means of relieving her necessity. We ask nothing that is not according to Thy will, but we know that Thou hast put her in Gregory's path through no action of his own, and therefore we feel that Thou dost mean him to help her in some way. So Lord, we leave it all with Thee, and we ask Thee to guide us through the day in every minutest action, and help us not to go a step of our own without looking to Thee. We ask it in the name of Jesus who died for us and for those for whom we are praying."

There were tears in Greg's eyes when he rose from his knees, and it was a minute or two before he could control his voice to speak.

"I wish I knew God like that!" he said at last.

"You may, dear Brother! I have no special influence in heavenly courts more than you can have. It is only through my Jesus who took my sins upon Himself that I dare ask that way. He died for you too. Will you take Him for your Saviour too?"

Greg stood at the window staring out but seeing nothing, thinking very hard, thinking back to the dying man in the train.

"I don't know how to go about it," he said at last in a husky voice.

"Do you believe on Him?"

"My mother brought me up to that belief," he answered hesitantly, "I accepted it more or less tacitly, but I've never done anything about it."

"Well, then do something. There's only one thing to do. Definitely accept Christ as your personal Saviour. You don't have to go into questions of intellectual belief and doubts. Just take Him at His word by a deliberate act. Kneel down and tell Him so, and then go out believing that you are saved because He said you were if you believe on Him. The moment you believe you are born again, and have a right to come to God through your Saviour Christ Jesus and talk to him as we have just been doing. Will you take Him?"

"I will!" said Greg solemnly.

"Then let's tell Him so," said Rhoderick Steele, and down

they both knelt again. So Rhoderick brought Him to the throne and introduced him as it were, and Greg found feeble voice in a few halting words to confirm the simple sweet act which made him a new creature in Christ Jesus.

When they rose again Rhoderick Steele took his hand in a warm grasp, and his own eyes matched Greg's, full of joyful tears.

"Now we are brothers indeed, Gregory!" said Steele. "I rejoice that I was allowed to see this day, and to be with you when you did this most important act of your whole life. I wouldn't have missed it for any pleasure I've ever known."

Steele's face shone as he put his arm about Greg's shoulders, and Greg told shyly how much this new friendship meant to him.

Suddenly the two discovered that it was getting late, and almost time for Steele's address at the conference hall, and they hurried away, Greg feeling for the first time in years that he had a real part in things worth while, a real new interest. He was half afraid to look the fact in the face that he had just taken Christ for His Saviour and pledged himself to a new order of things, yet shyly glad, thrilling every time he thought of it.

So Gregory Sterling went to the first Bible Conference of his life, and heard his friend speak.

But the first words he uttered so gripped Greg's attention that he almost forgot their speaker in amazement over what he was saying. For the man was answering authoritatively the question that had puzzled Greg in the wilderness, on his trip east, and increasingly since he had been living in the city.

"What's wrong with the world?" began Steele. "There are just four things wrong with the world today, four things that are out of place. First, the Jews are out of place. They belong in Palestine according to God's covenant, and they are scattered over the world because of their sin of unbelief. Second, the church is out of place. She belongs in heaven with her Lord Jesus Christ and she is settled down comfortably in this world. Third, the devil is out of place. He should be in the lake of fire and he is the ruling sovereign of this world. Although he is a defeated ruler he is still in office, ruling politics, economics, religion, every phase of life in the world. Fourth, the Lord Jesus Christ is out of place. He has defeated Satan as sovereign, and should be here, king of the earth, but he is still seated on His Father's throne, waiting for His inauguration day. *It will surely come!* And at about the same time the other three wrongs will be righted."

With a keen understanding born of eagerness Greg followed the explanation of Steele's astounding statements. And as he listened something within him seemed to relax. The prodding restless questioning of why, why, why? was satisfied at last. The fact of a majestic spirit ruling the world in opposition to God and His righteousness was sufficient reason for all the turmoil in the world. It gave Greg a strange sense of peace to realize that instead of seething with indignation over injustice, one must expect to take it for granted, and leave with God the responsibility of doing away with it.

Far into the night they sat and talked, and Greg was so stirred that he could scarcely bear to stop talking and go to bed.

It was a precious experience, followed by brief midnight worship together of the two young men, reading from the Word and praying. How Greg treasured the thought of it after his friend was gone.

And when Steele was finally sleeping by his side, Greg lay there thinking. Oh, if he had only known all this in his wilderness home! How it would have helped him through hard days and lonely nights and discouragements and disappointments! And then came the thought, would he have stayed there fighting for land and money and a chance to triumph over enemies and win success in the world when there was all this wonderful news to tell the world, and the world didn't know it? Certainly he would have had to go and tell. He meant to do that now, just as soon as he knew enough about it all to make it clear to others. Just where he would begin he didn't know, but he was ready to yield his life to God's guidance.

Then he thought of Margaret and wondered if she knew.

And so, with a prayer for Margaret he fell asleep.

12

RHODERICK STEELE had stayed three days and Gregory Sterling learned much, and found out how to learn more. In the bookcase of his hotel room was a row of books that his friend had said would be helpful to him, a big Concordance lay on his table beside his Scofield Bible, a commentary simple and clear of construction was at the other end, and several little papers and pamphlets that Greg had acquired at the Bible Conference were scattered about the room.

Greg had been introduced to a book store where such books could be found, and he had secretly sent down to his friend's Virginia address every book he heard him speak of wistfully as one he wanted to get some day.

But Rhoderick Steele's work was done at the conference and he had to get back to his church.

Greg couldn't bear to see him go. He begged him to stay another week and teach him, offered to send down a man to take his place, but Steele said there were some sick people in his parish whom he must see, and he knew his duty called him home.

He in turn tried to take Greg home with him, but Greg shook his head gravely.

"I can't go away," he said, "not till I'm sure Margaret won't need me. If I find her, and find she is well fixed and has no use for me, well then I can come. But not now."

Rhoderick looked at him tenderly.

"You must follow His leading," he said.

On the train he thought of the look in his friend's eyes and said to himself, "I wonder!" and then rested his head back, closed his eyes and began to pray for Greg, and the little lost girl.

Greg turned back to his hotel after seeing his friend off with a strange desolateness upon him. And yet it was not like the loneliness that had been his before Rhoderick came. He had a Saviour, he had a Bible, an utterly new book, and he had been given the key to unlock it. He knew there were wonders hidden there for him for he had had glimpses of some of them. So he went to his room intending to begin his study.

He had not been long at the strange new employment when his telephone rang and there was the voice of Nurse Gowen!

Nurse Gowen had gone back to her hospital work, and was put on a nervous case that required her constant attention. She had not been able to do much to help in the search for Margaret. She had not called up for several days. She had her living to earn of course, and though Greg had paid her more than she felt was right for the brief nursing case, and for the help she had given him the first day of the search, her pride had sent her back to work.

Now her voice was full of eagerness.

"Have you heard anything yet of Miss McLaren?" she asked. "I've had some pretty bad days with this nervous case and couldn't get a chance to get to the phone, but I've been thinking a lot about you and hoping you had found out something."

"Nothing yet," said Greg sadly. "I've sort of given up trying. There wasn't anything else to do, though I did plan to go down to Rodman Street tomorrow and ask again if she had been there. It seems strange that she hasn't gone for her clothes yet. She has the receipt for her back board. She wouldn't have to wait for that."

"Maybe she hasn't discovered it yet. Maybe she didn't understand what you said about putting it in her purse. Where did you put it? In the outer pocket?"

"No, inside with a letter from her grandmother that was in a little strapped compartment. She could easily miss it if she didn't know. By the way, you don't suppose, Miss Gowen, that Miss McLaren could have gone back to her home in Vermont, do you?"

The nurse was quiet for an instant and then she said:

"Well, that's an idea. I don't know why we never thought of that before. That would be the natural place for her to go, wouldn't it? And since she had money in her purse probably she did. But what about her things? It does seem strange that she didn't go for them immediately after you told her her board was paid."

"She's probably afraid of me, don't you see?" said the young man forlornly. "I suppose she's perfectly justified in her feeling after what that nurse must have said. But good night! It doesn't seem as if I could stand it to give this thing up! She never talked to you about where she lived in Vermont, did she? You don't remember the name of the town, or the name of her people do you?"

"Why yes," said Miss Gowen thoughtfully, "she did give me the address. I wrote it down on an old envelope. I told her I ought to have it in case she got worse or anything, and I wrote it down after you left on Sunday afternoon. Now whatever did I do with that envelope? Strange I never thought of that before in all our searching! It must be somewhere among my things. I'll go and look it up right away and call you again. Are you going to be there all the evening?"

"Right here!" said Greg.

Greg sat for the next fifteen minutes trying to put his mind on his study, but found he could not. Finally he put his head down on his book and began to pray:

"Oh, God, let me find her if you don't mind. If it's all right, let me find her and help her! Show me the way."

Suddenly the telephone rang again and he sprang to answer it.

"Well, I've found the address!" said Nurse Gowen.

"Yes?" said Greg, eagerly.

"It's Mrs. John Lorimer, Crystal Lake, Vermont."

"That's all?" asked Greg as he wrote it down.

"Yes, that's all. I'm dreadfully sorry I didn't think of it before."

"Don't worry," said Greg. "I think I'll find her now!" His voice was throbbing with excitement. "I'm not just sure how I ought to go about it, but I think I could telephone them and say she spoke to me about a job and I failed to get her address. That wouldn't startle her grandmother. You know she was terribly afraid I had telegraphed them when she was brought to the hospital."

"Yes, I know," said Nurse Gowen, "but I can't see how it could possibly alarm her, telephoning her that way. I think that's a good idea. Well, I hope you find her. I certainly do. I took an awful liking to that little girl. She was sweet! Well, I must get back to my patient now, but let me know if you get any news, and if there's anything further I can do just call me up."

"I will!" said Greg, eager to have her off the wire. "Thank you so much for getting the address. Good night."

119

Greg lost no time in getting long distance and putting in his call for the Lorimers of Crystal Lake. While he was waiting to be called back he thought of what he would say, wording it most carefully lest he alarm the good old grandmother. It thrilled him to think that in a few minutes he would be speaking with someone near and dear to the girl who had so stirred his interest.

But suddenly the bell rang and he found his heart beating very rapidly as he took up the receiver. Suppose she had gone home and it should be she who answered the telephone? What should he say at once to reassure her?

But it was only the long distance operator talking.

"Are you the party calling Crystal Lake, Vermont, name Lorimer? Well, that telephone has been disconnected."

Dismay entered Greg's heart.

"Are you sure?" he asked eagerly. "Perhaps it's only listed so because the bill wasn't paid. If so I'm willing to pay the bill at once right here at the telephone office in the hotel. This is an emergency call. It is most important!"

"Wait a minute!" said the voice.

Finally came a chief operator, and then a district superintendent, and Greg turned heaven and earth metaphorically speaking to induce the telephone company to annul that disconnection, but all to no purpose. They told him the telephone had been disconnected for six months, and the wires were down.

Then Greg begged to have the number of some neighbor of the Lorimers. But when they asked for the address he could give no street and number, and an hour passed away without his getting anywhere. All the patience and prowess and initiative that he had used in getting possession of his wilderness home and holding on to it, he brought to bear upon that telephone company, but could not get them to give him a number in Crystal Lake unless he knew the name. At last he asked if there wasn't a public telephone office or pay station there. He suggested a drug store, but there was no regular drug store. Finally it was disclosed that there was a telephone located in the postmistress's home, and Greg asked them to give it to him.

There was a moment's delay and then a big loquacious interested voice, tipped with curiosity, twanged vivaciously over the wire.

"Hello!"

"Is this the postmistress at Crystal Lake?" asked Greg hoping his voice did not sound too anxious.

"No, this ain't the postmistress. This is her Aunt Carrie Pettibone. My niece Lyddy Rice is postmistress. I'm just visiting her. I live over the other side of the mountain."

"May I speak with Miss Rice?" asked Greg.

"Why, she ain't here. She's down to the Baptist church."

"When will she be back?"

"Well, I can't exactly say. You see they're having protracted meetings over there, and she goes every night. She was pretty late last night. They had a long winded preacher. He's awful interesting. I'd be there myself if I hadn't sprained my ankle in the woodshed this afternoon, and I'm right hefty on my feet so I had to stay at home tonight. Was there anything I could do for you?"

"Why, I'm not sure, if you're a stranger there."

"Oh, I ain't a stranger. I've lived around here all my life. I was raised down to Crystal. I know everybody in this county."

"Well, then I wonder if you know Mr. and Mrs. Lorimer?"

"I should say I do!" triumphed the voice. "My mother and her mother used ta go ta school together. She was a Russell and they were old settlers round here. I remember I used ta hear my father say they was about the first folks around here that had a fine house. Their house was built over a hundred years ago. Has real oak beams. She inherited it from her folks, Rebecca Lorimer did, and that makes it all the harder for her now ta lose it. You knew they was going ta lose it, didn't ya?"

"Is that so?" said Greg patiently, with a troubled frown. The pencil which he had prepared to take down Margaret's address poised in the air an instant, then wrote "Foreclosure" on the pad beneath his hand.

"Yes, I guess there's no doubt about it! Elias Horner himself is giving out that he's give the Lorimers notice they got ta pay up the whole mortgage this time. It comes due four days after Thanksgiving, and he wants his money. It seems a shame doesn't it? Only three thousand dollars on thirty acres of land and that nice old house she was born in!"

Greg wrote quickly, "Elias Horner" "Three Thousand" "Four days after Thanksgiving" and frowned heavily into the telephone. He was getting more information than he had

121

bargained for, but it was all valuable. It made it all the plainer that Margaret needed him.

"Are you there?" challenged the garrulous voice.

"Yes, I'm here," said Greg.

"Oh, well I thought you mightta cut off. Well, as I was saying, Elias Horner, he's calculating ta make a Resort outta the house and the lake. The folks down in the village, some of them likes it and some of them don't. Of course it'll bring a lotta trade ta the store, and mebbe raise the price of land, but the settlers around here don't care fer having their ways broke up. They've lived here mostly a good many years just like the Lorimers. Mebbe I shouldn't have mentioned their troubles. My niece thinks I talk too much, but you asking for them made me remember about the mortgage. What was it you wanted ta know about the Lorimers?"

"Why, I wanted to speak with one or the other of them if I could. They tell me at the exchange that their telephone has been disconnected."

"Yes, that happened several months ago. About the time Mr. Pettibone's father passed away. I remember we had ta send somebody up the mountain ta tell them about it, them being old neighbors for so many years, only four miles apart, but the valley between of course. It makes it unhandy in these days not having telephones, especially in winter, but what can ya do when ya can't afford it? The Lorimers certainly have been hard up since the bank went up. They lost every cent they had, and they was counted well off in these parts."

"Well, I wonder if you could tell me," said Greg hopefully, "of someone who lives quite near them who would be likely to be willing to send for them to come to the telephone? You're not near enough are you? I have an important message for them."

"Mercy no," said Aunt Carrie Pettibone. "It's five mile if it's a foot, up the mountain from here. And the onliest neighbor they got at all is Sam Fletcher and he ain't got a phone. He never did have none, and it's a good thing I guess, too, fer his wife would be at it all the time and *never* get her work done. But you said an important message. It ain't any bad news is it? It ain't about Margaret McLaren is it? 'Cause I know they're terrible worried they ain't been hearing from her so often. They're afraid she's sick. They ain't had a letter at all except the telegram that come and hadta be sent up by mail cause

122

there ain't no delivery around here. I guess she musta heard about the foreclosure, cause she telegraphed something about money, that's how I come ta know the date four days after Thanksgiving. You see it come through by telephone and I happened ta answer the phone. I mostly do when I'm here, it saves my niece a lotta trouble. You ain't got bad news for 'em about Margaret, have ya?"

"Oh, no," said Greg, "I merely wanted to inquire her present address. You see she asked me a few days ago about a position, and I promised to get one for her, but I failed to get her present address. I wanted to speak to her grandparents tonight and see where she is so that I can let her know about this opening. I think it will be greatly to her advantage, and she will want to know about it at once. I thought perhaps I could get in touch with her family through another telephone and so find her address and telephone her tonight. I thought the postmistress would know someone near them. Of course I know the postoffice is not allowed to give addresses."

"Yes, that is a rule of course, and my niece Lyddy is awful closemouthed. She took an oath, of course, about their rules and regulations, and she takes it awful serious. So you wouldn't get nothing out of her. But me, I ain't took an oath, and I'm glad ta tell ya what I know, only of course it won't do ya much good as it happens 'cause the last time her folks wrote her they just addressed it 'General Delivery.' I know that fer a fact because I was helping distribute myself the day it come down and I took perticular notice."

"I don't suppose there's any chance you would know whether Miss McLaren may be coming home for Thanksgiving?" he hazarded suddenly.

"She couldn't," said the garrulous voice decidedly. "She wouldn't have the money ta come. They're awful poor. I heard say her gram'ma cried when she went away and said would she ever see her again. And you'd know by the size of the money orders she sends home. Sometimes only two or three dollars. Oh, I'm not *supposed* to know of course, but *I find out!*"

"I see. Well, thank you," said Greg. "I guess I'll just have to depend on writing. Sorry to have troubled you."

"Now ain't that a pity!" began Aunt Carrie Pettibone, and then stopped disappointed and gazed into the receiver.

"He's hung up!" she said aloud to the postoffice cat! "I declare some folks is hasty. I meant ta tell him she had a new

123

job, but I suppose he'll find that out. I 'spose mebbe he thought the bill was getting too big. He didn't say where he was. It musta been long distance of course. Well, I'm sorry I didn't find out. I didn't even ask his name! Now, how can I ever tell M's Lorimer about it? Well, it's just as well, mebbe. Lyddy might find I'd answered the phone again. It beats me how she thinks mortal woman can set and listen to that bell ring and know someone's on the wire, and not go answer it! I can't figure out why Lyddy don't trust me. I never tell people's private affairs. My mother always usedta say I had the best judgment of any of her children. Well, I suppose that's that! Mercy me, I do wish I'd asked him ef he didn't want I should send a message up ta the Lorimers tamorra. Mebbe he'd a opened up a bit more and left his name and address."

So Aunt Carrie sat down with a thump in the rocking chair that was a little too low for her bulk and her lame ankle, and picking up the county paper which she had filched for the evening from the Fagan post box, went back to her perusal of the county social column which had been interrupted by the telephone ring.

Miles away at the other end of that telephone wire, Greg sat staring at the little tablet he held in his hand, studying over the words he had written down while talking on the telephone. But at least he had learned one thing. Margaret had not yet gone home or this person would have known.

So, there was danger of the Lorimers losing their farm! Not quite two weeks away the time was, and what could he do? Of course he knew their location now, and could go up there and look into things, scrape acquaintance with the old folks perhaps, but would they not resent his intrusion into their affairs? And if he went away suppose that Margaret were to need him here? Oh, where was Margaret? He must find her first. And the time was so short! Not quite two weeks till Thanksgiving.

The trouble seemed suddenly to thicken about him too much for him to bear, and then he thought of his new friend and began to pray again. Some help would come. He was leaving it with God and there would be a way!

Then suddenly he sprang up, went to the desk and wrote rapidly. He had just remembered that he could at least try to communicate with Margaret McLaren through the General

124

Delivery. Perhaps she would be too afraid of him to answer, but at least he could try. So he wrote:

"My dear Miss McLaren:

"I do not blame you for having run away from me since I know what was said to you by that blundering nurse, but I am distressed that I have lost you. I have searched everywhere for you. Please be kind enough to let me prove to you that what you think of me is not true. That head nurse had just returned from her vacation and did not know what had been done in her absence. I am so sorry that you had to bear such a humiliating experience.

"I am hoping also that you will be interested to know that your new job is awaiting your coming. Work is waiting to be done as soon as you come. I would greatly appreciate an immediate reply,

"Very sincerely,
"Gregory Sterling."

Greg addressed his letter and looked at it wistfully.

"I'll mail that the first thing in the morning," he said to himself.

And then he went to bed.

13

GREG had been investigating the qualities of various automobiles for the last few days. Rhoderick Steele had assisted in the discussions. They had even tried out a couple. And one came that next morning for Greg to drive himself.

He was not an amateur driver, for before he went west he had worked as delivery boy after school hours for a couple of years and full time summers driving delivery trucks, and had often made a dollar or two driving ladies' cars for them for an afternoon, so that he took to the wheel quickly again. Somehow it eased his troubled mind that morning to be starting out with a vehicle of his own, not just a chugging taxi panting around corners and always having to be told where to go.

It was a little after nine when he turned into Rodman Street, drew up at the door of Margaret's former boarding place and stopped his engine.

He was just preparing to get out when the door opened and someone came out with a suitcase and two large bundles. He looked out the car window and there she was!

"Margaret!" he called in a strained voice, as if he thought she would get away from him before he could reach her. He sprang out, meeting her half way up the steps.

"Thank God I've found you at last!" he said, taking all three burdens in one hand and laying hold upon her arm gently but firmly with the other hand.

Margaret shrank back and looked up at him.

"Oh," she protested in a small frightened tone, "you mustn't carry those. I can carry them quite easily myself. They are not heavy!"

"They are *very* heavy," he said in a stern voice, "and you *may not* carry them. You are panting now with having carried them so far."

He led her down the steps and to the car, putting the packages in the back seat.

"But what are you doing?" she asked in a distressed voice, her eyes large with trouble. He noticed that there were great deep blue shadows under them.

"I am taking you with me," he said firmly. "I've combed the universe for you and now you've got to come with me and find out the truth. I'm going to show you that I'm not a liar and that I won't harm a hair of your head. After that you can do as you like. If you never want to see me again I'll clear out. It's entirely up to you. But I insist that you first find out the truth about me. I have a right to ask this of you. Get in, please."

His voice was cold and aloof. She gave him another furtive look and spoke in a troubled voice:

"But—I don't think—you are—a liar," she said. "After I had time to think at all I knew there must be *some* explanation. But —you don't understand. There were some terrible things said—"

"Yes, I understand!" said Greg grimly, "I know it all. I don't think there was a thing left out of the account I had. Get in, please!"

Margaret opened her lips to speak, looked into his set face once more and got in, her face very white, her eyes dark pools of uncertainty.

Greg drove very fast, threading his way through traffic skillfully, his face stern. He did not speak nor look at her.

Margaret watched him furtively, one hand gripping the arm of the seat. She wanted to explain, but his manner was so chilly that when she opened her lips to speak the words would not come. She held herself tense as if there were no cushioned seat there to hold her. Her knuckles were white with the strain of her grip. She felt suddenly faint and dizzy and told herself she ought not to have allowed this strange stern man to carry her off. It was the kind of thing her grandmother had always warned her against. And yet, even beneath the sternness, there was something so kind and trustable.

She felt the tears coming to her eyes and drew in her breath to keep them back. And then she noticed that they were drawing up before the hospital entrance!

"Oh, I can't go in there again!" she said shrinking back, her lips set thinly in determination.

Greg shut his own lips hard to hide the quiver that came about them.

"I'm sorry, but it's necessary!" he said.

He stopped the car, got out and came around to open the door for her.

"Your things will be quite safe here. I'll lock the car," he said. "We shall not need to be here long."

There was something aloof yet compelling in his voice and Margaret with a baffled look got out and waited while he locked the car, then went with him like a child who was being punished.

At the door she shrank back again, but he touched her arm lightly as any escort might.

"This way, please!"

He stopped at the desk and said a few words as if he had authority and the girl who was in attendance said "Yes sir," most deferentially.

They went up in the elevator and walked down the hall to the room that Margaret had quitted in such haste more than a week ago.

It was not until they reached the door that she saw the tablet, polished bronze, beautifully inscribed:

In Loving Memory of
MARY RUSSELL STERLING
For strangers in Necessity.
Donated by her son
Gregory Sterling.

Margaret stopped startled and read the words, a look of delight spreading over her astonishment, and then with a light in her eyes as she lifted them, almost a triumph, as if she had found her secret hope to be true, she gave him a rare smile. A smile that went over her face like swift sunshine, coming to its fullness as her gaze met his, lighting its fragile transparency into loveliness.

Gregory watched her with unchanged countenance, watched her as he used to watch a deer he was stalking, not losing an expression, a reaction, however fleeting, yet giving no sign of either displeasure or satisfaction. His look might almost have been called a jealous one, perhaps even a hungry one.

"Oh,—was that there all the time?" asked Margaret.

"No," said Greg still in that cool aloof voice, watching her. "It was put there after you left."

The thoughts and questions were chasing one another over her expressive face, and Greg missed none of them.

Then down the hall, her face chalk white, as white as her rattling linen uniform, came the head nurse. Came as if invisible chains were leading her against her will.

Greg introduced her.

"This is Miss Grandon, Miss McLaren! Miss Grandon, will you kindly tell Miss McLaren when this tablet was put here and why, and then make your apology to her."

Miss Grandon's hard lips were trembling nervously as she began to speak:

"Miss McLaren, I owe you an apology!" She tried to speak humbly as she knew was required of her by the institution, but her soul had been too long frozen and self-centred and an edge of haughtiness crept in.

"The arrangement about this room was made during my brief vacation and I had not been informed about it when I came on duty that morning," she said in her most frigid manner. "The tablet was put up about three quarters of an hour after you left, Miss McLaren, and that was the first intimation I had of it officially. It had been promised early that morning it seems, to be erected before you left the room so that you could see it. Before I left I had given orders that the room be put in readiness for an old patient who had engaged that room especially and I naturally supposed that someone had been usurping authority. And when you owned to me, Miss McLaren, that you were paying nothing for the room and felt that you belonged in the ward, I am not so much to blame perhaps for taking you at your word. There are so many impostors going about today—"

"I beg your pardon, Miss Grandon," interrupted Greg, "I believe you were going to *apologize*."

"Oh, it is not necessary in the least," said Margaret.

The head nurse swept Greg a look of bitter servitude and spoke quickly:

"I was just going to say, Miss McLaren, that I apologize most humbly for having made the mistake that I did, and I certainly am sorry if anything that I said caused you any annoyance. I am sure you will understand that in an institution like this, one meets with all sorts of emergencies, and one is not always infallible in judgment. I hope you will pardon my seeming discourtesy."

"Please don't think of it again," said Margaret regally. "I'm sure you were no more to blame than I was for being here. I hope you will forget it."

Greg could not keep a bit of satisfaction, of admiration from his eyes then as he watched Margaret. She had managed to show by tone and manner that she was a lady born, in spite of her shabby garments.

Greg did not keep her there long. He was dimly aware of nurses in the offing, peering around corners, opening casual doors into the hall. For it had not taken long for word to get around that the pretty little lost patient had been found and that "Grandon was getting hers."

Greg escorted her back to the elevator as if she had been a princess, and Margaret held her tired little head high and walked coolly away with such an air of unconsciousness that no one had time to study out her shabbiness, and even the little down-trodden shoes stepped daintily for the occasion. The shabby suit and the brave little feathered hat were royal apparel for the time being.

129

Gravely Greg took her to the office and showed her copies of the papers that had to do with the transaction of the room, saying little himself except to ask the young woman in charge to show the documents.

Gravely he took her out to the car again and put her in, and she, recognizing that the hospital steps, and the street in front, were no place for an argument, submitted to his courteous leading.

Seated in the car at last he turned to her, his keen gray eyes searching her face.

"Now, where were you going when I met you?"

Margaret started and flushed confusedly.

"Oh, you can just set me down on the avenue over there," she answered evasively.

"Meaning that you can then escape from me and never see me any more? Is that the idea?" His eyes were upon her compelling her to look up.

"No!" said Margaret earnestly, "not at all. I am not trying to run away. I am deeply grateful to you for all you have done for me and some day I would like to be able to repay your kindness in some way. But I do not want to be a further burden to you who have already done altogether too much for me. And while we are speaking of it I want to thank you—"

But Greg put up a protesting hand.

"Please, will you let that wait just a little till we have settled one or two matters? Won't you tell me where you were going?"

Margaret looked down at her hands folded in her lap and fumbled the fingers of her gloves, smoothing them out and trying to make them look less shabby. He saw that she did not want to answer him, but he kept his gaze on her until she had to lift her honest eyes to his face once more.

"I was going to the station."

He considered that a moment gravely.

"Were you by any chance about to go home to your people?" he asked.

"No!" she said quickly, "no, I couldn't do that. Not now! I wish it were possible, but it isn't. I've got to stay here and work."

"May I be so inquisitive as to ask why you were going to the station then? Were you moving to another city or to a suburb?"

"No," said Margaret, and then after another hesitation, "I was going to check my things till I could look up another room somewhere. You can check several things together for ten cents. You see I never discovered the receipt you had put in my grandmother's letter, nor the money, that wonderful twenty-five dollars, until this morning, and I went right away to get my things. I needed them badly, and wanted to get them out of that woman's house. Oh, you *must* let me thank you for that money! I really can't wait! You don't know how I had prayed for just twenty-five dollars! I needed it *so much!* And when I opened that pocket to look up the date of Grandmother's last letter there it was, just in my time of need! Some day I hope I can repay you, but until then I shall never cease to thank you for it."

"But," said Greg, "you don't mean you didn't discover it until this morning? Why, how did you live? Wait, let us get out of this noisy street somewhere where we can talk in peace. What time is it? When did you eat last? Did you have any breakfast? Answer me honestly. I thought not!" he said looking into her telltale eyes. "We'll go to a nice quiet place and have a breakfast luncheon. I'm starved myself."

"Oh, you mustn't do any more for me!" said the girl as he whirled the car around a corner and into another street, winding his way skillfully through traffic as he used to do with his delivery truck ten years ago.

"Why not?" said Greg gravely.

Margaret gave a hysterical little laugh.

"Don't try to answer till we get out of this bedlam," he said and whirled around another corner barely escaping a yellow taxi.

It was a quiet dignified tea room on the outskirts of the city where he brought up at last, with space to park the car safely, and an air of gentility about it that rested Margaret's sorrowful soul. She loved pretty quiet things and places. She loved peace and cleanliness and order, and she had seen so little of any of them during her stay in this great city!

He found a table in a secluded corner and there were little white pompon chrysanthemums in a slender brown vase standing at one side against the wall, and a great painted screen of bronze and green that shut them in from the rest of the room. The spicy fragrance of the flowers came like a reviving breeze to Margaret's senses. And there was warmth from a big fireplace near enough to send its glow around their screen. Margaret shivered deliciously as the warmth pervaded

131

her chilled body and brought a degree of comfort. Greg's keen eyes noted the shiver, and took account of the thin little jacket she was wearing.

"Now, first of all, what are we going to have? What do you want?"

"Just something simple," answered the girl resting back in her chair and taking in the beauty of the room like a soothing drink, "something hot, a cup of soup if it's not too expensive here."

"Is that what you've been living on?" he asked with another grave appraising look.

"Well, I didn't always have as much as that," she laughed. "Sometimes soup, sometimes coffee, seldom both." She was trying to make light of it.

"I think I'll do the ordering," said Greg, "this is my party. Do you like clam chowder, or would you rather have beef boullion for a start? We'll save the fruit cup till afterwards I guess. It's cold stuff to be putting inside, a day like this, when we're both hungry."

He made out his order at last, and when the waitress had gone to fill it he sat back and looked at her.

"Now," said he looking straight into her eyes, "if you only found the twenty-five dollars this morning what in the world have you been living on all this time? I know you hadn't another cent in that purse when you left the hospital."

Margaret flushed defensively, a bit of pride rising in her.

"Oh, I found a job for a while. It wasn't permanent, but I earned enough to keep me."

"What kind of a job?" asked Greg. "Perhaps you think I have no business to ask such questions, and I haven't of course, but I've been a good deal concerned about you since I lost you and I was somewhat comforted thinking you had that money to keep you for a little while. Of course if you don't want to answer my questions you don't have to."

"I don't mind answering," she said, lifting tired eyes and trying to smile, "only I don't want you to feel you have to worry about me. I got a job addressing envelopes. I did them by the hundred so it was up to me how much I earned, and I worked early and late and got seven dollars in all out of it." She lifted her head proudly.

"Seven dollars!" he exclaimed aghast. "But where—how

132

could you get along on that in a city? It's been some time since you disappeared."

He began to count the days on his fingers.

"I don't see how you could possibly get along on that unless you found a boarding place where they would trust you."

Margaret shook her head, and then lifting her eyes to his told him, half defiantly:

"Three nights I stayed in the station. There was a couch in the Ladies' Waiting Room and sometimes I got a chance at that, and there were rocking chairs. It wasn't bad. There are two stations you know. I moved about occasionally so I would not be noticed and asked to move on. Then I found a place where I could get a nice clean bed and coffee in the morning for thirty-five cents, and ten cents extra for a shower. That was better. And in the daytime I hunted for another job."

"But you must have had scarcely anything left for food," said Greg. "I've had some pretty tough times myself but I could always go out and shoot something. You can't do that in a city."

"I got along," said Margaret with a show of cheerfulness. "It would have been all right if I hadn't been worried. Even when it got down to the last two dimes last night I wouldn't have minded if I hadn't needed that twenty-five dollars so badly to send to Grandfather for the interest on the mortgage. You see Grandmother had written that they could raise all the interest but twenty-five dollars, and they were a little afraid the man who had the mortgage might foreclose if they failed to pay it on time. And last night I prayed and prayed, and I guess I didn't really expect I'd get any answer. I didn't see how God could possibly give me twenty-five dollars. And then when I opened that little bill pocket in my purse to get out Grandmother's last letter and be sure just what day she said they must have it, there was the twenty-five dollars, and the receipt for my room rent beside it! I just got down on my knees beside that cot in the dormitory and thanked God. It was the most wonderful thing that ever happened to me! And I can never get done thanking you for it."

"I guess I ought to thank God for letting me do it!" said Greg thoughtfully.

Margaret looked up wonderingly.

"I went out and sent the twenty-five dollars to Grandfather," she went on, "and then I went right away to Rodman Street to get my things. I wanted some clean clothes. You don't know how terrible it was getting on without clean things!"

Greg's eyes kindled sympathetically.

"But were you really going to spend ten cents to check your things when you had only twenty cents left in the world?" he asked. "Why, you would have only ten cents left for breakfast!"

"That would have been quite a lot for me!" she laughed. "But as it happened I wouldn't have had but seven left. You can get a peanut butter sandwich for five cents, and you can sometimes get an apple or a banana for two cents if you are not too particular."

She laughed gaily, though her wan expression quite betrayed her mirth, and the young man was wrapped in a deep sadness for her.

But the waitress appeared at that moment with the steaming cup of broth and there was no time for words. When she was gone Greg spoke.

"Well, I guess you're the bravest person I ever met."

"Oh, no," said Margaret drawing in a deep breath of the savory odor and picking up her spoon daintily, "I was never brave. When you *have* to do a thing it isn't brave. It's just that you have to."

"You are *brave!*" said Greg quietly as if that settled it.

They had finished the soup and the roast chicken with its accompaniments and were waiting now for the dessert that Greg had insisted on ordering against Margaret's earnest protest that they had had already far more than was needful for one meal. Greg suddenly leaned forward.

"I think perhaps I should introduce myself," he said seriously. "There seems to be nobody else to do it, and we don't want to have any more misunderstandings."

Margaret looked up with a smile.

"My father died when I was a little kid," he said. "He was a teacher, and there wasn't much money left. Mother died just after I got through high school and I went out west and took up some land. She was a good mother and I've tried to stick to the principles she taught me. I had to work too hard, and was too far out away from everybody to get into much mischief anyway. I worked like a hyena and fought to keep my land. And then suddenly just like a miracle I struck oil on my land, sold out and came east to try and live like other folks. This was my home town. I was lonesome. I landed here a few minutes

134

before I saw you fall off that park bench! I haven't done much since but hunt you. That's the story. Now, do you mind telling me where you were going after you parked your baggage at the station?"

Margaret flushed but gave him her steady honest gaze.

"Well, I was going to hunt another job and then get a cheap room," she owned.

"But you *have* a job," he told her. "I've been waiting to get to work till you got back, and I want to start at once. Unless of course you don't think I'm good enough to work for."

"Oh!" said Margaret, her eyes filling with tears, "I think you're wonderful. After all you have done for me how could I think otherwise? Of course I'll work for you if you've really got some genuine work for me to do."

"I have!" said Greg with satisfaction. "I have an office and I have work waiting. Some of it is parked on the floor ready to be taken care of right this minute, but the first thing that's got to be done is to buy a desk and some fixings for the office. It's just bare empty room now."

"We could use a box for a desk until you have time to buy the furniture," said the girl, her eyes kindling with interest. "I'm used to working anywhere."

"No, we're going to do this thing right!" said Greg. "You're going to make out a list of everything an office needs, everything down to typewriter, paper and pens and then you and I are going out to purchase them. That is, I'll go along if you don't mind. The picking them out is part of your work. I'm not up in those things yet. But first, you're going to have a good night's rest and get rid of those dark shadows under your eyes. Great Scott! I don't see how you think you can work if you don't take care of yourself!"

A shadow passed over the girl's face.

"I did the best I could," she said.

"Yes, I know," said Greg hastily, "I'm sorry I said that. But now you're going to have things so you can look out for yourself a little better. And just incidentally, you don't need to look for a room unless you want to. Your room's been engaged and a month's rent paid in advance, dating from the day you lighted out from the hospital."

"Oh!" said Margaret aghast, "how dreadful! You paying rent for nothing all this time!"

135

"Don't worry about that. I wanted to make sure and hold it till you came to see if it suited you."

"*Suited* me!" she exclaimed, "I'm not out trying to get suited!" she laughed with bitter gaiety.

"Well, will you go and look at it now? It's the place Nurse Gowen told us about. It's in the same house with the office and seemed quite attractive. I thought it would be easier for you than having to run out in the rain or snow. Mrs. Harris is a very nice little old lady and everything is clean as a pin. She will board you, too, and the nurse seemed to think that would be nice. You can try it out anyway, and if you don't like it you can find something better at your leisure."

Margaret looked troubled.

"It isn't a question of finding something better. It's a question of being able to pay for *anything,*" she said. "If it's nice I'm sure I couldn't afford it. And anyway, if it's a nice place I'm not fit to go to it. You can see just how shabby and disheveled I am. Any decent landlady wouldn't take me in looking this way. I'm a perfect tramp!"

"You don't look that way to me," he said, "but I can get your point and of course you know better than I. Equally of course you have got to be fittingly dressed. I had thought you might need some money just at the start and I arranged to give you your first month's salary in advance. I brought it along."

He put his hand in his pocket, brought out a roll of bills and tossed it down on the table before her. To the poverty-stricken girl it looked like a million dollars, a great roll! She drew back with almost anguish in her eyes.

"Oh, I can't take money before I have earned it!" she exclaimed.

"But you've got to be prepared for your work. Call it an investment, or a loan, or whatever makes you feel most comfortable, but I thought salary was best. Then when the month is over it's all paid and you don't have to think anything about it again."

"But I couldn't possibly earn all that in a month!" said Margaret.

"Wait till you see!" said Greg. "It's only what I offered you when you were in the hospital. You've got to pay your board you know. I went around to the different places of business and asked about salaries for the different work I want you to do, and then I added them all together and divided by the number of activities and this was the result. It's the salary I've decided to pay to whoever becomes my secretary. If you can't do the work right I'll promise to tell you, and if you want to leave at any time it's entirely up to you. Isn't that fair enough? You're not bound in any way."

"You're trying to be good to me!" said Margaret, her eyes downcast, her lips quivering.

"If I were would that be such a crime?" he asked half sadly. "I only wish I could help you somehow! But please remember I am being good to myself at the same time. I believe myself to be getting just the kind of secretary and assistant in my new business that I need. Now, will you please put that money in your purse? I think that waitress is coming back with the change and she might not understand it."

Margaret gathered the money into safe keeping at once.

"But I'm sure it isn't right for me to take this," she said dubiously.

"I'm sure it is!" said Greg, and got up from his seat.

As he swung into his handsome overcoat he gave a troubled glance at Margaret again in her little thin suit jacket.

"There's one thing," he said when they were back in the car, "you've got to go and get yourself a good thick coat with fur on it. All the women have fur on their coats and you need it to keep you warm today! I can see you are shivering this minute. That's the first thing you ought to buy. If you'd just get a good coat and put it on you could go to your boarding place right away and rest, and get the other things you need tomorrow. Can't you do that?"

Margaret looked doubtful.

"I have a coat at the pawnshop," she said. "I could get that out and do very well. It isn't grand and it has no fur, but I'm not used to fur nowadays. If you would just take back all this money except enough to get my coat out—they only loaned me three dollars on it—and enough to buy a decent pair of shoes, I could do very well until I have earned the money."

"No," said Greg, "I will not have you scrimping along that way. I want you to have the right things and begin right. You know people will come in the office, and you've got to feel comfortable to meet them. I've learned that clothes make a difference to some people. I'll tell you some day how I learned it. And I want you to buy that coat right away. It's got to be a good one too. It pays to buy good material well cut. I learned that out in Chicago one day. Come, now, will you be good and go and buy it? Because I warn you, I'll buy it if you don't. You'll be down with penumonia next thing if you don't have it, and I can't afford to wait any longer for my new secretary. And you haven't got one cent too much money. In fact I think you'll probably need a lot more before you get started right, and there's plenty more where this came from if you do."

"You are wonderful!" said Margaret. "It doesn't seem right at all. But if it really has to do with being presentable for your business I'll do as you say."

"Good girl!" said Greg as he drew up before the entrance of a large department store. "Now, I guess you can get what you want in here, can't you? Suppose I park right over there and wait for you. Don't hurry. I have a book in my pocket I want to read."

14

WHEN Margaret came out of the store she wore a lovely thick brown coat with a great beaver collar. Greg saw her at once and was satisfied. How pretty she looked! He was as pleased as if he had something new himself.

"Say, that's a corker!" he said, as she got into the car.

"I'm glad you like it," said Margaret smiling demurely. "And it was a bargain. Thirty-nine fifty! I never saw such a lovely coat at that price before. They were having a sale."

"You're sure it's all right?" he asked anxiously, putting out a tentative finger and feeling of the material. "It's warm enough, is it?"

"It's wonderful!" said the girl with her eyes shining. "I haven't been so warm in years."

"And you're sure there isn't anything wrong with it? It isn't out of style or hasn't any damaged spots or anything? There's usually something wrong with bargains, isn't there?"

"Oh, no," said Margaret wisely, "they have sales now and then to attract people to the store, and they usually have a leading special that is really a bargain. I've had to watch for bargains so I know."

"Well, it's a peach!" he said, relapsing into the vernacular of his school days. "Say, that makes you look like a princess!"

The color came into Margaret's cheeks and her eyes were starry with pleasure. Greg suddenly grew embarrassed. He had to be careful saying things like that to this girl. She might run away again. He must watch his ways. She wasn't like those girls in the train. She was a lady.

"You like it, do you?" he asked in a sphere tone, "you didn't just go and buy it because it was a bargain?"

"I love it!" said Margaret. "I never dreamed of having such a marvelous coat! Not for years and years anyway." She was like a child in her pleasure.

"But you are very tired," he said. "You are going straight home and lie down. Promise me! Or I shan't let you work tomorrow!"

"I could work some this afternoon," she assured him seriously.

"No," he said sternly. "You're going to lie down till dinner time."

"Dinner!" said Margaret, "after such a meal as you ordered!"

"Dinner," said Greg sternly. "You must learn to eat three meals a day. Now, here we are. I hope you'll be comfortable."

Margaret was suddenly silent with awe, looking up at the big old brownstone mansion that had become a rooming house in its old age.

"Comfortable!" she said. "Comfortable? Well, I should hope! But I never expected anything so grand!"

"I guess it used to be grand," said Greg as he stopped the car and helped her out.

The little old lady who came to the door had white wavy hair combed down over her ears, and wore a gray wool dress with white collar and cuffs. She looked as if she came out of a book of long ago. She welcomed Margaret primly.

"Another package of books came for you this morning, Mr. Sterling," she said turning with great deference toward Greg.

"Oh, that's good! Then we can get to work soon. Step this way, Miss McLaren, and see what you think of the offices."

He took out a bunch of keys, unlocked the door to his right, and Margaret stepped into the big old double parlors and looked around.

"What delightful office rooms!" she said, secretly contrasting the stately walls of the beautiful old rooms with the low-ceilinged, dirty, cobwebby place where she had addressed envelopes a few days ago. What wonderful lot had befallen her to be allowed to work in a place like this!

Mrs. Harris beamed upon them with tiny dignity and was most deferential.

"I'm glad you've come, Miss McLaren," she said, "it'll be company for me. There's nobody else in the house but the boy that's taking care of the furnace to help himself through college, and he mostly isn't here. It's been real lonesome!"

Margaret had to blink to keep sudden tears from coming into her eyes. To think of anybody but her own family feeling that way about her coming.

"Oh, you make me think of my grandmother!" she said suddenly, and Greg turned and gave Mrs. Harris a quick keen glance.

"Well, that's nice," said the landlady. "Now what time would it suit you to have dinner? We can arrange meals within reason to accommodate your hours at present. You are the only boarder I have yet."

"Please don't change your habits," said Margaret. "For the present at least it will make no difference to me. Unless Mr. Sterling might want me for some reason."

"There might be an occasional day when Miss McLaren would have duties that would keep her," said Greg in a business-like tone, "but she could always let you know in plenty of time I should think."

Then Mrs. Harris took her boarder up to her room, a large second floor back sitting-and-bedroom, nobly furnished in old walnut with a bath adjoining. A wide bay window looked out into a court at the back as clean as the inside of the house. There were handsome well preserved old lace curtains at the windows and some pots of scarlet geraniums on the window seat. A canary hung from a long hook in the middle window.

"I left Dick in here till you came," apologized the old lady. "He's always been here and he likes the sunshine, but I can take him down in the kitchen just as well. He's lots of company."

"Let him stay here," said Margaret. "I'd love him, unless you'll miss him yourself."

"Well, we'll see," said the old lady. "Now, you'll find towels and soap in the bath room, and I guess everything is here you need. If you want anything else you can just let me know. I'll run down and get the dinner started."

When Greg came upstairs with the baggage he found his new secretary standing by the bird cage with tears in her eyes.

"What's the matter?" he asked in alarm setting down his burden and coming over to her. "Don't you like it? You don't have to stay here if you don't like it you know."

He cast a swift look about the room to see what could have disturbed her.

"*Like* it!" said Margaret, brushing away the tears and bringing forth a bright smile. "It's just like heaven! I was just thinking it couldn't possibly be me. It must be a dream and I will wake up pretty soon and find it isn't so!"

"Oh!" laughed Greg greatly relieved. "Well, you can see you need a good rest or you wouldn't be crying about being in heaven! Now I'm leaving you—and don't waste any time getting started on a good sleep. Can I open your suitcase for you?"

"Oh, no!" laughed Margaret, "it opens all too easily of itself. It had a rheumatic catch. I'm surprised it stayed shut so long!"

"Well, then I'll be seeing you tomorrow morning. About what time? Would nine o'clock be too early? And oh, yes, here's my telephone number if you need to call me for anything. Now, can I depend upon you not to run away before I come again?"

"I give you my word of honor I will stay right here till you come."

"All right, Casabianca," he grinned, "I'll absolve you from that in case of a burning deck, nothing else. But suppose you give me your hand on that."

Laughingly she put her hand in his and he went away thinking what a little soft hand it was! He remembered about it all the way home, the pleasantness of having a little hand like that in his.

He didn't even remember that Alice had small soft hands also.

When he was gone Margaret took off her hat, hung up her new coat, and went fluttering around her new abode. All this room for herself! What luxury!

She opened her baggage and put away the few things that were usable, realizing in this palatial surrounding how pitifully old and worn her things were. She had pawned the best of her

141

wardrobe long ago, and it had been scanty in the first place. Well, she was glad that she had bought the little brown crêpe. It hadn't taken a minute to try it on and it was so very cheap. She would put it on tonight for dinner, and yes, wear it tomorrow. Her suit really wasn't fit to use even for work until it was cleaned. Then as soon as there was a chance she would buy another cheap little dress or two, just so that she would not disgrace her employer. After that she would save and send home all she could. Oh, if she could only do something to save the old house! Well, she mustn't think about it. She would pray that God would touch Elias Horner's heart and make him willing for them to have a year or two longer to pay in. Anyway, she was rejoiced that she had sent that twenty-five dollars that morning! And to think of having all that roll of bills after buying a coat and dress and shoes! It was marvelous!

So Margaret put away her few things, took a hot bath and lay down.

She came up from the far depths when the silver bell rang for dinner, flew into her new brown dress with a couple of motions, smoothed her hair and went shyly downstairs. Somehow she felt like an invited guest instead of a boarder.

She marveled at herself that she could eat another meal, but she did. Everything was delicious. A delightful soup of chicken and rice, a chop and a baked potato, stewed tomatoes cooked with onion and celery the way Grandmother made them, and seasoned with plenty of sugar and pepper and salt. A piece of translucent apple pie and a neat square of velvety cheese! Well, there was no question but that she was going to be well fed if she stayed here!

When Greg came at nine o'clock she had her list ready, made out in neat rows under different headings. "Furniture," "Machines," "Stationery." She had forgotten nothing from a filing cabinet to a pencil sharpener. There were a few things which she had marked with a question mark. For example the manifolding apparatus. Did her new employer need to manifold anything? How could she be sure about anything without knowing more of the business?

But Greg was delighted. He ordered them all, with no exception. "We might need it in a hurry some day. Better get it," he answered to every questionable article.

They made a full day of it, having told Mrs. Harris that Margaret would not be at home to lunch. They lunched in a

142

small tea room in the shopping district and worked over their shopping list while they waited, discussing the different makes of typewriters, the different kinds of carbon paper and pens, the best kind of filing cabinet for their purpose.

But Margaret's pleasure came when they chose rugs and chairs for the offices.

"It wouldn't be necessary to have rugs," said Margaret practically. "The rooms have lovely hardwood floors, and an office doesn't need to be furnished like a parlor, unless you want to make it luxurious."

"I think I do," said Greg thoughtfully. "I've never had much of that sort of thing. I have a notion it's an asset in some ways to have things beautiful and restful. I had a couch once. I always meant to get it a new cover. It's too late now, but I think I'll have some leather-covered chairs instead. Big deep ones. I've been to two or three really fine offices this last week, and I'd like to have a room like them. I have a notion we could work better."

So Margaret reveled in lovely old oriental rugs, and finally selected two Serapis, lovely in soft pastel blendings of old blue and coral and jade and white. The leather chairs they chose were dark blue and deep with comfort. There were two desks, one for the front room for Greg, one for the back room for Margaret.

"And when I'm not here you will sit in the front room and receive any callers," he said. "The back room will be for work of course."

So the desk for the back room was arranged to drop its typewriter down and out of the dust when not needed, and the desk for the front room was large and polished and had many deep drawers.

The filing cabinets matched the desks, and everything was quite like a dignified office. There were raw silk sash curtains for the windows in deep cream. It did something sweet and satisfying to Margaret's artistic soul to have the pleasure of selecting these things and she went back to her boarding house that night feeling that she had been on a pleasure excursion.

The next day seemed almost like her childhood's anticipation of Christmas with all those packages coming. It was tremendously exciting, meeting the delivery trucks, directing where the things should go. She had a niche in the rooms marked out for each article. Then when they had all come, putting away the paper and pencils in the drawers and cabinets, arranging everything as it should be. It all seemed a lovely dream in which she was moving, everything delightful, if only she had not that pang at her heart about her dear grandparents. She was eating the fat of the land, doing only pleasant things, and they were living mostly on cornmeal mush and—did they even have milk with it now if Sukey was sold?

Then her heart would cry out. Oh, if only this wonderful position had come a little sooner, and she might have saved Sukey! Perhaps too, even the twenty-five dollars had not been enough to make up the necessary interest. Perhaps they had failed in some of their calculations; some of the furniture didn't sell, or the man hadn't paid for the cow yet. She must find out exactly how much she was paying for her board and parcel out her money. Perhaps she might dare to spare five or ten or even twenty more dollars before Thanksgiving, just in case they might need it. Of course she must keep enough on hand in case Mr. Sterling asked her to get something else. He would not like it for her to take the money he expected her to use in clothes and spend it on her relatives, and she must not risk her position even for them, for in the end if this lasted she could help them more abundantly of course.

So she went about arranging the offices, even singing a line of an old song as she polished off the tops of the desks with an old bit of silk from a worn-out slip she had discarded.

Then came Greg breezing in happily, smiling good afternoon. He had been off on some business that morning and came in now with papers and a big bundle under his arm.

But he stopped at the door and exclaimed.

"Say! This is great! I wouldn't have believed it would turn out this way. I couldn't have done it. I wouldn't have known how it would look! And you've even got some of the curtains up! Here, I can help at that!"

He went from one new article to another, admired and touched it. He saw down in all the chairs, felt the leather, delighted in the colors of the rugs.

"I'm going to enjoy these a lot!" he said with his face a glow of pleasure. He was pleased as a child.

Then he turned to Margaret who stood watching him.

"I certainly selected the right assistant," he said with a look that made her glad. "You have made a picture of these rooms.

144

You needn't worry about earning your salary. I'll have to be raising it after people see this, to hold you. The interior decorators will all be after you!"

She took it with a laugh and motioned him to the other room to see how well the filing cabinets fitted into their allotted space.

"But what are we going to put in all these?" she asked. "That's what I want to know."

"Oh, I'll show you!" said Greg.

He went to the big bundle and took out a lot of pamphlets and little paper-covered books.

"These are to put on the shelves in those glass front book cases," he said, "and there'll be more tomorrow. And here is a list. I was fortunate in getting it. It has the names and addresses of all the ministers and churches in the city. We're going to send out some little pamphlets."

"But what is it about?" asked the girl picking up the list. "Is it an advertisement of something you are going to sell?"

"No, not at present. We're going to give these away first, and then if people want more we'll help them get them. They are little books that the world needs. They explain things that are vague in the minds of most people. The world is full of troubled people now, I've discovered. They need to understand about it. I never did till a few days ago, and I want to tell people where they can find out. There they are, look at them. Perhaps you won't understand—unless you've known about it before."

Greg stopped in a muddle of words. He didn't know just how to explain the unique ministry which he had talked over with Rhoderick Steele.

Margaret took up a handful of the little tracts and booklets and examined their titles.

"Why!" she exclaimed, her face lighting up, "these are religious tracts and books!"

"Yes," said Greg looking at her shyly, wondering if she would laugh at him. Alice Blair would laugh, he was sure of that. But this girl was different from Alice Blair. Why! He hadn't thought of Alice Blair in days! "Are you acquainted with things like that?"

"I certainly am!" said Margaret with a ring in her voice. "I've been brought up on things like this. But I didn't know you were a Christian. Anyway not a real one like this! Why this one tells the way to be saved! It's wonderful! I've heard of the man who wrote it. I took a correspondence course in Bible Study once, and he was one of the teachers!"

"That's why you are different then!" said Greg thoughtfully.

"Perhaps that's why you are different yourself!" said Margaret with a great light in her eyes. "Oh, if I had known you knew the Lord Jesus and cared about things like this I wouldn't have been afraid of you ever!"

"I haven't known Him long," said Greg reverently.

Their eyes met and there flashed between them something, a bond that seemed to bring them nearer to one another because of this common interest they had discovered in the things of another world.

"Oh, this is wonderful!" said Margaret. "It's better than all the rest! To think I am going to work for a Christian man, and do real Christian work! It's what I've always wanted to do, but never thought I could because I have to help my dear family. But, Mr. Sterling, how are you going to make it pay? You can't really make money selling things like these can you? At least there must be a very small profit in it."

"I'm not trying to make money," said Greg, "I've got enough of that for the present at least, for all I need and a lot over. I've been figuring it out that if other people who have money can afford to retire from business and just travel around the world and play games and buy expensive nothings for a collection or a fad, why couldn't I afford to enjoy my income in the way I please? So, for a little while at least, I'm going to make it my business that a good many people shall know more about how to be saved. I want to make people get interested in the Bible too. Not that I've ever read it much myself, though my mother used to love it, but I've just heard about prophecy, and what wonderful fulfillments are going on in the world today, and I don't believe many people who call themselves Christians really know about it. I think they should, so I'm going to help some of them at least, to know. People are wondering what all this trouble in the world means and I've just found out that the Bible tells, and that if everybody knew that it's all in the Plan, they wouldn't take things so hard."

"Oh, I think that will be marvelous!" said the girl.

"There'll be some other things too, when I get them worked out, or prayed out. I think maybe I can do a little at giving a few people some work. That will be a great deal better than giving them charity. I don't believe in charity when people are able to work. It takes away self-respect and pauperizes them."

"And yet look at all you've done for me!" said Margaret. "And you say you don't believe in charity!"

Greg suddenly grinned.

"That wasn't charity," said Greg, "that was pure selfishness. I just did that to enjoy myself and get a good secretary."

The next day Margaret started in to work in earnest, with piles of envelopes and a long list of addresses, stacks of tracts and little booklets to slip into the envelopes and send out.

Greg was in and out a couple of times during the day, but seemed busy and a trifle distraught. Margaret wondered, but worked on happily, and life seemed settling down into a delightful routine with an ideal employer.

Then the second morning about ten o'clock a smart cream colored car trimmed with lines of scarlet drew up before the house and a startling little lady with golden hair and very red lips got out and came in. She was presently ushered by the disturbed Mrs. Harris into the front office. Mrs. Harris was wondering if she had been mistaken in her renter after all and if this was the kind of visitors he was going to bring to the house. She had distinctly smelt cigarette smoke on the lady's breath as she had let her in. On her *breath*, mind you, not her garments!

Margaret came from the inner office to greet her and was a bit startled also, recognizing the type instantly.

The visitor turned a sharp curious gaze on the secretary and put on her most offensive air.

"Who pray are you?" she asked disagreeably.

Margaret drew herself up sweetly and looked the other woman in the eye.

"I am Miss McLaren, Mr. Sterling's secretary. Is there anything I can do for you?"

"No, certainly not. I wish to see Mr. Sterling. Where is he? In that other room?" and she marched to the arched doorway between the offices and peered behind a handsome leather screen that partly sheltered the other desk.

"Mr. Sterling has not come in yet," said Margaret, ignoring the rudeness and standing just where she had been when the woman entered.

"How soon will he come?" asked the visitor. "Doesn't he have regular hours?"

"I am not sure. He is very busy outside of the office just now. He came in for only a few minutes yesterday. He might come at any minute of course. But—can I give him a message?"

"Of course not!" said the invader, flinging herself into a big chair and taking out her cigarette case. "I'll wait awhile."

Margaret went back to her typewriter in the other room. She was typing a few letters this morning to accompany certain booklets. But she was within range of the lady in the chair who was now smoking languidly and staring around the room. Presently the visitor got up and went over to the desk, pulling open a drawer and peering within. She picked up the booklet on the top, read its title and flung it down.

"Holy Cats!" she exclaimed amusedly, "can you beat it? Greg Sterling! My word!"

Margaret was just arranging carbon paper for a duplication and heard her words and wondered. Was this one of her employer's intimate friends? If not how did she dare go through his desk this way?

For now the visitor was opening every drawer and laughing immoderately.

Ought she to stop her, Margaret wondered? But what harm could she do? As yet there were no private papers in that desk, only Christian literature to be given away. If this person chose to take some she was welcome.

So Margaret held her peace and went on writing, greatly troubled in her heart however to know what standing such a woman as this could have with Gregory Sterling.

But the morning hours went by, and the visitor stayed on, smoking innumerable cigarettes, dropping her ashes on the Serapi rug, tapping her foot in annoyance, and yet staying on. And still Gregory Sterling did not come.

Several times the lady got up from the chair where she was sitting and pranced restlessly around the room examining things in detail, feeling of the quality of silk in the curtains, of the leather of the chairs, turning over the silver desk set to look for the hall mark, even stooping down to look at the rug on the floor, turning the corner of it over to examine the back. Margaret happened to notice that and wondered. She knew that was the way an oriental rug was judged, by the closeness of its knots, the number to a square inch. But even if she was interested in fine old rugs she was rude. One could see that at

148

a glance. Or else she must be a very close friend who felt privileged to do what she pleased here. She couldn't be a relative for he had said he hadn't any living relatives that he knew of.

About half past two, having smoked up all the cigarettes she had with her, the lady went so far as to ask Margaret for some more. Margaret told her courteously that she didn't use them. The visitor looked her up and down contemptuously and said, after a pause, "No, *you* wouldn't!" Then she whirled on her heel and went to the desk, sitting down and taking a sheet of paper out of the drawer. She wrote rapidly for a minute, and then flinging the pen down on the blotter took an abrupt leave.

15

MARGARET had been working steadily all the morning ever since her arrival. She had not stopped for lunch. She did not even like to go across the hall into the dining room. She'd had a feeling that the visitor would examine every nook and cranny if she did, and there were a lot of papers in the back office that she did not want disturbed. Besides, who was this woman? What right had she in here anyway? Mr. Sterling might blame her if she left her alone. So Margaret stayed.

Mrs. Harris had rung the little silver lunch bell and waited five minutes. Finally she opened the door of the back office softly and sighed to Margaret with uplifted brows that lunch was ready. Margaret gave a noiseless signal that she understood but could not come at present, and in a few minutes the good little landlady appeared as silently as a bird might have entered the room, with a nice lunch on a small tray and set it down noiselessly beside Margaret, departing as soundlessly as she had come—a feather could not have trod more lightly —but with an expression on her face that spoke volumes.

Margaret had managed a bite now and then surreptitiously, noiselessly, a bite to chew on, a swallow of the delicious milk, and worked on, making her fingers fly over the keys in constant monotony.

When the lady at last took her leave, and she heard her car

start away from the house, she sat back in her chair and drew a sigh of relief. Then she got up and went into the front office. There on the desk lay the paper the lady had written and without intending to read it her eyes took in at a glance the few words it contained:

"Darling Greg:

"Come for a cosy little dinner tonight at eight entre deux. I need you! Am in awful trouble!

"Love,
Alice."

There it lay in letters so large that anyone coming into the room could not fail to catch its gist. If Mrs. Harris should come in she could not help seeing it!

Margaret went to the window and stood looking out with troubled eyes for a minute trying to think what was her duty. Then she came back, folded the paper and slipped it inside an envelope, laying the envelope on the blotter where Greg would not fail to find it. Now he need not know that she had seen it. Then she went back and finished her cold lunch, eating slowly, thoughtfully, a cloud over her face.

Presently came Mrs. Harris for the tray.

"Well, is she gone at last?" She peered cautiously into the other room and finding it empty stepped through and went and looked out the window. Margaret was glad she had put the note decently into an envelope.

"Yes, she's gone," she said, trying to make her tone casual. She would protect her employer as far as she could.

"Do you know who she is?" Mrs. Harris came back to the inner room.

"No," said Margaret, still brightly casual. "I think somebody perhaps come for advice. Maybe somebody in trouble. She seemed awfully restless."

"Oh," said Mrs. Harris, considering that view, "you don't think then that she's any of his *friends*—or relatives?"

"I shouldn't suppose so," said Margaret, "she doesn't look like his kind."

"Well, I should hope not," said the little old lady setting her lips firmly. "I certainly never had a woman like that in my house! She didn't really look respectable. Such red lips! And those long earrings! She looked outlandish!"

"People do dress that way nowadays," said Margaret thoughtfully. "A great many people do."

"Not *nice* people!" said Mrs. Harris. "All that *paint!* My! I can't see how they can bear themselves! I think they look just grotesque, don't you? You don't wear paint!"

"No, I don't care for it," said Margaret.

"Did you see her car?"

"Why, no! I didn't happen to go to the window. Did she have a nice car?"

"Nice! Well, it wasn't ladylike. It was painted white with a red stripe around it, and it was one of those queer low kind of cars that sporting men drive. I really felt kind of ashamed to have a woman like that coming out of my house and driving away in a car like that. Did she say she was coming again?"

"She didn't say," said Margaret. "She asked when Mr. Sterling was coming back and I told her I didn't know."

"H'm!" said Mrs. Harris. "Well, I'm glad she's gone! Poor thing, you look all beat out! Eating your lunch ¬in that piecemeal way. Well, I sincerely hope she doesn't come again!"

Greg came in about four o'clock. He seemed happy and a bit absent-minded. He sat down and began to read some small books he had brought with him. Margaret told him about the caller, gave him the note, and he looked annoyed.

"How long did you say she stayed? Heavens and earth! Where's that telephone book? Thank you."

He applied himself to the telephone and Margaret vanished into the other room trying to rattle her machine so that she wouldn't hear the conversation. She wondered if she ought to go upstairs for a few minutes and give him privacy. Then she reflected that he could close the doors between the rooms if he so desired. Anyhow she was only a secretary. He probably wouldn't think it mattered what she heard. Perhaps it was just as well she should know what attitude he took toward her so that she would know what to do in case the woman came again.

And then she heard Greg's voice booming out clearly over her machine's clatter.

"That you, Alice? Too bad you had such a long wait this morning, and I'm sorry, but I can't make it to your dinner tonight. You'll have to get somebody else in my place. I've

151

made other arrangements for the evening. No, I can't make it tomorrow evening. You'll have to excuse me. I'm awfully busy these days, and I don't fit into that kind of thing anyway. . . . What's that? . . . No, not then either. . . . I just haven't time for social affairs. . . . No, not possibly! But what is the trouble? Just give me an idea. You aren't sick are you? Nothing happened to your mother or sister? Nobody dead? . . . Oh, money! I see! . . . Debts? What kind of debts? Debts of honor? What does that mean, gambling? . . . Sorry, but I haven't any money to pay anybody's gambling debts. Don't believe in them. It's God's money, not mine, and I can't use it that way. . . . Yes, perhaps I am old-fashioned. I don't mind. . . . What night? Sunday night? No, I'm going to church. . . . Yes, I suppose *that* is old-fashioned too. . . . No, not any night, Alice. I'm a busy working man and can't turn night into day. To tell you the truth I don't like the crowd you run with. They're too speedy for me. And I don't care to go to places where everybody is drinking. It's disgusting to me. . . . No, I haven't changed my ideas on that subject either. . . . What? You're afraid they'll sell you out? Your *friends* sell you out! Seems to me I wouldn't call them friends. . . . Oh, you mean you might lose your apartment? You mean your landlord might *put* you out? Well, I'm not sure but that would be a good thing for you. You know, I think it would be a lot better for you if you went home with your mother. . . . Oh, yes, I know you always used to say you didn't get along, but that's not right either. One only has one mother you know. Listen, Alice! You really oughtn't to be living alone that way. It isn't right, especially in your position. You might be misunderstood. . . . Oh, well, you can laugh, but I'm telling you. . . . You really ought to go home. People would think a lot more of you. . . . All right, you can laugh if you like, but it's the truth. . . ."

Suddenly Margaret heard that sharp peculiar click of the telephone that indicated an angry conversationalist at the other end of the wire had reached her limit and hung up, and then she heard Greg chuckle amusedly and sit back in his chair. When she glanced through into the next room a few minutes later he was deep in his book again, his brows drawn together in concentration.

Margaret went on with her work, an undertone of relief in her mind. Nevertheless she wondered who was this lady to whom he had talked so frankly, obviously admitting a past in which he had known her well. A wild idea that perhaps she had once been his wife and was divorced, came to her. Greg had told her his brief story, but hadn't mentioned any girls. There hadn't been any place in that brief autobiography he had given her in the tea room for any episode of this sort. Had he been merely reassuring her? Yet he seemed so frank. Well, it was none of her business of course how many wives and sweethearts he had. He was only her employer, and as an employer she had no fault to find with him. What did it matter? She would just forget it and do her work and be happy.

But the subject would keep coming back, and troubling her. It wasn't just curiosity. She wanted her Mr. Sterling to be all that he seemed to be.

Of course she knew that there were men who had a great many girl friends of different kinds and thought nothing of it. But a friend like the woman who had been in the office that day was not consistent with his profession of Christianity, or with the unique business he was trying to establish. Still, he couldn't help how old friends turned out of course.

Well, he hadn't gone to her dinner anyway! He had told her plainly that he didn't like her crowd, and wouldn't drink! What more did she, a mere secretary, want to reassure her?

So she tried to put the subject away from her mind.

Mrs. Harris tapped at the door just as dusk was coming down to bring a special delivery letter that had just arrived, and Greg looked up from his book to thank her.

"By the way, Mrs. Harris," he said with a boyish grin, "could you take an extra boarder for dinner tonight? I've got some work I want to do here in the office this evening and a man is coming here about eight o'clock to see me. I don't want to waste the time to go out and get something to eat."

"I certainly can!" said Mrs. Harris in pleased dignity. "We're having a beefsteak and there'll be plenty to go around."

"That sounds good," said Greg with another grin, and went back to his book.

Margaret in the other room paused in her work and wondered.

At dinner he was just like a merry boy, asking for more fried potatoes and string-beans, praising everything on the table, saying a great deal about the strawberry jam which he declared was just like his mother's. Mrs. Harris was immensely pleased.

After dinner Margaret hesitated a moment at the door.

"Shall you need me tonight, Mr. Sterling?" she asked, quite formally.

"No, not tonight, thank you, Miss McLaren!" he said with a pleasant smile. And then looking at her more keenly.

"You'd better get a good rest. You look as if you'd had a hard day."

"Oh, no!" she protested. "I enjoy my work."

As she went upstairs to her room she found that she was a trifle disappointed that she was dismissed this evening. She must deal with herself about this, she told herself severely. He was only an employer, and she was only a secretary. She had been looking on the business with as much interest as if they were partners, and she must just realize that she was a hired servant. That was probably what that dreadful woman had been sent to the office for today, to make her realize that she must guard herself. Her life was such a lonely one that she would be greatly in danger of getting too much interested in a man who had been so kind to her as Sterling had been. She must look out for herself. He was a very attractive man and he didn't seem to be aware of it either. So many were.

So Margaret worked demurely through Saturday, shepherded her thoughts on Sunday, and went back again to her work Monday morning quite rested and refreshed. She had written a long letter to her grandmother. She had been figuring out her necessary expenses, what she must buy to be presentable at her work, how much she could save, and she was overjoyed to find that she would soon be able to give her grandparents quite a substantial sum toward paying the mortgage off. She only wished that she were at home for a few hours that she might find out if they were really getting along all right otherwise. It seemed so awful to have to have them away off there alone. But it must be in God's plan that she should be here. She would trust it to God.

There was no letter from Vermont on Monday morning, and Margaret was grave and a bit sad at her work.

Greg breezed in near noon and told her he had joined a class in a Bible school. He was very enthusiastic about it. He said there was a great deal about the Bible that he never knew he didn't know, and it was going to be great, studying it this way.

154

He couldn't go regularly of course, at least not every day, but he would run in when he could, and study their books between times. He had just come from a class that morning.

He sat down at his desk a few minutes and read his mail, dictated a letter or two in his brief direct style, asked a few questions about some books he had ordered that hadn't arrived, then picked up his hat and overcoat to go out again, and Margaret went back to her typewriter.

"By the way," he said, stepping to her doorway, "I've got to be away for a few days this week. I'm going up to Vermont on business. Just where does your family live? I was wondering if you wouldn't like to drive up with me and spend Thanksgiving with your grandmother! I could drop you at your home and pick you up the day after Thanksgiving, or maybe Saturday if I couldn't get through sooner."

Margaret's hands lifted from the keys of her machine and flew to her heart, her eyes grew large and her face was fairly white with delighted wonder.

"Oh, but I couldn't let you do that for me after all the rest!" she said.

Greg's eyes lingered almost tenderly on her. "Poor little girl," he thought. "She must still be afraid of me!"

"I know," he hastened to say shyly, "I know I'm only a stranger to you still, and perhaps you think it isn't quite the thing for you to take such a long ride with your employer, especially when you haven't known me very well. I'd thought of that and I wondered if you would like someone to go along, a sort of chaperon? Only I wondered where we'd park her until we got ready to go back. Your people might not want anybody else around when they have you only a day or so. They might want you all to themselves. I'd thought of Mrs. Harris. I heard her say once she used to live up in New England. But she told me last night her folks up there are all dead, so of course she couldn't go and visit anybody, and besides she says her niece is to be here with her over Thanksgiving. Then I thought of that Nurse Gowen. We might be able to get her if she's through with that nervous case, but —what would you do with her when we got there?"

"Oh," said Margaret in a little awed voice, "what a simply wonderful thing for you to think of! Why—I—I don't think of you as a stranger, really. But—" Suddenly Margaret's head went down on her two hands that rested on the frame of her

155

typewriter, and for just an instant her shoulders shook. Then she lifted her head and her eyes were all dewy like rain in a sunbeam.

"I know I can't go of course. There are all those circulars to be got off at once! I know I mustn't allow you to do it. But it's just heavenly of you to think of it, and oh, you don't know how much I wish it were possible."

Greg blinked at her perplexed for a minute. He had a wild desire which bewildered him, to take her into his arms and kiss away those tears. But he had never had a desire like that before, not even with Alice. Alice had always been the one who took the initiative in such things and rather embarrassed him.

He wasn't just sure what was Margaret's reason for demurring. Probably she thought it wasn't proper or something. Maybe she still didn't quite trust him. But if she wanted to go as much as that she was *going* if he had to upset heaven and earth to bring it about.

He watched her for a minute wistfully and then a determined look came over his strong jaw and nice pleasant lips, and a sudden cunning to his eyes.

"Just where is your home town?" he began with a politic air. "Here, I've got a road map here somewhere in my drawer!" He swung the upper drawer of his desk open and there it was, quite as if road maps were the only proper thing to keep handy in the top right hand drawer of a man's business desk.

"Come here and let's see how near I'm going to it!" he said flipping the map out on the desk and purposely avoiding Margaret's eyes. He wasn't at all sure she would come. He might have to look up that home town by himself.

But she came, eagerly, surreptitiously mopping away her tears with a little inadequate handkerchief.

They bent over the map together. Margaret placed an accurate finger on the exact spot where Crystal Lake was located, although it wasn't large enough in reality to get its name on the map, but Margaret knew its surroundings and began to point them out, tracing the journey wistfully, as if her mind had often gone that way.

Greg took in the situation at a glance and selected a city at random an inch or so above the spot to which Margaret was pointing.

"It's not so far from Rutland, then, is it?"

"About forty miles away," said Margaret, unsuspecting.

"Well, say, now, that's nice," he said, trying to look innocent. "Because that's where I'm going. I've been looking up the mileage and I figured we could get there in one day, perhaps before dark if we started early enough."

"Oh!" said Margaret, her eyes glowing thoughtfully, wistfully. "And of course it wouldn't be much out of your way," she added gazing down at the map and thinking hard. "You could leave me down in the village at the Pettibone's or the Williamses' for overnight and I could get someone to take me up in the morning. I could probably get a chance to ride up with Sam Fletcher, or if he didn't happen to be down I could easily walk. I've done it many a time. And it would be such fun to walk in on them! They've been worried about me I know. But, I oughtn't to lose so much time here. And I know I oughtn't to let you bother with having me along."

"Say, what bother are you? Why you can keep me from losing my way! I've never been to Vermont in my life and you have. Don't you see I need you? Besides, it's deadly lonesome on a trip like that with no one along."

"But isn't there someone else you ought to take?" asked Margaret fearfully, and then remembered the painted lady and grew shy.

"Not a soul!" said Greg earnestly. Then noticing her hesitation he added artfully: "You see I thought we might combine business and pleasure if you went along, that is if you don't mind working when you're on a pleasure trip. I thought we could work out the wording of those other circulars and also a few important letters I want written. I haven't had the time to think them out, and I thought if you didn't mind we could get those out of the way and then they would be all ready for you to type when we got back."

Margaret's eyes began to sparkle now and her conscience retired beaten.

"Oh, if it's a business trip that's all right," she said. "I certainly won't have any more hesitation or any compunctions if I can be of service. I'll be delighted to go. It's the best surprise I could have."

"All right then, we'll call that settled," he said in a business-like tone. "How about starting tomorrow morning? Would that be too soon? This is Monday. Thanksgiving is Thursday. We'll get there Tuesday night and I could drop you and go on to

Rutland. I'm not sure whether I could finish up my business in one day or not. I'd have to see when I got there. But I'd probably come for you Friday morning, or maybe not till Saturday. You wouldn't mind if you had a day or so longer at home would you?"

She smiled delightedly.

"No, I certainly wouldn't mind," she said.

"I envy you!" he said looking at her like a little hungry boy. "You've got folks, and one likes to have folks on Thanksgiving Day. A holiday doesn't mean a thing when you haven't anybody to share it with."

"Oh," said Margaret with a troubled glance, "wouldn't you, —couldn't you get through, and come back to spend Thanksgiving with us? I know Grandmother and Grandfather would be delighted to have you, and I'd like so much to have them know you. It would make them feel a great deal better about having me off away from them in a strange city if they knew the man I was working for."

"Say! That would be great!" said Greg, grinning delightedly, just as though he hadn't been fishing for an invitation with all the arts he knew. "But perhaps it would upset them terribly to have a stranger coming unannounced."

"No," said Margaret, "it wouldn't upset them. They don't upset. And they would like it. The only thing is, I'm afraid maybe you wouldn't care for it there. It's very plain, and rather lonely up on our mountain. We love it, but others might not. And then—well, you see they haven't very much money and they won't have grand things to eat."

"Say, young lady, what do you think I am? A pampered pet? Don't you know I've subsisted on canned beans and salt pork weeks on end? And don't you know I'm just hankering for a bit of the wild loneliness I left out west? You can't scare me off that way. How about it? Can you get ready to go in the morning? Would five o'clock be too early to start?"

"I'll be ready!" said Margaret joyfully, "but I must finish those letters and get them off before we go."

"Let the letters go hang till we get back!" grinned Greg. "We're going off on a bat and we don't want to be bothered with letters! Anyway the men they're going to don't even know they're going to get them, and they wouldn't read them Thanksgiving Day if they came, so why not mail them next week?"

Margaret laughed gaily.

"You're just like a child tonight!" she said and then checked herself. This was her employer. She mustn't be too free with him.

"Well, let's!" he said and gave her a happy boy's grin again.

"All right!" she answered rising to meet his festive spirit.

"That's great! Now, I'm going out on a few errands. Is there anything I can get for you? Or would you go along?"

Margaret gave swift wistful thought for a moment and then resolutely shook her head.

"No," she said firmly, "I'll stay and get ready."

So he went whistling off down the hall and out the door, and she heard his car drive away. She stood still a minute looking thoughtfully after him, trying to keep her heart from being so wildly happy at the pleasure that was before her. Trying to tell herself that he was only being nice and that it was really a business excursion. She just mustn't think so much about him. She *mustn't!*

Then she went back to her typewriter and made her fingers fly over the keys. He might be willing to have those letters finished next week, but she wasn't. She wouldn't enjoy her outing if she left unfinished work at home.

So before he got back she had them all typed and ready for his signature. And after dinner she hurried breathlessly upstairs to put her small necessities into the old suitcase. For just a moment when he had offered to take her out shopping she had thought wistfully of getting a new suitcase, or bag or something. This one was so shabby. Then she remembered how much her dear family needed money, and she desisted.

But she was happy as she went about her small preparations, and crept into bed at midnight so excited she could hardly sleep. She was going home tomorrow! Would tomorrow never come?

16

IT was still quite dark the next morning at five o'clock when Greg parked his car in front of the house and opened the front door with his latch key. But he found Margaret standing in the hall hatted and cloaked, her little shabby suitcase on the floor by her side and Mrs. Harris just coming from the dining room with a neat box in one hand and a thermos bottle in the other.

"It's just a few chicken sandwiches and a sup of coffee," she said as she extended the two to Greg. "I thought they might come in handy before you get there, for you know she scarcely ate a bite of breakfast. Just drank some juice and took one bite of toast."

"You're not sick, are you, Miss McLaren?" he asked anxiously. "Maybe I shouldn't have asked you to start quite so early."

"No, I'm not one bit sick, Mr. Sterling," she declared. "I'm just so excited about going home I couldn't swallow, that's all. I tried not to disturb Mrs. Harris. I begged her not to get up at all. I could easily have found something myself, but when I stole carefully downstairs I found her here before me."

Greg grinned.

"She's a winner as a boarding house keeper I should say. I didn't find anybody having lost sleep on my account at the hotel. I was told the dining room wasn't open yet and I had to get a bite at an all-night restaurant."

"You don't say!" said Mrs. Harris indignantly, "well you just come right in here and drink this other cup of coffee and eat an egg and some of this nice hot toast. I left it on the top of the toaster to keep hot."

"Thank you, Mrs. Harris, I'll just take a swallow of your wonderful coffee so I can forget what I had at the restaurant. It was awful stuff, bitter as gall. Too bad you had to get up so early, but we're profiting by it all the same."

"Oh, I'm expecting my niece today. I had to get up early anyway to get ready for her."

"As if you weren't always ready," laughed Greg. "Well, I

guess we'll be going along. No thanks! Nothing more to eat. I haven't got any family or home to be going to. I'm taking my fun by proxy you see. But I guess I'm too excited to eat, also. Well, good-bye till Saturday probably. Too bad you couldn't go with us, but we'll be thinking of you when we eat the sandwiches. Thanks for your thoughtfulness."

They went out into the cold crisp morning air and got into the car.

"Would you prefer to take the back seat, Miss McLaren?" asked Greg quite formally. "You could lie down and take another sleep before daylight really comes. Or would you like to sit up front and be chummy?"

"I'll sit up front and be chummy if you don't mind," said Margaret her eyes sparkling. "You don't think I could go to sleep now, do you? Why this is the first time in my life I ever started off for an all-day automobile ride! And you talk about sleeping! I want to see how the stars go to bed, and listen to the world wake up."

"Well, it's the first time in my life too," said Greg. "There's a pair of us. Oh, perhaps I'm mistaken. I used to get up at five to drive the milk delivery truck when I was in high school to make extra money, but that doesn't count."

So Margaret got into the front seat and Greg stowed her suitcase into the back along with a big hamper and his own suitcase, and they started off.

They were out and away from the city before the day began to break faintly. Margaret saw her stars go to bed, one by one, saw the night put out its lights and day creep dimly into the east, and her heart was so happy it seemed almost bursting.

It was a crisp bright morning when the day really got awake, and the road stretched before them like a smooth white ribbon. They were out from the city now and past its suburbs, into the real country, with fields of huddled corn and heaped up pumpkins on every hand, and here and there a gnarled apple tree with a single brown apple hanging by a long stark brown stem. A place of wide spaces, and fallow fields, here and there a space of fall wheat standing out with startling emerald brightness against the frostiness of all the other brown-tinged world. A place of great spreading barns, mostly painted red, and small cosy white houses green-blinded and sheltered by a group of tall elms or pines.

"This is what I like!" said Greg, pointing out a lovely old

white farmhouse that wore a homey look. "There's some space to breathe out here, and it's quiet. I don't know how long I could survive in a city. It didn't used to be that way when I lived in the home town. Things were farther apart and there weren't so many of them."

Margaret's eyes lighted.

"Oh, maybe then you will like my home," she said. "It's very still there. You can hear the trees whisper and hear the clouds go by. When anyone comes driving up the mountain it sounds like an army with banners and we all rush to the window to see who it is. It's an event you know."

"Will they do that when we come?" asked Greg like a little pleased boy who was getting ready a surprise.

"Oh, yes!" said Margaret. "They will. They'll be so surprised. And pleased! This lovely car! I don't think they've ever seen a car like this close by. Of course in the summer we have lots of cars down the mountain where the hotel is, but of late years Grandfather hasn't been going down so much. Not since the old horse got lame. And now he's sold of course, and they don't go down at all. They will be proud to see me riding in such state."

"But if it's night when we get there," said Greg, "they can't see the car. Will they perhaps be frightened?"

"Oh, no," said Margaret, "they are not easily frightened people. They will think it is some stranger perhaps who has lost his way. They will come out with lamps, both of them, and hold them high, and expect to bring any stranger in and offer hot coffee and a place to sleep."

Greg beamed.

"Had you lived there all your life?" he asked wistfully.

"No," said Margaret. "I was born in India. My father and mother were missionaries. They both died of fever when I was only four years old and I was sent home to my mother's parents. They brought me up. I only dimly remember my parents. So my grandmother and grandfather have been everything to me. They moved to Rutland when I was old enough for high school. Before that I was in the country school. Then when I finished high school they sent me away to college. It was very hard for them to spare the money. They had to mortgage the farm. But they've lived up on the mountain in the old farmhouse ever since, and when I was graduated and came home I was so happy to be with them

162

again! But it didn't last long. A little over a year ago the bank where Grandfather had everything closed, and then I had to come to the city to earn something. It's been rather hard to be separated from them now when they're getting old, but they are so sweet about it, and they are going to be so delighted when I come in tonight. It's going to be just wonderful! I feel as if I ought to have some special words in which to thank you for giving me and them this great pleasure."

"Please!" said Greg. "I'm enjoying this as much as you are! You don't know how empty my life has been since my mother died. When I came east I guess I somehow felt there'd be something left of the old life for me to come into, where I'd be happy and contented and could live as I knew my mother would like me to live. But when I went down to our old house —it was the day I'd made up my mind you were lost hopelessly —I found everything gone fluey. I had always thought I'd buy that house and fix it up just as Mother had it and live in it, but there's a boiler factory back of it now, and the noise and dirt and squalor are something fierce. There was even a pig in a pen in the back yard grunting at me, and a lot of dirty squalling children in the front yard, and mud, mud, mud everywhere! Not a spear of our old lawn left! The people on the street all looked dirty and discouraged and slipshod.

"I went down to my old school and sat in my same old desk and tried to feel at home. It looked the same, only everything was grimy from the boiler factory and the other industries that had grown up around. Nothing was the same.

"Then, there was a girl I used to go with in high school. Mother never liked her but I thought Mother didn't understand her. But when I saw her—well, she's a *mess! You* know! She's that girl that came to the office the other day. She ran away and got married but she's been divorced twice since. She's just a mess! That's all there is to say!"

Margaret's spirit suddenly soared aloft.

"So, perhaps you can understand," went on Greg, "how kind of lonely and disappointed I felt till I got this idea of business and doing something worth while in the world. There just wasn't anything to tie to! You see I had a wonderful mother and we used to do a lot of things together, and I've always been lonesome since she died. So it's mighty nice to be going to a real home and seeing people together who love each other and are living a decent life. I know I don't belong there, and I don't intend to hang around a lot and get in the way, but I'm mightly grateful for a little glimpse of home life on Thanksgiving Day at least, if you're sure your folks won't mind having me. I don't suppose there'll be any business I can transact on a holiday."

"Oh, I know they won't mind," said Margaret eagerly. "The only thing is they'll feel badly that they haven't any turkey to offer you. Grandmother has had to give up raising turkeys. She wasn't strong enough to look after them right. They take a lot of coddling you know. But they'll roast some chickens, and Grandmother certainly does make wonderful roast chicken. It's almost as good as turkey. That is if they haven't had to sell the chickens too!" she added soberly.

It occurred to her that they might have had to kill the chickens for their own food lately.

"Oh," said Greg, "you needn't worry about that. I brought along a turkey! I couldn't go out to dinner and not bring something. It's back there in the hamper with a lot of stuff that the man said goes with it. I didn't know but I was carrying coals to New Castle, but it was the only thing I could think of that I could take, and I couldn't just invite myself to a Thanksgiving dinner and not bring something."

"How very wonderful of you!" said Margaret sitting back and drawing a deep breath of relief. That lack of a turkey had been secretly troubling her mind ever since she started. If she could have hoped at four o'clock that morning to find a food shop open she would certainly have gone out and purchased one, but it hadn't occurred to her the night before, and there was no way to get one so early in the morning.

"I think you must be related to a fairy godmother!" she said, her eyes starry. "I never saw anybody with money before who used it in such beautiful ways!"

"I'm glad you're pleased!" said Greg. "I got to thinking maybe you would think I was presumptuous! But of course you didn't have to use the things if you didn't want to. That's why I told you before we got there. If you aren't perfectly sure they won't be offended I can stop at some poor little cottage on the way and leave it, or even sling it out on the road. I wouldn't hurt your people for the world."

"I'm perfectly certain that they will think that the Lord sent it!" said Margaret solemnly.

164

"He did!" said Greg as solemnly. "I asked Him last night what to do about it, and He told me to take it."

"Then why did you ask me?" asked Margaret with a twinkle in her eye, and then they both laughed heartily.

"Well, you see, I'm rather new at praying," explained Greg, "and I wasn't sure that perhaps I had understood the Lord aright. But say, wouldn't this be a good time for those chicken sandwiches? I believe I'm hungry."

Margaret produced the box and the thermos bottle and they had a merry time at the side of the road on the edge of a little grove which was mostly bare branches now, with an evergreen here and there. There were paper cups and plates, and the contents of the box was ample and delicious.

"That Mrs. Harris is a crackerjack cook," said Greg as he finished off with a big piece of Mrs. Harris' spice cake and a large hunk of cheese.

"She certainly is, and she's a wonderful woman. I can't think how it ever fell to my lot to board with her after all the terrible places I've been since I came to the city. Why, when I think of where I stayed last week this time and how I scrimped along hungry all the time, I have to pinch myself to believe it's myself riding along in state today. It doesn't seem possible!"

"And a week ago today I didn't know where you were!" mused Greg. "Gosh, I'm glad I found you! I couldn't forget how sick you looked and how you needed somebody to take care of you! And—I couldn't see going all my life and thinking you thought such rotten things about me!"

Margaret's spirit soared again. He cared what she thought of him! Later she told herself that any decent man would care about having any girl think things like that about him of course. But at the time she was just happy about it and the day seemed bright indeed.

"It was good of you to care!" said Margaret gravely. "I guess if it hadn't been for you I might not have been alive by now. Or at least, maybe I'd have been very sick somewhere in a hospital, nobody knowing where I was. That last morning before I found the twenty-five dollars in my purse I was just about as near desperate as any human being could be. I had prayed twenty-five dollars, and thought twenty-five dollars till I couldn't think of anything else, and I hadn't eaten anything for a whole day. I could hardly topple along the sidewalk and I wasn't in any condition to work if I had found a job. And then when I'd just begun to realize it, after bringing my baggage down from the third story, God sent you! He sent the money and He sent you!"

Greg gave her a look then, a look that went away down deep into her soul, and seemed to come from deep in his soul. And the look was followed by a smile that seemed to enfold her and take her right to his heart. It filled her with a quivering joy, and her conscience flew right up and told her to choke it. Told her it was all her silly little sick imagination and she must not be glad like that for a man who was really a stranger, just an employer, who had done all this for her merely because he was a Christian and wanted to help her, had just been sorry for her, that was all.

The little glad quiver lay down in her heart ashamed, but every time he looked into her eyes it rose up and soared again, and finally she gave up and decided she was having a nervous breakdown or something, and must try to take things as they came along and be glad and not be so self-conscious.

They stopped for lunch early in the afternoon and Greg made her take a rest on the couch in the empty parlor of a country hotel while he went to a garage to have the car looked over.

Late that afternoon they fell to talking about their childhood days, she telling how she used to skate and swim and trudge to school across the mountain, and how on rainy days her grandfather took her to school with the old horse and buggy. Then Greg told little anecdotes of his own boyhood, things he had not thought of for years, precious sweet little memories about how Mother had oyster soup on a cold night when he had been out shoveling sidewalks all the afternoon.

They began to feel as if they had known one another for a long time. They had come into Vermont now and the mountains towered about them. Here and there a little mountain stream rushed away making hurrying melody over great boulders, or cascading down a cut in the hillside. Now and then they came upon a casual railroad rambling out of the dense forest of hemlock and spruce, and into it again on the other side of the road without any warning whatsoever. On and on they went without meeting anyone for an hour or two at a time. Impressive silence reigned.

"I didn't know we had any such vastness unoccupied in the east," said Greg. "And yet they say that there is danger of the world getting over-populated! Plenty of room right here for a good many thousands to live comfortably for several eons to come I should say. It reminds me of the west. I'm glad I came up here. I had a feeling that all the east was one city after another. I guess I need to do a little traveling around my home parts and find out where I'm living. But this is great! I'd like to come up here summers! Yes, and winters too. This would be splendid with snow on the ground and branches."

"It is," said Margaret, wistfully. "It's wonderful at Christmas, with snowshoes. We used to have an old sleigh, too, when I was a child."

"It must have been wonderful! But say, we've come a long way since morning and I believe we're going to get there before dark," said Greg taking a look at the map.

"We are indeed!" said Margaret excitedly. "We're coming into Booker's Corners, and that's only three miles from Crystal, the foot of the mountain where the station and the postoffice are."

"Booker's Corners!" said Greg looking around. "Is that a town?"

Margaret laughed.

"It's a township. There's a schoolhouse on a cross road, a company store and a little station, but people live all about on the mountains, and they come together for school entertainments, and sometimes protracted meetings in the schoolhouse. They have to go to Crystal to church. Here we are. This is Booker's Corners, and this is the Company Store. Take the turn to the right here. There, there's the schoolhouse. Now, it's only three miles to Crystal."

Margaret was watching every tree and familiar turn as they drove through the rough dirt-road into a dense thicket of pines and tall forest trees, some of them still hanging onto their brown dead leaves of summer and rattling them sepulchrally.

"How still it is!" exclaimed Greg. "The motor sounds almost irreverent!"

As they drew near to Crystal Greg was watching the girl by his side. Her eyes were starry with excitement, her cheeks were flushed, her lips were parted with her eagerness.

"There! Now you can see the postoffice. That brick building. After it burned down they built it of brick!" she explained, her voice sweet with interest. "And there! There's somebody just coming out. Oh, why, that's Aunt Carrie Pettibone! What would she say if she knew *I* was in this lovely car! But oh, don't let her see me! She'd never let us go till she had found out everything about us and why we are here. She has eyes like a ferret and a tongue like perpetual motion. She is quite capable of holding us up to find out who we are."

"Aunt Carrie Pettibone!" said Greg with a grin. "How are you, Aunt Carrie!" he called out with a low bow as the car swept on by.

Aunt Carrie, a little shoulder shawl thrown over her bulky shoulders, paused in her progress down the street to Mrs. Silas Manley's house, and stared after the elegant car and the courteous gentleman who had called out her name. Who was he? She couldn't place him. Must be a summer visitor of course, but who? How maddening not to have recognized him in time! Her reputation as a newsmonger was at stake and what should she do? Well, at least whoever she heard of as being in town she could tell how he called out to her.

Margaret was convulsed with laughter.

"Now, she won't sleep all night trying to think out who you are!" she giggled.

"Well, she looks as if she could stand the loss of one night's rest," grinned Greg. "Aunt Carrie Pettibone! She looks like a character!"

"Oh, she is," said Margaret. "She's the world's worst talker. But here, this is our turn. That house up the road there is Elias Horner's. He's supposed to be the richest man in Crystal, and the crookedest. He's cheated everybody he came near all his life. And just beyond in that little white house in the field lives his sister-in-law, Kate Lavette. She used to own the big house he lives in and was left well off when her husband died, but he made her think he could handle her money better than she could, and there she lives in a little shack and he lives in hers. Everybody in town is furious about it, for Kate Lavette is a lovely old lady, but nobody could ever do anything. He got it fixed somehow so he had the law on his side, and he is posing as being very good to her because he lets her live in the shack on her own land that he stole from her."

"Elias Horner!" said Greg thoughtfully. "He must be a charming old egg. I'd like to meet him on a dark night and give him a good trimming!"

"Well, he needs it!" sighed Margaret, "but I expect Providence will have to give it to him. Nobody else has ever beaten him in anything he set out to do."

"Well," said Greg still thoughtfully, "Providence sometimes uses human instruments. Now, is this your mountain? Say, this is a wonderful view. And there's your lake, isn't it, snugged away in that valley? Say, this is a great place! My! I'd like to spend a summer here! Ah! And there's your house! What a view? Why that's worth coming all the way, just that view! And what it must be in summer!"

Margaret's heart swelled with pride and her eyes were starry with joy. It seemed just the nicest thing that could have happened that she should be bringing this best of all possible employers up to see her home and her lake and her view.

And then even while they watched the dear old house grow larger to their approach, till every old-fashioned small-paned window was visible, a light sparkled out in one window.

"They're lighting the lamps!" said Margaret excitedly. "No, it's the lantern! Grandfather must be going out to the barn to milk! See! The door has opened and he has the lantern in his hand. Can't you see it swing? And that other bright spot is the lantern light on the milk pail. Oh, they can't have sold Sukey yet! I wonder—!" her voice trailed off into puzzled silence.

"And who is Sukey?" asked Greg.

"Sukey is the cow," answered Margaret absent-mindedly. "They were selling her for thirty dollars to help pay the interest on the mortgage. But she can't be gone yet—!"

He could see that she could scarcely wait until they reached the house, was scarcely aware how much of the family troubles she was letting out. How pretty she looked in the twilight, her face flaming out clear against the dark background of the woods, the light in her eyes almost like a lamp. How glad she was to get back! His heart turned a bit lonely at the sight. He wished he belonged somewhere.

"Grandmother has come out on the step!" she cried. "She has seen the car and she is watching!"

Then they rounded the curve in the road, came up to the level on which the house was built, and the car stopped.

17

MARGARET was in her grandmother's arms. Greg stood behind by the car and waited, his hat lifted, as if he stood before a holy thing. Grandfather came back from the woodshed, his milk pail in one hand, the lantern in the other. His hearing was still good. He had heard the car. He held the lantern high, so that it shone in Greg's face. He had given one glance at the two women locked in each other's arms, a swift sweep of his eyes over the beautiful shining car, and then his scrutiny went to Greg's face.

Greg sensed that the old gentleman wanted to know what kind of man had brought his precious Margaret home. He knew that his whole history would be ferreted out by that look and he would be held in judgment. Gregory Sterling stood up and took it gravely, like a man, and when it was over he grinned, just a big boy grin, and reaching out took the lantern and the milk pail from the old man's hands.

"Can't I help?" he said. "I'm fine at milking!"

His voice brought Margaret back from her grandmother's embrace to a sense of her duties as hostess.

"Oh, Grandmother, Grandfather," she cried, "I'm so excited I'm forgetting my manners. This is Mr. Gregory Sterling, the man I am working for now. He was coming up this way on business and offered to bring me for Thanksgiving!"

Then the old man and his old wife put on their best smiling dignity and welcomed the young man cordially.

"We are greatly indebted to you!" said the old man.

"I shall be grateful to you forever for bringing her back to me!" said the old lady reaching out her two hands and taking Greg's in a warm clasp.

"It was a pleasure I assure you," said Greg with his nicest smile. "And now, I'll just unload the baggage and then I'll be getting out of your way. It isn't right to break up a family meeting like this with the presence of an outsider."

"We do not count our Margaret's employer an outsider," said the old man with old-time courtliness in his manner that sat graciously upon him even in overalls and a ragged overcoat. "Come in. Come right in the house. Rebecca, my dear, you have no shawl about you. Won't you hasten inside? You know you have had a bad cold and the air is crisp tonight!"

"Yes, please don't stand out here talking. I'll bring the things in. Miss McLaren, do induce your grandmother to go in out of the cold," urged Greg.

Margaret thus roused drew her grandmother inside the house and helped her to light the lamps, stopping every minute or two to exclaim over being at home, and how wonderful it was to see them both. Margaret had lost her head just the least little bit. She wanted to laugh and to cry both at once, and she wanted to tell them how wonderful her Mr. Sterling was, but she couldn't find the words.

It was Greg however who took the initiative. The rest of them were dazed with happiness. He went out to the car and brought in Margaret's suitcase and then the big hamper and set them down in a corner of the kitchen. For it was to the kitchen door they had driven, and it happened that the kitchen was the only place in the great wide house that was warm. The two old people were economizing on fuel. Grandfather couldn't chop wood as well as he used to do, and Sam Fletcher wasn't always available.

"Now," said Greg when he had brought in the baggage, "where's this Sukey cow? My hands are just itching to do some milking again. Please show me the way!"

"Oh, but Father, he mustn't milk in clothes like that! You mustn't let Margaret's employer do the milking!"

"It was not my proposition, Rebecca," said the old man smiling. "It's just being taken out of my hands."

"But I want to milk," said Greg earnestly. "And you needn't be afraid I don't know how. I've milked many a cow. I won't make Sukey cross. She'n I'll be friends in no time. You'll see! Just lead me to her. In fact I believe I can find her without being led!"

"But not in those clothes!" protested the grandmother. "Margaret, he mustn't. He *mustn't*. Get your grandfather's clean overalls! They're in the bottom drawer. You know!"

Margaret flew to do her bidding and returned as Greg was going out the door with the lantern in one hand and the pail in the other, divested only of his hat and coat. She presented him with the overalls and he accepted them with a grin.

"All right," he said, "I'll put them on when I arrive at Sukey," and he threw them over his arm.

Grandfather had taken over the lantern, and was leading the way happily. Somehow it seemed like old times, Margaret home and this nice genial young fellow who was her employer! Just fitting into the home life. Queer, he seemed too young to be employing anybody, but if Margaret said it was so, it was so of course. However, it was just as well he should look him over before he brought him back to the house. Mother would want to know what he thought of him.

The mountain night drew close and shut down about the old farmhouse, with Margaret and her grandmother scurrying about getting supper in the kitchen, and Greg and the grandfather doing the milking and telling funny stories to each other in the barn, much to old Sukey's annoyance, who couldn't understand what all this excitement was about.

"Who is he? What's his business?" asked Grandmother as soon as the two men were gone. "Rutland? Then he'll have to stay all night of course. When do you have to go back? Not *Friday!* Oh, coax him to make it Saturday. He seems very nice. Are you sure he's all right? Not like that last man you were sort of afraid of! Yes, I know you were, Margaret, child! You can't deceive your old grandmother!"

"Grandmother, I think Mr. Sterling would like us to ask him to dinner Thanksgiving. Would you mind? He's very lonesome. He hasn't any relatives living and he's crazy about farms and the country."

"No," said Grandmother considering. "I wouldn't mind at all if I only had a turkey. It's too bad we haven't any turkeys this winter. And there are only two tough old hens. Your grandfather has been wanting me to kill them but I had a sneaking desire to have them left till after Thanksgiving. Of course I hadn't an idea you would come home. But I just thought we might need them. They don't lay any more, but Sam Fletcher brought us up a dozen eggs and we've been eating those instead of meat. It doesn't seem like a company dinner on Thanksgiving without a turkey."

"Well, he's brought a turkey, Grandmother. He went out and got some things last night. No, I didn't put him up to it. He did it himself. I didn't know he was going to do it till we were on the way. I didn't have any time to go out and get anything or I'd have brought one myself. I knew you weren't

172

raising turkeys this year. You see I didn't know till last night that I was coming. He just came in the office where I was writing on the typewriter and told me he had to come to Vermont on business for a couple of days and where did my folks live? Didn't I want to come along and spend Thanksgiving with them? It was just like that, as if he had asked if I wanted some ice cream."

"I've got a can of mince meat left," said Grandmother thoughtfully. "Oh, I'm so glad you've come! What a wonderful time it's going to be! And there's dried corn and beans! We can have succotash! And some of our lovely rutabaga turnips are left, and a Hubbard squash, and plenty of our own potatoes of course, but we haven't got a cranberry!"

"Don't mind about the dinner, precious," said the girl, stopping to hug the old lady. "He doesn't mind what he eats. He's quite old-fashioned. He's just delighted to get up here! He's been alone out in the west on a cattle ranch or something and he knows how to rough it. He won't mind anything. He's a good sport."

"But how long have you known him, Margaret?" asked the old lady anxiously. "Where did you meet him? How did you happen to get such a good job?"

"Well, I didn't meet him," evaded the girl. "He came after me. At least I guess God sent me the job. It's a long story and I'll tell you when we have more time."

"You won't go and get ideas about him in your head, will you, child?" said the old lady in a sharply anxious tone.

"Oh, no, dearest! How absurd! Why should I? And if I did he wouldn't think of such a thing. Now don't go and spoil this nice time thinking up things to worry about!"

"No, I won't, you precious!" said the old lady with a contented smile. "Here, you fry that mush. Make plenty. I'm going to whip up an omelette, and have it ready to flip in the pan by the time they come in. He'll have to sleep in the south bedroom. Your grandfather put up the little sheet iron stove there this fall, thinking we would sleep there. But we didn't bother making another fire. There's plenty of heat coming up from the cook stove, so we use the kitchen chamber. It's nice and cosy, and the fire keeps up all night. There's a fire already laid in the south bedroom. All it needs is to touch it off, and after supper you and I will run up and make up that bed with clean sheets and plenty of blankets. I'm glad you brought him.

It'll be good for your grandfather to get in touch with the world for a few hours. He's always cheerful but there have been so many anxieties this winter!"

"Oh, Grandmother, what about the mortgage?" asked Margaret eagerly, "I suppose you don't know yet? Has Grandfather sent in the interest?"

"Well, no," said the old lady evasively breaking eggs with a snap, "the fact is he hasn't got it all in yet. That twenty-five you sent was wonderful! Even Grandfather was almost discouraged till that came. The man that bought the cow hasn't paid for it yet. He hasn't even come to take her away. We don't know whether he's trying to back out or not. We heard he lost a lot of money in a bank up in the next county. And the woman that said she wanted my walnut set hasn't answered the letter at all though I've written twice and told her the offer was only for a short time. I don't know what we're going to do, Margaret. Sometimes—well—it almost seems as if God had forgotten us! But I know He hasn't of course! Only I can't see ahead!"

Margaret's arms were around her again in a minute.

"No, dearest, He hasn't forgotten us! I thought that too, last week, but just look at this wonderful job I've got! And to work for a Christian man! And in Christian work!"

"Oh, is he a Christian? Well, that makes all the difference in the world. That is if he's *real*."

"He's real!" said Margaret with conviction. "But there they come! Just hear Grandfather laugh? Shall I make the tea?"

Greg came in bearing the milk pail with an air of ease that made Margaret stare. Strange he seemed to be at home anywhere! She looked at him with admiring eyes, glad that the lamp light would not give away her admiration to him.

"Now," said Greg, setting down the pail, "do I get a drink of this milk before I go on my way to Rutland? Where's the strainer? I want to finish the job up thoroughly."

"You're not going to Rutland tonight!" said Grandmother firmly. "You're staying right here with us! You'd lose your way going down the mountain in the dark. In the morning it'll be nothing to go."

"Well, you can't make me feel bad asking me to stay all night," said Greg, with his disarming grin. "I was hoping you'd do just that, but I didn't like to say so. Not that it would matter about going to Rutland in the dark. You can't lose me. I've knocked around ten years in the wilderness and I guess I can

174

find my way to Rutland. But I'd *like* to stay here if I may. It's the first place I've found that looked like home since my mother died!"

"Bless his heart!" said Grandmother, thoroughly won over. "Of course you'll stay. John, is there plenty of wood up in the south chamber?"

"Well, I wouldn't say plenty but there's some. I'll just run up and start the fire and then it'll be warm by the time he wants to turn in. I'll take up a couple more sticks!"

"I'll take the wood!" said Greg. "Where do I find it? But I'd be comfortable just rolled up in a quilt on that couch. You don't need to fuss up a bedroom for me."

"We're not going to fuss," said Grandmother, "but you're going to sleep in the south chamber. The wood is there in a pile right by the woodshed door. Father'll show you the way up. Margaret, light a candle. John, you'll need to take up a pitcher of water so he can wash his hands. He'll likely want to wash after driving all day. When you come down supper'll be ready. Father, show him where the towels are, and see if there's soap on the wash stand. Don't be too long for I'm making an omelette."

"That sounds good!" said Greg as he mounted the old oak staircase, his arm full of wood and carrying a candle to light him on the way.

"Fried cornmeal mush, and home-made maple syrup, omelette and fresh brown bread, applesauce, tea and carroway cookies. Does that seem enough, Margaret?"

"Plenty, Grandmother!" said Margaret with a lilt in her voice.

"Well, now run and wash your face and smooth your hair. I'll finish the rest. I want to have another pan full of mush going. They always want a lot. Run child, quick! I'm just putting in the omelette and it will be heavy if it isn't eaten right away!"

The omelette was a golden brown when the two men came downstairs, and Greg ate his share and said he never had tasted anything better. But it was to the fried mush that he gave the greatest attention. He said he had not had any since his mother used to make it. He had tried his own hand at it in his wilderness shack, but it hadn't turned out right. It had lumps in it, and wouldn't get brown, just turned a sort of a dirty green.

Grandmother laughed at him and told him he let the grease get burned in the pan before he put it in, and then and there she took him over to the stove and gave him a lesson in frying mush.

They had a merry supper, and afterward Greg opened his hamper and brought out things that he didn't know were in it himself. He had given the man in the store some money and told him to make up a hamper with everything in it that went toward the making of a Thanksgiving dinner. The man had done his best. There was a turkey big enough for a regiment. There were cranberries and sugar and flour and baking powder and loaves of bread and pounds of butter. There was seasoning of all kinds and vegetables, some of which Grandmother Lorimer had already, and some of which she had never seen. Broccoli, for instance. She had never eaten broccoli, but she had a canny idea of how it ought to be cooked. There were nuts and raisins and candied fruit, and a great five pound box of chocolates. There were a great many things that couldn't possibly belong in a Thanksgiving dinner, but Greg had given the man so much money that he had to fill the hamper up with everything he had, so he put in crackers and cakes and cheese, and a lot of canned goods, until Grandmother thought in her secret heart that it would take them quite all winter to get it all eaten up, and some things she meant to save till next summer.

They had a delightful time putting the things away, and Grandmother Lorimer beamed happily and asked Greg how soon he could get back from Rutland. She said that they would need him to help eat up everything.

It was very late for the Lorimers when at last the old farmhouse settled down for the night, and the old man said to his wife as he got into bed at last:

"Well, Rebecca, what did I tell you? Didn't our Father send us a nice surprise? He never forgets His own."

"Yes, John," said Rebecca fervently, "I know. I was wrong of course. I found a little piece of poetry in that book Margaret sent me last summer. It just fits me. I found it several days ago but I didn't tell you because I was afraid you would rub it in. Listen. I can say it now because I feel it. I *know* it:

" 'He was better to me than all my hopes,
    Better than all my fears,
  He made a bridge of my broken works,

176

A rainbow of my tears.
The billows that guarded my sea-girt path
But bore my Lord on their crest,
When I dwell on the days of my wilderness march
I can lean on His love and rest.'"

"Yes," said old John, "that is good. You must say it to me many times, Rebecca. We may not be out of the wilderness yet, but we'll always know He is getting ready some of His best for us, after the hard times. Well, how do you like the young man our Margaret brought home?"

"He's not a young man, John, he's just a nice boy. I feel as if we'd always known him."

"Well, yes, he does fit right in," mused the old man. "It would have been nice if Margaret had had a brother like that!"

Rebecca gave a sniff.

"Brother, nothing!" she said with asperity. "If he just doesn't break her heart I'll be thankful! He's too good-looking for an employer and too young, but I don't see as there's anything we can do about it except to pray."

"And isn't that enough, Rebecca? Come, now, remember we're having a real Thanksgiving, and don't let's borrow any more trouble, not for five more days anyway."

The old lady sighed deeply.

"Yes, I know, John." And then after a moment of silence, "You don't think you could just ask him if he knows of anybody that could give us a new mortgage, do you?"

"No," said the old man firmly, "I'd rather lose the farm than go around hinting for help. That's what he would think it was."

"Yes, I suppose so," sighed the old lady.

"Now, then, Rebecca, what was that about a rainbow out of your tears?"

"Well, John," said his old wife with a twinkle, "it was the *tears* He made the rainbow out of. If there weren't any tears how could there be a rainbow?"

"Well, Rebecca, that's so, too. So perhaps the hard things He's giving us are so we may have more rainbows! Who knows?"

Greg tore himself away from the farm about half past ten the next morning and went on his way to Rutland. He didn't know a soul in Rutland, and he didn't have any business there, but just to be speaking the truth he went to the postoffice in

177

Rutland and mailed a few of his little books to the ministers in town after carefully inquiring their names from the postmaster. After that he drove back to Crystal as fast as his automobile could travel, and went stealthily by a back road he had figured out on the way down, to the house of one Elias Horner.

Elias Horner was out, so he sat himself down to wait, and spent his time wondering what Margaret and her family were doing at the farm and how soon he could plan to get back without exciting their suspicions.

Elias Horner had seen the shining car from afar as he drove up to his house and had expected to find one of the city syndicate who were interested in making Crystal Lake a summer resort. So when he entered his house and found a strange young man whom he had never seen before, who introduced himself as a friend of Mr. Lorimer, he frowned heavily and set out his ugly under jaw. This upstart from the city was probably some young puppy from a law school who had been sent here to intimidate him, or to wheedle him into not foreclosing on that farm. So he set his jaw and spoke with a snarl.

"So you've come from Lorimer, have ya? Well, it's no use your wasting my time and yours trying any smooth words on me. I want my money, and if I don't get my money I'm going to foreclose at once! Money's the only thing that'll speak to me!"

"That's entirely satisfactory to me, Mr. Horner," said Greg with a smile. "That's what I've come for, to pay you your money!"

"What?" the old fighter's jaw shot out like a serpent's tongue, and Elias' little beady slippery black eyes tried to pierce him, but Greg didn't pierce easily.

"I said I had come to pay the mortgage for Mr. Lorimer. You know it's not easy for him to get down the mountain, so I've undertaken to attend to the matter for him."

"Who are you? How do I know your check is good?"

"Why, did you want it in a check?" asked Greg innocently. "I've brought it in cash."

Cash! the old man snapped out the word incredulously, "I guess you don't know how much that mortgage is."

"Yes," said Greg steadily, "I know. Suppose you bring on your papers. I'm prepared to pay the whole."

Reluctantly Elias Horner went to the safe back of his desk and got out his papers. He saw his dreams of wealth from the new syndicate melting away, and yet there was nothing he could say. He had demanded his money and this casual young stranger had produced it. The farm which had been all but in his grasp, which had been his highest ambition and aim for several years, in fact ever since his old neighbor had come to borrow of him, had slipped away from him in a moment, and so unexpectedly! Better it would have been to have let the mortgage run on a little until Lorimer got so far behind in his interest that he had to give it up, sometime when there was no rich young friend at hand to help. Perhaps it was not too late yet. He would try.

He returned with his papers in his hand, but sat down and looked at the caller:

"I've been thinking it over," he said, clearing his throat noisily to adjust a philanthropic smile on his hard old grizzly lips. "If Lorimer feels that he would like to let this mortgage run on a year or two more, at a little higher rate of interest say, I'd be willing. I don't like to press an old neighbor too hard in these times!"

"No," said Greg decidedly, "Mr. Lorimer wishes to have this mortgage paid off at once."

The old jaw shot out again and the smile disappeared.

"You making a new mortgage?" he asked with a sharp look at Greg.

"No," said Greg calmly, "Mr. Lorimer wants his property clear. Now, are these the papers?"

Greg left presently with a long envelope tucked in his inside pocket and Elias Horner sat by his fireside fingering the pile of hundred dollar bills ruefully, and thinking that he had made a bungle of the whole affair. Now, what would the syndicate people say to him? He had been so confident, and they had gone ahead with their plans just as if the land was theirs!

18

GREG had always been close-mouthed, therefore he had no trouble in going back to the farm and enjoying himself hugely all the rest of the day, saying absolutely nothing about his business of the morning, with all the time that long envelope in his inside pocket.

They gave him gingerbread hot out of the oven, and a glass of Sukey's creamy milk for lunch when he got back because it was so near dinner time he mustn't have a regular lunch.

He pulled off his coat and put on an old pair of trousers from the west that he had put in his suitcase, and chopped wood, carried up a lot of it into every bedroom in the house where there was either a fireplace or woodstove, filled up the wood boxes in the parlor, the dining room, the kitchen, and stacked a lot by the woodshed door. Grandfather told him he could cut wood faster than any man he ever saw.

He went out to the barn and tidied up things for Sukey and the two hens that were left, and then he did the milking again. He enjoyed it all too, getting back to hard work again. And while he worked he did a lot of thinking. He'd got to get a place somewhere where there was some real work that would tire his muscles and make him sweat. It wasn't good for any man just to stay in the house and use his brain. He ought to have to work physically for at least a few minutes every day. He would have to see about that just as soon as he got this book and testimony business well under way.

He thought a lot about Margaret, too, as she had been when he came back from Rutland. Her cheeks were flushed from the oven, her hair—one wavy lock had escaped from the knot at the back of her neck and kept falling down over her ear. Her eyes were starry with welcome. There was a smudge of flour on her cheek, and another on her arm below her rolled up sleeves. She was wearing a dark blue calico dress that she had found in her closet, a relic of her school days, that made her look like a little girl. What a lovely girl she was!

And to think of a girl like that getting her night's rest in a railroad rocking chair, or even a rooming house cot! To think of her sitting starving on a park bench! Proud and sweet and dear! The thought of her surged over him like a wave that would engulf him. He had to whistle to keep the tears back.

They had another lovely supper table that night, sitting long about it, telling stories, getting to know one another like old friends.

They touched on many things, including the faith of their fathers—and mothers,—for Greg spoke of his mother's faith, and of how she had always read the Bible and prayed with him every night of her life until she was stricken with illness and had not the strength to speak.

After the supper dishes were cleared away, Margaret and her grandmother tiptoeing softly around and listening to the talk, Grandfather read a psalm of praise, and asked Greg if he would pray.

Greg got red to the roots of his hair, and then got white again, but he answered after an instant of hesitation, "Yes, sir, I'll try."

Greg on his knees praying in public for the first time in his life, haltingly, but with a childlike confidence in his new found Saviour that stirred the hearts of the others and brought tears to their eyes! Margaret thrilled anew as she heard his petition. It didn't seem real that there was a young man like this, so attractive and strong and true, who could pray that way.

Thanksgiving Day dawned bright and clear.

They had talked it over and decided to have a late breakfast and then Thanksgiving dinner about four o'clock. But Margaret and Greg took an early walk about the mountain, while the frost was yet powdering the brownness of the hillside, and rimming the mossy rocks. Margaret showed him all the haunts of her childhood. Here she used to play tea party on this flat rock with acorns for cups and saucers, and little pine cones for food. Here was where she brought her cornstalk dolls to play school, and there was the path down over the mountain where she used to walk to school when she was little.

They went to the lake, and saw the old canoe turned over on trestles and sadly needing paint. Margaret told how she skated and swam here, and how the stars shone at night in its deep blue depths as if the sky were turned upside down on the earth.

When they got back there were scrambled eggs and toast

and hot doughnuts and coffee. Then Greg put them all in the car, Grandmother in her old well-preserved bonnet with the grosgrain ribbon strings that she rolled up carefully and pinned every time she took it off, Grandfather in a somewhat threadbare but still dignified black overcoat, looking every inch a gentleman. Then Greg drove them to church.

"This is the first time in five years that I've been to Thanksgiving service," said Grandmother happily as she took her seat on the soft cushions, and touched the upholstery of the car with appreciative fingers. "And the first ride I've ever had in an automobile," she added.

"Except once in the station flivver, Rebecca, don't forget that," laughed her husband.

To Greg that service in a little country church by the roadside was a sacred thing. He worshipped in the song and prayer entering into the spirit of true worship; and he thrilled to look at the faces of his companions, the older ones sweet and chastened and yet peaceful, the younger one strong and brave and lovely! He felt a real happiness welling up within him. And though the preacher was old and weary and a little bit monotonous, and the singing was anything but cultured, it all seemed beautiful to Greg.

There never could have been a better turkey more perfectly cooked than the one they ate that afternoon, for nobody could make better stuffing than Grandmother Lorimer, and Greg had provided everything possible in the way of materials so that she lacked nothing to her hand. The mashed potatoes were like velvet, but no smoother than the deep yellow of the baked Hubbard squash, a dish which Greg had never tasted before. The cranberries were clear like rubies, done in the old-fashioned way with plenty of translucent juice and the skins cooked tender and candied and left in. Rebecca Lorimer's mince meat was delectable.

"I am sure we shall need nothing more to eat for a week!" said Greg as he finally refused another helping of pie. "It's been wonderful! It's been a dinner to remember. Now, would it be in the nature of a crime if we all just left this table as it is for a couple of hours and took a ride? There's going to be a fine moon coming up and I thought we could stay out and see it rise."

So they spread a fine old linen tablecloth over the table and left it, though there wasn't such a thing as a mouse in the whole of the old house, and they had a wonderful ride about the country and over the rugged hills, ending with the panorama of the moonrise.

Margaret sat in the back seat with her grandmother, her hand softly folded in the old lady's. Just for that happy Thanksgiving Day the shadow of the impending mortgage was banished and there was a look of great peace on the old lady's face.

When they reached home and the dishes were done there was that sweet family worship again. Greg treasured every minute of it, the psalm that was read, and the old saint's prayer, leaving everything in the hands of the Lord. Greg thought he could vision the shadow of that mortgage behind the earnest petition, and the paper in his pocket almost burned its way out, but he bided his time. He knew the old man did not have the money for the interest, and there was still four days before it was due. He would like to have relieved his anxiety at once, but he was afraid lest the sweet old pride would be hurt, so he refrained.

Greg did a good deal of thinking and planning that night as he lay in the south chamber with a real feather bed under him, and homespun blankets over him, the wind whistling around the corners of the house. It must be cold indeed up here in the mountains when real winter came down.

Greg had not the heart to take Margaret away from the old people at once or he would have hastened away in the morning to begin to work out his plans. So he let himself be persuaded to stay another day and he and Margaret spent much of the day together out of doors. Sometimes when he had to help her up a steep place he thought how very sweet it was to be with her, and he held her hand close to help her and kept it just a little longer, perhaps, than was necessary. Then he would remember how she had once run away from him, and he would release her quickly and try to make it seem that it had not been.

Margaret, with her grandmother's warning in her ears, and her own conscience alert to warn, yet felt the joy of his touch, and the strength of his arm beneath her own, and could not but think how wonderful it was to walk thus with a companion so attractive.

Then when that great thrill of joy would rush over her as they walked close together through a narrow pass, and he

183

seemed to be guarding her so carefully from the roughness of the way, she would reproach herself and remind her heart that he was just a nice boy on an outing and that she was really his secretary, just his secretary and nothing else, entertaining him in payment for his having brought her home for Thanksgiving. And they would walk demurely into the house, with only the shine of her eyes and the rose of her cheeks to tell tales to the sharp old eyes of the grandmother who watched her beloved child so anxiously.

That evening he told them of Rhoderick Steele and his friendship and then of his own business and how it had grown out of a talk that they had. The old man listened and nodded approval, added his word concerning prophecy and the signs of times, prayed again that night at worship for Greg and his work, and for the part their precious grandchild had in carrying out such a wonderful testimony for the Lord Jesus Christ.

"And now," said Greg, as they were about to retire for the night, "I'm inviting you both to a Christmas party! Will you come?"

The old people beamed on him lovingly. They thought he was joking.

"But I mean it," he said, "I'm throwing a party Christmas. It's a house party and it's going to last quite a while. I'm going to try to get Rhoderick Steele to come to it too. I want you to know him."

"Well, that would be wonderful, Son," said the old man smiling wistfully, "but I guess that's impossible. Maybe you can bring him up here to visit us some day when summer comes and it's nice and pleasant here. You know Mother and I are old people and we aren't much at traveling around any more. Besides, we haven't the money. We may as well tell the truth. We'd enjoy it, I know, but it wouldn't be possible."

Grandmother said nothing, only just stood wistfully smiling and trying not to let tears show through the smile.

"Oh, but," said Greg, "you know Margaret and I are coming up after you. Aren't we, Margaret?" He had not been calling her Margaret before and it made her cheeks rosy to hear it. "We're driving up a week or so before Christmas, and we're going to take you back with us. We'd take you down with us tomorrow only I haven't got my place fixed up yet and perhaps you'd want a little time to put away your things and park Sukey down with Sam Fletcher!"

"Oh-h-h!" breathed Grandmother in a kind of awe.

But Grandfather continued to smile as at an impossibility.

"Well now, my dear fellow! That's a wonderful offer for you to make, but of course we couldn't let you do it. What would you do with two old parties like Mother and myself. We're antiquated you know and as shabby as if we came out of the ark. We haven't even money this winter to buy suitable clothes for a visit to the city. We thank you with all our hearts —don't we, Rebecca?—and appreciate your suggestion, but we'll just have to wait till you can come and see us again, and we hope it will be mighty soon."

Grandmother's eyes grew suddenly cloudy with the old question that troubled Eve in the Garden of Eden. She looked down at her seedy black alpaca dress and realized that she was unfit for house parties.

But Greg was not to be put off thus easily. He sat down again and began to explain.

"You see this isn't a regular house party. It's not a fashion show, and we want you just as you are. We're not inviting people who have fine clothes. My friend Steele I hope can come, but he's quite hard up himself, so you needn't mind him, and if we have anybody else there it will be sure to be somebody who is poor and needs a little cheer at Christmas, and we want you to come and help make it pleasant for them. But most of all we want you for yourselves. I've not had any Christmas myself for ten long years and I want one. You are necessary to my plans for a real home Christmas. I've never known a grandmother and grandfather of my own, and now I want to adopt you if you'll let me."

They argued for nearly an hour and Margaret had to add her pleadings, before the old couple finally gave in, and gave a tacit consent to at least think about it. But the last thing Greg said as he took his candle and went up the winding old stairs to his room was:

"Then that's settled. We'll come up for you. And we'll come in plenty of time to have a few days of real snow in the mountains. It must be great here in winter!"

Grandmother was up early, having plotted silently the night before to have a good hot breakfast. She already had a wonderful lunch put up, and she was bustling about, trying to smile and keep back the tears when the rest came down.

They made a merry time of it getting off, though Margaret and her grandmother had much ado to keep from weeping.

"It won't be long," said Margaret, smiling brightly as she got into the car at last. "We'll be coming back after you very soon you know, and we're going to be together Christmas!"

So they drove off into the dawn, and the old people stood at their mountain door shading their eyes and watched them away. Then they turned back to their empty house once more and tried to get back the sense of content they had had together before those two young things came to surprise them.

"He's a fine young man," said Grandfather, sitting down to drink another cup of coffee, for he had been too excited to really eat much breakfast. "He's going to do a great work. He's left me a lot of his little books that he's circulating among ministers and church members, trying to give a real message to people who have been lulled to sleep by the modern preaching. It's a wonder, too, for the dear fellow hasn't known much of the truth very long himself. That man Steele who brought him to the light must be a great fellow. I'm looking forward to meeting him at Christmas myself."

So Grandmother knew that Grandfather really was contemplating the Christmas party, and she hugged the hope to herself and the house no longer seemed desolate. She would go to work that very morning getting ready. She had thought of a way in the night that she could turn her black alpaca, put one breadth upside down and make it quite wearable again. And there were some of John's shirts that needed to have their collars and cuffs turned to make them respectable. She would sponge and press his suit, too, and mend his overcoat. Oh, they would make out! And perhaps there would be some little things about the house that she could hunt out and burnish up that would do for Christmas gifts. That little leaved table that Mr. Sterling had admired so much. Perhaps they could manage to take that along. Or some of the old books! Oh, there would be ways to find Christmas gifts, and Grandmother cleared off her table quite happily, even humming a little tune softly. Grandfather smiled as he came in from the barn. Mother wasn't going to grieve after her girl after all. And she seemed to have forgotten the mortgage entirely. Well, the Lord would provide somehow.

So Grandfather got out the old Bible, hoping for a word of guidance. There were three days now till the mortgage was due. Should he take what money he had, the twenty-five dollars Margaret had sent, and the thirty she had left her grandmother at leaving, and go down to Elias Horner today, or should he wait another day? It wasn't half enough for the interest, and he had very little hope that the man who wanted Lukey was going to be able to pay for her, or that the woman who had wanted the furniture was going to respond to their offer, but perhaps he ought to wait another day.

So he sat down with the old Bible and opened it to the one hundred and twenty-first psalm they had read before the children left, and there to his surprise was a long manila envelope lying between the pages! He took it up and turned it over curiously, wondering how it got there. He had seen Greg looking again at the psalm after they had finished worship. He had told him it was the psalm of the traveler and Greg had said he wanted to remember that.

"Why, Rebecca, what's this?" said the old man in great excitement. "Here's an envelope addressed to me. Did you put it here?"

"No," said the old lady coming quickly to look over his shoulder. "What is it? Is it something Mr. Sterling left behind?"

But even after his trembling hand had opened it and taken out the contents it was some minutes before the old man took in just what it meant, and the old lady gazed at the legal document in bewilderment.

"Is it something important?" she asked. "Should we get Sam Fletcher to see if he can ride down and telephone somewhere to stop him?"

"Rebecca!" said the old man, suddenly reaching out his arm and drawing his old wife to his side, "Rebecca! Do you know what this means? It means our mortgage is paid off! It's *paid!* Rebecca! Every cent! We don't even have to pay the interest! The farm is saved! Praise the Lord. Let's kneel right down and thank Him!"

So down they got and the old man thanked his Heavenly Father with tears in his eyes and a song in his voice.

"But I don't understand," said the old lady as they got up from their knees. "Who did it? Who paid it?"

"Why, our Heavenly Father of course," smiled the old man.

"All the silver and the gold is His, and the cattle upon a thousand hills!"

"Yes, of course, but how did He do it? Who did He work through?"

"Well, I suppose through that dear young fellow," said the old man, brushing the mist from his eyes and studying the paper again. "His name isn't on it, but he's the only one who could have done it. Margaret was as much troubled as you and I. She didn't have the money."

"You don't think she got it fixed with a new mortgage, do you?"

"No," said the old man, "she couldn't. I'd have had to sign a new mortgage because I'm the owner. No, it's paid off all right, and I don't believe Margaret even knows it yet!"

"You don't!" said the old lady. "Well, he is just a precious young man. How wonderful! And he knew he'd done that all the time he was urging us to visit him at Christmas! Well, we'll *have* to go now, won't we, John?" she asked eagerly.

"Well, yes, I guess we should go," he said thoughtfully. "In fact he really seemed to *want* us, and I guess it is God's leading."

"I wonder why he does it?" said the old lady. "Do you think he's getting fond of our Margaret? Is he doing it to please her?"

"I don't know, Rebecca," said the old man cautiously, "I wouldn't get that idea in my head. It might bring disappointment. Our girl is a good levelheaded girl. She won't let her heart get her into any trouble. Don't you worry. And they just seemed to me like a pair of sensible young people. I think that young man is just trying to be kind. But I've been thinking, Mother, if we go down to visit him at Christmas maybe I could find some kind of a clerical job and make enough to pay him a little every month till we get it paid off."

"Maybe you could!" said the old lady. "Margaret would help too! That would be wonderful! But you ought to sit right down and thank him."

"That's just what I was going to do."

So the old man sat down to write his letter, and the old lady went about her housework with a song on her lips. It was an old tune of her childhood she sang, but the words her heart fitted to it were:

"He was better to me than all my hopes,
    Better than all my fears,
He made a bridge of my broken works,
    A rainbow of my tears."

19

THE two young people driving down the mountain had another glorious day together. To Margaret it was like draining the last luscious drop of a marvelous vacation. She had adjured herself in the watches of the night that she simply must not presume upon a thing that happened while she was in Vermont. There had been quiet intimate talks, glances of sweet intimacy, a touch of their hands now and then that had thrilled her, little dropped phrases that seemed to mean so much to her eager thoughts and yet might just have been casual friendship. They were comrades, that was all, she told herself severely. When she got back to the office she must not act as if any of them had happened. Particularly that last night when he had called her Margaret! How that had gone to her heart to hear him speak it, and how cross she had been to herself afterward that she had let it matter so much. Why should he not call her Margaret? Likely he didn't even realize he had done it. He was hearing her called that all day and he likely just miss-spoke himself.

He had called her that one other time, too! That day he found her in Rodman Street! He had called out, "Margaret!" but he had not acted afterward as if he knew he had done it. He was just under the excitement then of finding her. Well, likely he had only called her so last night playfully. Still, it brought the bright color to her cheeks to remember it.

So she had resolved to take the beauty of this one day and not let it cloud the more formal days that she knew must come afterwards in the office when they should return to the world of real work.

So they rode down the mountain gaily, and continued their comradeship throughout a happy day, eyes meeting in sweet understanding of mutual likes and dislikes, happy awareness of each other.

Once when they came to a long stretch of smooth quiet road where there was little likelihood of meeting anyone, to her great delight Greg put her at the wheel and began to teach her to drive. His hands over hers now and then, his strong guiding presence, his foot touching hers occasionally, once when he leaned over to show her just how to step on the clutch his hair brushed her cheek. But he did not seem aware of it. She drew long deep breaths and refused to think of it. He had to put his hand over hers to show her how to turn the wheel. So she took it all calmly, and just enjoyed the day to the last minute.

A few slow lazy snowflakes were zigzagging down as they neared the city, with a promise of more to come, and the streets had a slushy dismal look. Margaret glanced out and suddenly realized that her beautiful interval was over. Tomorrow and the rest of the days she must go back to considering herself an employee in a reserved and dignified atmosphere.

"A man is coming for me tomorrow," said Greg in a sudden business-like tone as they drew up at Mrs. Harris' house. "He wants to take me out to a place ten or fifteen miles from the city and introduce me to a little group of ministers and Christian workers. I probably shall not be back till late Sunday night. I'm supposed to go to one church in the morning and another in the evening. So I shan't be seeing you till sometime Monday. If anybody comes in Monday morning you'll know what to say to them. If I were going to be at home I'd ask you to go to church somewhere with me."

He helped her out and carried her suitcase in for her. Mrs. Harris and the niece who was still with her came out to meet them, and there was no chance for a parting word. Just a good night and a smile before everybody, and Margaret felt suddenly the let-down after the wonderful day of companionship. Well, it was just as well perhaps. No lingering delusions to take her mind off her work.

With a somewhat dreary feeling she ate the nice supper that Mrs. Harris had prepared for her, told cheerful pleasant anecdotes of her visit at home, gave Mrs. Harris the messages her grandmother had sent, and then went up to her room and put away her things.

Outside the night had settled into thin sharp crystals of snow, half-heartedly coming down and coating the ground with white. She thought of the mountain and wondered if it was snowing there. She thought of the dear old people alone in a storm and wept a few tears, she thought of the dearness of the last few days and turned her mind away from it.

Finally she sat down and wrote as cheery a letter to the home folks as she could write, a brief one, went out to the post box on the corner and mailed it so they would know as soon as possible that she was safely back, then shook the snow out of her hair and went to bed. But she did not go to sleep. She lay there for several hours and tried to think of the mortgage and work some way out to pay it. She prayed about it at intervals, and resolutely turned her mind away from memories that would keep haunting her.

She wrote another long letter to her grandparents on Sunday, went to a strange little church where the worship was most formal and didn't seem to help her, came home and read some of Greg's little books, and was glad when the day was over and she might go to sleep again.

Monday morning she went to work. There was a great stack of mail-orders to fill, letters from ministers asking about literature, letters from people asking eager puzzled questions about the literature they had received, and one personal letter for Sterling. Strange he hadn't thought to look the mail over Saturday night. But he hadn't likely expected anything that required immediate attention. It was postmarked Virginia, and written in a strong hand. That must be from his friend Steele about whom he had talked so much.

Greg didn't come in until after eleven. He had met some men at the hotel who had been interested in his work and he had been talking with them. He came with a brisk business-like way, and though there was a pleasant light in his eyes when he greeted Margaret, there was nothing more to remind her of the comradeship they had shared those delightful few days. It was just as she had told herself it would be and she was glad she had herself well in hand. He would see that she had no intention of presuming upon his kindness of the past week.

She handed him the mail with the Virginia letter on the top and he tore it open eagerly. She watched his face for a second as he read. How it lighted up! How much he thought of his friend!

Then suddenly he swung around to her.

"My friend Rhoderick Steele is going to be married to-night.

191

He wants me for best man, and the only way I can possibly make it now is by airplane. That's my fault. I should have got this mail Saturday night. Well, it can't be helped. Will you call up the airport and find out what time a plane goes? I'll sign those letters while you do it and make out a check for you in case there should be need for you to pay for literature that may come."

He had scarcely finished the letters before she brought him the memoranda. He glanced at it and then at his watch.

"I can make it," he said, "if you will telephone him I am coming. I'll have to run over to the hotel and get some evening clothes. They may not be needed of course if it's a quiet affair but a best man would have to be ready I suppose. If you get him at once phone me at the hotel, but if you have to wait I'll be gone and you can just leave a message for him that I'm on my way."

He handed her the signed check and started for the door, then suddenly turned back and came to her again.

"Good-bye!" he said and half put out his hand. But before her hand could go out surprisedly to meet his he suddenly stepped close and put his arm about her, drawing her close for an instant and kissing her softly, tenderly on her lips.

"Good-bye—Margaret!" he said again, and was gone before she could recover from her amazement.

Margaret stood there in the office trembling from head to foot with joy and awe. The thrill of his kiss was still on her lips. The joy of his arms about her enveloped her like a garment, and the blood went pounding through her veins.

Presently her senses began to assume some degree of their normal poise and she was able to think connectedly. She had been so careful and dignified, and *this* had happened! Without any warning he had kissed her! And she couldn't by any sort of juggling make herself feel that it was just a casual brotherly kiss. There had been devotion and tenderness in it. It was precious to remember. And yet, she had no right to presume upon it. Perhaps he didn't feel the way she did that people mustn't go around kissing promiscuously. He hadn't seemed like the kind of a young man who would kiss a girl just from friendliness because he happened to be going away, but perhaps that was it. She simply mustn't count it anything else. Her grandmother's words were still ringing in her ears, and she must guard herself from allowing any playing with holy things. A kiss was not a thing to be given lightly. If he ever came back from his ride in the air she would have to make him understand that—that is if he ever attempted such a thing again,—unless—! Well she mustn't consider any unless. She must keep her principles and make them clear. Yet she knew in her heart that if he never came back, if some dire disaster should happen to him on the way, she would treasure that kiss through the rest of her life and count it the most precious thing that earth held for her. Well, life was full of a strange lot of complications, and she suddenly roused to the fact that she had an immediate duty. So she rushed to the telephone, her cheeks rosy now, her heart crying out to her, fairly screaming to her, that she loved Greg, and she never could undo it. She loved him with all her soul, and was glad, glad that he had kissed her good-bye.

And yet when a few minutes later, having held a brief converse with Rhoderick Steele, she called Greg's hotel, her voice was cool and impersonal and she was prepared to let one Gregory Sterling know that she had ignored that kiss. That she wasn't even considering it as a fact in her history.

But unfortunately for her resolve she was told by the hotel clerk that Mr. Sterling had just left for Virginia. She was too late after all, and she was glad of that too. Nothing he or she could say could change that kiss or spoil its beauty for a few days at least. Probably not until he came back. And for that brief time it was hers to think about, at least when she couldn't possibly help doing so.

Greg came back Wednesday morning, briskly, joyously. He looked her fairly in the eyes with a radiant smile. He spoke eagerly on business matters at once.

"I'm going to need you this afternoon," he said. "Can you arrange to go with me right after lunch, about one o'clock, say?"

Margaret had schooled herself to be calm when he came but her voice was a bit tremulous as she answered. She decided in a flash that he had forgotten that kiss, and she would forget it too. It was likely just an impulse he had, and she wasn't going to bring him up standing. He might think she had an evil mind if she did.

"I could go," she answered quietly, "but there were some people telephoned this morning. They are coming in to look the books over. And there are still some of those envelopes not addressed yet."

"That's all right," said Greg confidently. "How about that niece of Mrs. Harris'? Isn't she here yet? Mrs. Harris was worried that she hadn't any job. We'll just commandeer her, and let her try her hand addressing envelopes and meeting the people. And if she's got any brains at all she ought to be able to tell people about the books. Of course it's better to have a Christian person do it, and maybe she is, but we can't tell till we find out. Suppose you call her in and I'll give her a little dope about the literature. We may need her help from now on if I carry out some of my plans, so we'd better see how capable she is."

In amazement and some trepidation Margaret called Jane Garrett and then went back to her desk. She sat there trying to finish what she had been doing when he came in, but her thoughts went wild and her hand trembled. It wasn't going to be so easy to ignore what had happened if she had to go out with him alone.

But she need not have been afraid. Greg was not going to trouble her with any attentions. He was all intent on his business.

"We're going shopping," he told her gleefully as she came out to the car wearing her very best secretarial manner. "I need quite a good many things at once."

But he turned the car quite away from the shopping district and rushed out into the country as fast as he could go.

"Oh, I thought you said you were going shopping," said Margaret at last in a small voice when the silence had lasted quite a while. Greg had seemed absorbed in his own thoughts.

"I am," he said pleasantly, "but I didn't say where. You see the first thing on my list is a house. I'm going to throw a party you know, and I have to have a house to have it in."

"Oh," said Margaret quite startled. "Are you really serious about that party? But you aren't going to have to find a house just to have a party in surely! Why, I presume Mrs. Harris might take in my people for a few days. They could have my room and I would sleep with Jane Garrett. Then you could take your friend to the hotel if he came."

"My *friends!*" said Greg emphatically. "He's married now you know and they are both coming. Then I thought we'd ask Mrs. Harris and Jane, and Miss Gowen the nurse, and perhaps a few people who haven't any nice times and need them. We'll want a few children for Christmas Day at least. I guess we can scare some up somewhere. Christmas wouldn't be Christmas without a few children. How could one do that in a hotel? Mrs. Harris' house is all right, but that's my place of business. I couldn't see having a house party there. No, I've got to have a house. I may need it later myself anyway."

"Oh!" said Margaret in a meek voice.

After a few more minutes of silence Margaret spoke again. "Did you have a pleasant wedding?"

"Some wedding!" said Greg. "I'd like mine to be like that. No fuss and feathers. They only had a few friends of the family, and it was in a little white church almost two hundred years old. The bride wore a dress that her great great grandmother wore, but nobody else was dolled up much. She's lovely. I want you to know her. You'll like her I know. She's the only girl I ever knew that I thought was some like you."

Margaret's cheeks glowed at that, but she answered gravely. "I shall be glad to know her."

They swept into a long smooth road bordered with high hedges on either hand.

"There are two houses on this road for sale, and one for rent. One of them is furnished. I don't know whether I'd like that or not. You might not think the furniture was right. I like your ideas of furniture."

"Thank you," said Margaret trying to smile formally, "but I should think you were the one to be suited, not I."

"Well, you see I prefer your taste to my own, so that makes it all right," said Greg.

Then suddenly he brought the car to a stop before a tall iron fence bordering a hillside slope with a beautiful low-spread stone house at the top set against a background of deep dark pines and hemlocks and spruces. Rhododendrons and laurel clustered about the stone terraces, making the place look alive in contrast to the dead brownness of the fields and trees about.

"Oh, isn't that beautiful!" exclaimed Margaret, shaken out of her gravity. "I never have seen a more wonderful place!"

"It suits me all right!" said Greg. "Let's go in!"

"What?" said Margaret. "You don't mean—"

"Yes, this is one of them. This is the one that's furnished. The family has gone bankrupt and they've taken what they've

195

hoarded and gone to Europe to live more cheaply. It's for sale at a song, compared to what it cost."

"Oh, but even at that it must be some song!" said Margaret awed. "You don't mean you would buy a house like that just for a *house party!* You aren't entirely crazy you know!"

Greg laughed.

"Not for a house party alone. Not just for one house party! If I went there to live I'd have a good many of God's kind of dinner parties I'm thinking. The poor and the halt and the lame and the blind. It looks as if there is room enough and that's what I want. There are several acres of land here and that leaves room for some of the things I want to do, building small pretty houses not too close together to give men work, and people houses they can afford where they can get out of the city. I've got a vision too of a Bible School somewhere in the offing and the little houses will do for the students to live in while they are studying. I mean to make every workman take an hour's Bible study too, evenings, while they work here. That'll be a condition of being hired. I don't intend anybody to be helped here in a financial way without knowing the truth about salvation and what's the matter with the world today and a few other things before they leave us."

"Oh! Wonderful!" breathed Margaret as they turned into the great stone gateway and swept up the smooth drive. She began to look at Greg in a new light now. She forgot to wonder what his attitude toward herself was. She suddenly went under and out of sight. She was one of God's children listening to the plan of a remarkable testimony, glad to be one of the smallest units of that plan.

"There's a stone chapel up the road a little way. It used to be a church, but it's been abandoned for a long time. I thought maybe I could get hold of that, and I want to get Steele and his wife up here. He can teach and preach there, for a beginning, and maybe a school will grow out of that. I hadn't naturally much time to talk it over with him, but he'll be up here Christmas."

They swung up to the porte-cochère and Greg stopped the car. He took out some keys, got out, and began to fit one in the door.

"You are really going in?" asked Margaret in awe again.

"Surely. I got the keys from the agent and some of the facts, but I wanted you to pass on it first."

He flung back the massive door of the mansion and led her in.

"It's rather cold here," he said looking at her sharply. "Are you warmly dressed?"

"Oh, yes," said Margaret enchanted with the vista before her, "I won't be cold!"

Before her a great room stretched to low broad windows at the other side looking into the deep green of the woods. An enormous fireplace almost filled one end of the room with a wide doorway at either side, and the other end was equally occupied by the leaded panes of a vast bookcase filled with books. Soft tones of oriental rugs put color into the scene, and here and there a great painting held one's attention. A gallery ran across one length of the room showing other vistas of rooms with latticed windows opening into the gallery. It was a place to make one exclaim and Margaret exclaimed.

"Oh, I'm glad I have seen one such lovely house!" she said delightedly. "It looks like a palace, and yet it looks like a home!"

"It does, doesn't it?" said Greg watching her face tenderly. "And yet the people who owned it had several other homes. One in the city, one in Palm Beach, one in the mountains, one in Maine and a castle abroad."

"How could they bear to leave this when they had brought all these lovely things together!" said the girl, putting her hand out and touching the soft texture of a drapery.

"I suspect the getting these things together was the work of some interior decorator like yourself," said Greg. "It is only people who have the home vision who could really make a home out of a palace. Now, come let us look through the rooms."

He took her arm and led her through the rooms, up the stairs, and finally down again.

"Now," said he looking down in her face, drawing her arm a little closer in his own. "Tell me, Margaret, will this house do, or must we look farther?"

"Do?" she echoed wonderingly, painfully conscious that he had called her Margaret again. "*Do!* It is wonderful! It is marvelous!"

"Yes, it is all that, but could *you* make a *home* here, a real home, where you would be happy, and where your dear family could be with you and feel at home?"

"Oh," said Margaret trying to keep her balance. "Could *I*? Couldn't *any*body? I am not the one to be considered of course, but I can't see why anybody wouldn't think a home here would be the next thing to heaven!"

"But you *are* the one to be considered, Margaret! You are the *only* one. Don't you know that if you won't consent to make a home for me somewhere then I'll never have one on this earth? Don't you know that I love you better than my own life, and want nothing better than to have you always by my side? Darling, you don't know how I've missed you these last three days. Oh, Margaret, could you love me?"

He held out his arms and Margaret went into them and hid her face against his. Then all the joy of her dreams, all the thrill of sweetness that real earthly love can have for two human beings who also know the love of the Lord Jesus, seemed to be revealed to these two in that first precious moment.

Suddenly Greg realized that the house was cold, and that it was dangerous for them to stay there any longer, and reluctantly they tore themselves away from the enchanted place, which seemed to have become in the last hour their own, and already filled with pleasant memories.

"We've shopped enough for one day," said Greg as he took his place beside Margaret in the car, stopping first to draw her into his arms once more and press his lips to hers. "Oh, my darling! To think you're mine, and I'm going to have you with me all the time! No going back to a lonely hotel at night! When can we be married? Would you like it to be at Christmas in the little chapel, with your people here, and Steele to marry us? Or shall we just go and get married right now to-night by any preacher we can find?"

Margaret laughed joyously.

"Oh, you child!" she bantered. "Of course we'll wait till they all come. It would be beautiful that way! Shall it be on Christmas Day?"

"Yes, on Christmas Day after we've opened our stockings and had our gifts, and we'll have the tree the night before. On Christmas Day in the morning! How will that be? I'd like you to be my Christmas bride. Do you think your family will be satisfied with me?"

"Satisfied!" laughed Margaret nestling close to him. "You don't know how they adore you. I'd be almost afraid to tell you all they both said about you, it might spoil you, and I wouldn't have you spoiled for the world."

When they got back to the office they found some people there and it was not for half an hour that they had the room to themselves. Having dismissed Jane Garrett to the other part of the house they discovered there were letters for them both from Vermont. They read them sitting on the big leather couch, Greg's arm about Margaret, her hand in his.

Suddenly Margaret looked up from her letter her face all a-sparkle.

"You've paid the mortgage off! Oh, Gregory, you darling angel! If I never loved you before I'd love you now. What a *wonderful* surprise to give them!"

Then she drew Greg's face down to her own and proceeded to reward him tenderly.

"That's wonderful!" he said emerging from her embrace at last, "but you don't need to lay so much stress on that mortgage. Don't you know I'm figuring to go up there and spend all my summers, and sometimes get there in the winter also?"

Then he caught her in his arms again and drew her close.

"My darling! My little Christmas bride!" he whispered. "Oh, God has been good, good to me! I can never thank Him enough!"

There is no telling how long they would have sat there talking, planning what they would get for Grandmother and Grandfather for Christmas, how they would have the wedding, who should be invited, and all the precious details of such an affair. But suddenly they heard footsteps, the footsteps of prim little Mrs. Harris coming along the hall briskly, to find out why Margaret didn't come when the dinner bell rang.

Greg had presence of mind always. When Mrs. Harris opened the door the light had been snapped on and Greg was sitting decorously at his desk reading his letters. Margaret was at her typewriter putting in a sheet of paper.

Mrs. Harris went her way, and Margaret presently came to supper, her cheeks rosy, on her lips a smile. She was thinking how that first kiss he had given her would *always* be hers now, anyway. And how his voice had sounded when he had called her his little Christmas bride.

20

THERE were busy days for the next three weeks for both Greg and Margaret.

Every morning Margaret would take the first two hours at least in the office, inducting Jane Garrett into the work, opening the morning mail, answering the telephone, and talking with various callers who came. For Greg's intensive distribution of literature throughout the city and vicinity was beginning to bear fruit. Hungry people,—hungry for the Word of God, were coming like bees to the honey, and there was no day in the week and scarcely more than an hour or two of the business day when there was not someone to ask for more free literature or to examine the rare collection of devotional and helpful books and pamphlets. Jane Garrett was proving an apt pupil, and getting her eyes open at the same time to a good many truths that she had never heard of before. And Mrs. Harris beamed with pleasure. To have a prospect of keeping her precious niece near her instead of letting her go back to the middle west to an ill-paid job, was all that Mrs. Harris now asked of life.

Incidentally, too, Mrs. Harris was getting her eyes open to a lot of things, and it was quite a common occurrence for her to run into the office toward the close of the afternoon and look out a new book or paper to read that evening.

Greg came breezing in every morning for a few minutes, as if he knew just when he was most needed, bringing new supplies of literature, pausing to discuss a new book with some customer, taking down the name and address of people who needed enlightenment.

Then every day sooner or later he would give a quiet signal to Margaret, and she would presently come down with her hat and coat on and they would hurry away together. Sometimes to the house to measure for new curtains for some room that didn't have the kind of curtains that pleased them. Sometimes to the store to purchase something for their Christmas plans. Mrs. Harris had found a middle-aged English woman who made it her business to go out doing housecleaning, bringing two able and trustworthy helpers with her. These were put into the house to clean and the work went forward with remarkable rapidity. Each time they came back to it the two householders found another room nearing completion, sweet and clean and dustless, with shining windows, freshly laundered curtains, everything in perfect order.

"We shall need to be hunting up some servants I suppose," said Greg one day, looking around on the spotlessness with satisfied eyes.

"Oh no, not yet, anyway," protested Margaret. "We don't want a lot of strange servants around to bother us at Christmastime. We want it homey and cosy. I know how to cook and clean. Grandmother and I can do the cooking."

"Yes, but this is a very big place to keep clean, and if you spend all your time in cooking where will there be any left to have good times in? And especially at Christmas we want plenty of good times. I'll admit it's more homelike without a lot of servants, but we want to have time to give to our guests. Besides, we want our grandmother to have a good rest and not to have to work hard."

Margaret nestled her hand in his and smiled up at him.

"You are dear!" she remarked irrelevantly. "And yet you never had a lot of servants in your life! Well, I'll tell you, we'll compromise. Suppose we get these cleaners to come in every so often, as often as they are needed, and just go through the house putting it in order, making it immaculate, and then by and by as we see the need, and find the right person or persons, we'll get one or two. I wouldn't ever be happy having a lot of servants managing my home, would you? I'd rather manage it myself. And if we don't do our own cooking at least I can train the one who does it, or Grandmother can, which would be far more to the point."

"That would suit me all right if it doesn't make you work too hard," said Greg. "I agree that the servant question ought to be worked out gradually, step by step. I had thought maybe we could put a gardener in that little cottage down by the side road, and if we could get one with a wife who could cook so much the better. Then we'd have the house to ourselves except when she was needed."

So gradually with the help of Mrs. Harris who knew many

trained workers of various kinds they worked out their problems together.

"We're not going to be a fashionable rich family," smiled Margaret, "we're going to be a real family with a home and a home life! We don't have to do as the world does. Even though we have a mansion for a home we don't need to live in the manners and customs of the fashionable world."

"I should say not!" said Greg contentedly. Then he suddenly stooped and drew Margaret into his arms and kissed her.

"You precious little girl!" he said, his voice full of feeling. "How is it that you were kept so unspoiled from the world? How is it that God kept a girl like you for me? Just me, Greg Sterling? Why, if I had known when I left my ranch and traveled east that there was such a girl waiting for me I'd have come in an airplane all the way. The train wouldn't have been fast enough for me!"

She lifted her happy face to his and smiled joyously.

"What about me?" she said. "Don't you think I've got something to be thankful for in you? I'd rather have you than any man I ever met. I'm so glad you're just what you are! I'm so glad you don't want to make a big show with your money."

"Well," said Greg thoughtfully, "I suppose if you'd wanted to go into the world and shine and have parties and all that I'd have forced myself to be willing somehow for your sake, because I love you so much, but I'm mighty thankful you don't! Now, shall we go upstairs and see if there's anything more we need to get for our grandmother and grandfather? We must have things pretty perfect before they get here, for I've a hunch they won't be willing for us to spend a great deal on them if they know it beforehand. They're that way, aren't they?"

"Yes, they're that way!" smiled Margaret. "But I know they're going to enjoy everything you've arranged for their comfort."

Greg had planned that one charming wing of the big beautiful house should be set apart for the grandparents, whether they would consent to spend all their time in it or not. He said they should make their home with them, if they would, and then in summer they would all go back to the old farmhouse on the mountain, maybe sometimes in winter too, just to have a good time together. How Margaret's heart leaped with joy at the idea!

So the lovely apartment had been made as homelike and comfortable as possible. There was even a little room which had perhaps been intended as a dressing room in the original plan of the house that Greg had had fitted up for a kitchenette, with a tiny electric stove, a sink and an electric refrigerator, in case Grandmother should sometimes want to get up a little meal for Grandfather and feel independent now and then. It was just across the hall from their bedroom, living room, and delightful tiled bathroom. Not near enough to make them feel they had to use it all the time, but near enough to be convenient any time Grandmother was seized with a desire to do her own cooking. But of course all that was contingent on a time when there should be servants in the kitchen and Grandmother wouldn't feel at home in the big kitchen downstairs.

At the other end of the hall was another group of delightful rooms, the master apartment of the house, and Margaret went through them wonderingly, looking about on the beauty and comfort there prepared, and put up a little prayer of thanksgiving. This was to be the hallowed place that she would share with Greg. They two were to be one! What a tremendous, wonderful mystery! After all her desperate need and loneliness and peril God had brought her out to a large place like this, and let her see such joy and luxury this side of heaven! Ah! She would walk softly before the Lord. She would ask Him constantly to keep her heart right with Him, to let her use his wonderful gifts in the right way, to witness for Him!

By this time Margaret was wearing a beautiful clear diamond like a drop of dew on the third finger of her left hand, and Mrs. Harris was most respectful to her, and did all in her power to make her comfortable. Jane Garrett was her adoring slave, looking at her worshipfully, studying her every wish, anticipating any little need she might have, and working in the office as if it were a holy calling. There was no longer any question but that Jane was a Christian and eager to learn everything she could of Bible truth, eager to pass it on to others. There was also no longer any question but that it would be perfectly safe to leave the office in Jane's care while they went after the grandparents.

At last the house stood shining and ready. Mrs. Harris had offered her services to get dinner ready for them the night they should return from Vermont. There seemed to be nothing more to be arranged for a happy homecoming and a joyous time at Christmas. They had even found the children for a Christmas children's party, children from a forlorn little country orphanage, whose endowment had melted away with the failure of a big Trust Company. They had invited the children for a feast at five o'clock and the Christmas tree on Christmas Eve, and made glad the heart of their attendant by promising to look after the children that day and let her go visit her old mother. They were planning eagerly for gifts of clothing and toys for each child and a gay time generally. They had even gone so far as to get the name of each child, fifteen boys and seventeen girls, with their ages and sizes, and Margaret was doing individual shopping for them just as if they had been real children in a real home. Margaret felt that it was the most wonderful thing she had ever done to be allowed thus to brighten these dreary little drab lives.

So the morning dawned that they had set for their return to Vermont, and Margaret came down very early, her hat on, her coat on her arm, and found Mrs. Harris and Jane ahead of her, with breakfast almost ready. Greg was already in the office awaiting her, having been invited to breakfast.

He met her with gladness in his eyes. Margaret's heart gave a leap of joy as he stooped to greet her. Was life going to be one continual praise from now on? Oh, for grace not to be spoiled by such beautiful devotion! She felt constantly her own unworthiness. How recently she had been in despair, yes and doubt of God's love for her, when all the time He had been planning this wonder in her life!

They did full justice to Mrs. Harris' breakfast this time, and then Margaret hurried to the office to get her coat. But Greg followed her, came up behind her, took her coat from her hand, and held it. She turned and reached out her arm to put it in the sleeve but the lining did not feel familiar. It was soft slippery satin, instead of the dull finish of her own coat, and as he folded it about her and whirled her around to fasten it, she suddenly saw Mrs. Harris and Jane standing in the doorway. Something in their eager expectant faces made her look down at herself, and lo she was arrayed in a soft beautiful coat of gray squirrel!

"Greg!" she said "Oh, *Greg!*" and her eyes were shining like stars.

"Does it fit?" he asked anxiously, his face one broad grin.

"It fits like the paper on the wall!" said Mrs. Harris, as excited as anyone. She and Jane were all too evidently in the secret and enjoying that presentation as much as if the coat had been theirs.

"Oh, Greg! How wonderful!" she said again lifting her eyes full of delight to his, and right then and there before those two adoring startled females he took her in his arms and kissed her!

Mrs. Harris lowered her eyes and went scuttling off embarrassedly, but Jane backed off to the other side of the hall where she could continue to drink in the wonderful sight and registered a vow that if she couldn't marry a man as good and fine and devoted as Mr. Sterling she would remain single all her life and just be glad that she had been permitted a sight of what real love could be like.

Margaret looked down at her other coat and hesitated.

"Yes, take it along too," said Greg, reading her thoughts. "You may want it for walks in the woods if it isn't too cold. Now, all set? Let's go!"

He picked up her suitcase and the other coat, called good-bye to the Harrises, and they went out to the car.

"Yes," said Margaret still thinking about the other coat, "I can let Grandmother wear it back over her other one. I was afraid she would be cold. Her coat is rather thin!"

"Is that so?" said Greg frowning. "I thought you were going to get her some things."

"Well, I did. I got Grandmother a plain wool dress, and some new collars and cuffs. I didn't dare get too much lest she would think it was going to be too grand for her and would back out of going. I thought when we got there I could get her the things she needed."

"That's right," said Greg, but there was a hidden twinkle in his eyes that belied his close-shut lips.

Greg had brought another big hamper along but there was no turkey this time, instead there were chops and beefsteak and everyday things that hungry people would like. There were also several big boxes and packages in the back seat, but Margaret had some of her own, new shirts and warm underwear for her grandfather, a lot of little necessities she knew they had long needed, and she did not notice what Greg had. In fact she was too happy to be started out alone with Greg again to notice much of anything else.

"Do you realize, young lady, that this is really our wedding trip?" he asked when they had traversed the lonely early morning streets of the city, inhabited only by milk carts and bread wagons, and were finally out on the smooth highway.

"Oh, it is, isn't it?" said Margaret slipping her hand inside his arm and squeezing it close. "Oh, I'm so happy, Greg."

He leaned over and kissed her radiant face.

"You haven't got a thing on me!" he said joyously. "I'm the happiest man in the United States! But say, do you realize that we're going to be different from everybody else? We're taking our trip beforehand instead of afterwards. That's what you call unique, isn't it?"

"It's lovely," said Margaret resting her head against his shoulder and looking dreamily off over the frost-touched fields. "It doesn't matter *when* it is!"

"But aren't you going to mind not going off on a wedding trip afterwards like everybody else? You know we couldn't invite a party and then go off and leave them."

"Oh, I wouldn't want to go away!" exclaimed Margaret. "I want to stay and enjoy the new house and see what Grandmother and Grandfather say to everything, and begin to *live*. We can go off again sometime, can't we?"

"I'll say we can!" said Greg. "We've got all the time there'll be you know."

"I shall thank my Heavenly Father every day all my life for sending you to love me," said Margaret softly.

All too soon the bright day fled. Precious hours ever to be remembered. Hours as near as earth can come to heaven.

They came into the region of snow presently, hard glittering deep snow that had already settled down to stay and make a bed rock creaking sound for tires. Greg stopped and put on the chains as it became increasingly difficult to drive without them. And then suddenly they were at the farm and being welcomed by the old couple, eagerly, lovingly, Grandmother taking Greg in her arms as if he had been her own son.

No, they didn't know yet. Margaret hadn't told them. She had wanted the pleasure of being there to see their faces. And so when the welcomes had been said and they came within the wide old kitchen, lighted now by many lamps all shiningly ready for an illumination when they should arrive, Margaret took Greg's hand and stood beside him.

"He loves me, Grandmother, Grandfather, isn't that wonderful?" she said with a lovely glow over her face and her eyes starry bright.

"No," said Grandmother with a light of satisfaction on her face. "No, it isn't wonderful, but it's *beautiful!* I'm *glad!*" and she said it in a tone of great relief, as if she had been so afraid he wouldn't.

Swiftly the week sped away in the snowy woods, and they had such a blissful time, those two who were so soon to be married, going about from one spot to another saying: "Here it was that you took hold of my arm when you almost fell, and I wanted to pick you up and carry you up to the level, only I didn't dare!" and "Here was where you gave me such a beautiful look and called me Margaret!"

Breathlessly as the days went by they enjoyed every precious moment, meanwhile working along with the old people to help get the house ready for hibernating, and to help them get ready for the journey.

It was Greg who solved the question of baggage.

"Why, you won't need a trunk!" he said, when the old people were suggesting sending a little old haircloth trunk by express because they had no bags or suitcases but some too shabby to take to a city. Margaret was greatly troubled that it hadn't occurred to her they would need something of this sort.

"You see," said Greg, "there's a trunk on the back of the car, and it is made up of three mammoth suitcases. You can have one apiece and one over for extras. Here, let me show you!"

He brought in the big suitcases and opened them and Grandmother sat down and examined them in great delight.

"It's going to be nice, John," she said as pleased as a child, "to go back where they have things again. It's almost ten years since we've been much of anywhere except Rutland."

But the morning of going finally came, and the house was closed and shuttered, the fire put out, the oil taken out of the lamps, everything safe for leaving, and in a kind of delicious trepidation the old people went out, down the snowy path to the car and climbed in.

"Now," said Greg, "you'd better put on those coats before we get going. It'll be hard for you to get them on comfortably when we get started, and it's a right snappy morning. You'll need them. Of course we have a heater in the car, but I'm sure you'll need them."

"Coats?" said Grandmother looking down in astonishment at

the furry heap that lay in the seat where she was about to sit down.

"Coats?" said Grandfather, getting on the running board and gazing at the neat cloth bundle with furry edges and collar on his side of the back seat.

"*Coats?*" said Margaret as she tried the door for the last time and flew over the path to see what was going on. And then her face blazed into brightness that vied with the glint of the rising sun from behind the heavy snowy clouds in the east.

For Margaret suddenly understood and she paused to breathe,

"Oh, you Precious!" as she brushed past Greg.

"I'll help you, Grandmother!" she called with a lilt in her voice. "You might as well take off the other coat and hang it on the rack, and that sweater too, you won't need them. Here, let me unbutton it."

Margaret unfastened the old threadbare coat that had seen service for almost twenty years, stripped off the old gray sweater, and slid the frail little arms of the old lady into the satin-lined coat of fur before she even felt a breath of air. Grandmother stood up in the car and looked down at herself in amusement, soft dark fur from her neck to her toes!

"But I don't understand," she said breathing on the ripples of fur and touching her cheek softly to its silky surface. "Whose is it, Margaret? I shouldn't feel comfortable borrowing anything fine like this. Something might happen to it. It might get mussed."

"But it's yours, Grandmother! Greg got it for you! See, how nicely it fits you! Isn't that wonderful? And he never said a word to me about it. Not a word! Sit down, Grandmother dear, you can't hurt it. It's sealskin and it won't muss. It looks so pretty on you. Look at her, Grandfather, doesn't she look sweet?"

There was great excitement and even a little more delay before they could get those two dear old saints to realize that the coats were their very own, but Greg finally coerced the old man out of his thin shabby old overcoat that he had worn for years and into the splendid fur-lined coat that made him look like a prince.

"But this is too nice for me," he said surveying himself before he got into the car. "Too nice for an old superannuated farmer."

At last however the sun shot a real ray of light into the dimness of dawn and startled them all, they had planned to get such a good early start. Then Greg did manage to get them both in their seats, with the car doors shut, and they started down the mountain.

Margaret watched from her vantage of the front seat with the little mirrors arranged so that the two sweet old faces were reflected perfectly, and presently she signed to Greg to look also, and they saw the looks of admiration that passed from one old lover to the other. Finally, Grandmother in her sealskin wrapping nestled her head furtively down on Grandfather's furlined shoulder, and he stooped over and placed a tender kiss on her wrinkled cheek.

It was better than any wedding trip a couple ever took to watch the joy and delight of the two old people as they began to come again into the world. They enjoyed every minute of the way and did not seem to be in the least tired. Greg's quiet joy in their pleasure finally expressed itself vocally as he turned around and grinned at them both.

"Oh, boy! I'm glad I've got a family!" he said joyously.

There was no snow on the ground when they reached Greg's home city, but there were signs of its soon coming in the lowering clouds that banked themselves above the dark of the pines as Greg turned the car into the driveway and swept up to the house.

The night was coming down and lights were twinkling from many windows as Grandmother looked out from the car.

"Is this a hotel?" she asked as the car stopped under the porte-cochère.

"No, dearest!" said Margaret happily. "This is home. At least it's going to be. It's the house that Greg has bought for us all to live in."

"But I don't understand," said Grandmother in a small frightened voice. "This is like a palace. This must be a very expensive place. I don't understand, Margaret."

"You don't have to now, dearest," said Margaret taking the hand that Greg held out to help her and springing lightly to the pavement. "We'll explain it all out to you afterwards. Come now into the house and see how pretty it is, and how homelike."

Into the beautiful home walked the little old lady in her rich fur garment and her ancient bonnet. She stood looking about her as perhaps she will look again when she first sees heaven. She saw the wide vistas, as roomy as her mountain birthplace, she saw the great fireplace with its burning logs and leaping flames, she saw the comfort and the beauty everywhere, and then she turned to her old husband and buried her face in his new overcoat, shedding actual tears.

He patted her head happily and smiled down upon her.

"What's the matter, Rebecca! Don't you like it?"

Then she lifted her tear-wet face.

"Like it?" she said. "*Like it!* John, it frightens me it's so grand! It's as if when He saw I was dissatisfied with things as they were and Margaret away off from us and everything dark, that He should have flung down the finest they had in heaven and said, 'There, child, take that! If you will be growling all the time take the best!' It's the way He had to reprove the children of Israel when they grumbled."

But the old man patted her soft fur shoulder and shook his head smiling.

"No, Rebecca, you're quite mistaken, my dear. It's not like that at all. Why, this is the rainbow made out of your tears, don't you see, Mother, don't you see? It's God's love giving you a glimpse of something as near like what heaven's going to be as they have here on earth."

21

EVERYTHING worked out just the way they had planned it beforehand.

The days preceding Christmas week were not many but they were filled with delightful bustle and excitement, into which, after a day's rest, the two old people entered heartily, fully persuaded at last that they were about to acquire the finest grandson-in-law that lived on earth. After they understood that the house they had come to live at least part of each year in, was not for show, but for the service of the Lord Christ, they were content, and spent much time going about it and "telling the towers thereof."

There were still presents to be tied up with tissue paper and ribbon and cards, and Grandmother just loved it all. She took a lesson from the way the orphans' presents were being tied up and got some paper and ribbon for her own little gifts which she had selected so carefully from her storehouse of the years.

Early in Christmas week Rhoderick Steele and his bride arrived and became at once a part of the harmonious family, entering into all the plans.

Mrs. Prentiss, the English woman who did the cleaning was on hand with her helpers as the festal day arrived, but Grandmother and Mrs. Harris who came up with Jane part of every day, was an important factor in making arrangements. Grandmother made the mince pies and the stuffing for the turkey, and Mrs. Harris did the plum pudding and fruit cake, so there were plenty of helpers. Margaret had so many other things to look after that for the time being she was glad to relinquish the culinary arrangements into such very able hands.

Rhoderick Steele's bride Mary had a face like a madonna, and she and Margaret became instant friends and went about together with their shopping secrets.

Grandfather and Rhoderick Steele found great interests in common and spent much time with their Bibles open, sitting about the fire talking, Steele opening up new thoughts to them all whenever there was time for any of them to sit down and listen. Grandfather, too, showed himself to be well informed in the deeper truths of the Bible and they had sweet converse together.

Packages arrived and were unwrapped and rewrapped and labeled. One day a grand piano came and was set up in the great entrance hall in a niche that seemed built for it, and after that they sang hymns in the evening, Greg at Rhoderick Steele's suggestion producing a lot of hymn books.

The Christmas tree was set up and trimmed, all the family helping. Nurse Gowen arrived, and Mrs. Harris and her niece came out from the city to stay till after Christmas.

The day before Christmas in the early afternoon the orphans came and were escorted to the great room at the top of the house, probably intended for a ball room, but now consecrated to the Lord Jesus Christ.

Here were electric trains and a whole little village of toy houses and delightful contrivances such as children love, also indoor swings, trapezes, dolls, tea tables and games galore.

Here for three delightful hours the children old and young played and enjoyed every minute. Then as dusk began to come down and the lights came on, they went downstairs and were served a Christmas dinner fit for a king. Turkey and filling and vegetables, cranberries, ice cream and pie, nuts and candies. One wondered where they put it all.

Then they all filed into the big room with the fireplace at one end and the sparkling tree at the other, and screamed with delight at the wonders set before them.

The gifts were distributed and they grew quiet with their pleasure, each wondering perhaps what a home would have been with fathers and mothers like these people. And then when the last present had been handed out, the last drop of ecstatic delight squeezed from the moment, Greg told them all to turn around and face toward the fireplace.

They had not noticed before, their minds were so filled with the wonders of the tree, but now they saw in miniature on the mantel a little village stretched out before their eyes, built upon soft green hills where little white sheep clustered about their shepherds, or lay huddled under tiny palm trees.

There was a deep midnight sky above the village sprinkled with stars. They did not know that it was only crepe paper with silver paper stars; the little village clustering on the hillside looked very real to them. Queer eastern houses with outside stairs, the kind of place that belonged to Bible times. A low khan with a wall about it, built of tiny stone blocks, flat-roofed houses, a watchman on a housetop here and there, three camels with turbaned riders, and suddenly a great electric star above all flashed out, and they saw what it was. Bethlehem!

While they were looking, exclaiming, wondering, over the picture that Margaret and Greg and Rhoderick and Mary had built there on the mantelpiece, Rhoderick began to tell the story of that night so long ago, of how the Son of God the King of Glory left His throne and came to earth to be born a child that He might live and suffer and die to save us all from the penalty of our sins. Just a touch of Calvary at the end, a picture of that Saviour, without a sin of His own, yet borne down by agony because of our sins which He took to set us free from their penalty!

It was very still when the brief prayer came, and each child was brought face to face with his Saviour.

Quietly, gratefully, fervently they said their thanks and

went out, with their wonderful gifts, new dresses, suits, toys, candy and oranges. They had never had such a Christmas before.

Then the tired workers sat back and rejoiced for a little, ate a quiet little supper of their own, and hung up their stockings around the fire, with only the firelight and the twinkle of the Christmas tree lights to guide them. They stole back and forth putting their gifts into the stockings, knelt in a brief prayer and went to their beds.

Christmas morning dawned bright and clear with a heavy fall of snow upon the ground, weighting the branches of the pine trees, picking out every bare branch of the other trees, making the world into a Christmas mystery of beauty.

They all came trooping merrily down, a bit later than they had planned because the snow had fallen so softly in the night that it seemed to have muffled their sense of time, and like so many children they went for their stockings and had a wonderful time opening them about the fire. Just a happy homey family time, for it seemed as if they had always belonged to each other.

Everybody had a present for everybody else. Some of them were very trifles, but each had some significance, some thought behind it that made it valuable. There were bits of jokes and delightful amusing rhymes wrapped with each gift, and before they had read them all and admired everything the time was hurrying by and it was almost nine o'clock. Suddenly breakfast seemed desirable and they went gaily to the dining room where there were sausages and buckwheat cakes, coffee and a great pan of sugary doughnuts, Grandmother Lorimer's doughnuts, the traditional doughnuts that always went with a Lorimer Christmas breakfast.

While they were eating the doughnuts, Margaret in her simple dark green dress slipped quietly away for five minutes or so, and as they all came out from the dining room she came down the stairs attired in white, just a little hand-knit white dress of simple lines and quiet mode, lovely in its texture of heavy silk threads, and most becoming. She was carrying a great armful of white roses and smiling at Greg who stood at the foot of the stairs looking up.

Grandmother and Grandfather suddenly dropped into two chairs that stood at hand and sat there smiling, and Rhoderick Steele came forward and stood before them.

Then Greg took Margaret's hand in his and led her down the last step to stand beside him, and so in a solemn simple service they were married.

It was not like other weddings, truly, for the bride and the groom went about among their dear friends all day long and had a happy time. The Christmas dinner eaten late in the afternoon when the doughnuts were fully forgotten, was the best Christmas dinner, Greg said, that he had ever tasted, and they all assented eagerly.

They lingered about the board telling stories, eating nuts and candies, just lingering, loth to stir and bring this happy day to its close.

They came back into the great living room then, gathered about the piano, and all sang. They had their hymn books out and were singing first the Christmas songs, "Silent Night," "O Little Town of Bethlehem," all the dear old Christmas carols, and then they opened the hymn books and began to sing others, about the coming back of the Lord Jesus for His own. "He is coming again!", "Jesus May Come To-day!", "It May Be At Morn!" There were some good voices among them and they sang from the heart. The old people felt as if they were almost at the gate of heaven, and it did not seem strange to realize their Lord might come at any minute now and call them all away.

Then, while they were singing, the doorbell rang.

Nobody heard it but Jane Garrett, and she slipped quietly to the door and opened it.

There on the portico stood a little company of gaily dressed people, and outside were a couple of big cars.

The Christmas air was keen and cold, and a sharp little businesslike wind was at work outside with the fine powdery snow. It blew in Jane's face with stinging little pricks, and it wafted in the clean outside air on the edge of which was a breath of exotic perfume, and a taint of liquor on hot breaths mingled with a strange oriental hint of smoke.

A woman with gold hair and a startling scarlet dress led the oncoming visitors, and afterward Jane remembered wondering how she got her dress to match her lips so perfectly, and how strange it was her eyebrows were so thin and highly arched. She wore long flashing earrings of deep red like drops of blood, and her fingernails were stained to match her garments. Jane shrank back and wondered at her.

"Is this where Gregory Sterling lives?" demanded the lady in a shrill high voice as if she were speaking to a person far beneath her.

Jane shrank still farther and admitted that it was, and suddenly the whole troop of visitors flocked past her as if she were nothing and surged into the great beautiful Christmas room beyond, that still echoed with the sentence: "Jesus may come today!"

The lady paused on the threshold and looked about her, a smile of amusement on her lips, looked from one member of the Christmas party to another, her eyes resting for just an instant on the white-clad girl standing by Greg's side. Then she called out noisily:

"Hello, Greg! Merry Christmas! We heard you'd bought this place and we just dropped in to get a drink. We're all simply perishing with thirst, and we happened to know that this house has a fine old wine cellar stocked with the real thing. Open up, won't you and pass it around. Be a good sport and don't be a dog in the manger!"

It happened that just as these interlopers entered the singers had come away from the piano and grouped themselves about the fire, and now they all looked up in startled amazement.

Greg whirled about sharply at the sound of that voice and faced the girl he used to go with in his high school days, faced her with a stern white face, a deep look of indignation in his eyes, faced her with the look he wore once when he faced a bear in his wilderness home and the odds were against him.

Just an instant he looked at her, then he spoke quietly, coldly. Not a flicker now in his face, even the anger under control.

"Sorry to have to disappoint you," he said clearly so that everyone in the room could distinctly hear, "but I emptied every drop of that old poison down the drain the first day I owned the place, and then smashed all the bottles and sent them to the dump. But let me introduce you to my friends. This is my grandmother and grandfather Mr. and Mrs. Lorimer. This is Mr. and Mrs. Steele,—" Greg went around the circle, and then suddenly drew Margaret's hand within his arm, "And this is my wife, Mrs. Sterling," he said, with a something in his tone that hushed the amusement on Alice Blair's lips and for the instant held her scorn in abeyance while she studied the girl in white with the saintlike face. Then her eyes traveled around the circle again with the look of a keen appraiser.

"And now," said Greg without attempting to name the rest of the intruders, "Mrs. Blair, we were about to listen to my friend Mr. Steele read to us. If you will be seated we shall be glad to share the pleasure with you."

Greg indicated a long deep-cushioned, built-in seat that ran along the wall between the windows, and something compelling in his voice made those gay strangers sit down. Was it curiosity that made them linger, or something outside of themselves that restrained them?

And instantly Rhoderick Steele took his little book out of his pocket and began to describe a scene at a well outside an oriental city. A few vivid sentences, and the attention of the whole little company was upon a majestic figure seated on the edge of the well, watching the approach of a woman, an outcast from society, coming for water at the hour when she would be sure not to meet any who would scorn her and spit upon her.

In the same conversational voice Steele read and explained:
" 'Jesus saith unto her, Give me to drink.'

"The woman was amazed that anyone, especially a Jew, should speak kindly to her. Then the Man went on, 'If thou knewest the gift of God, and who it is that saith unto thee Give me to drink, thou wouldest have asked of him and he would have given thee living water. . . . Whosoever drinketh of this water shall thirst again. But whosoever drinketh of the water that I shall give him shall never thirst.' "

When Steele had finished and closed his little book the guests drew quick sharp breaths and there was a stir among them. Greg sensed the tenseness in the air and dared not look toward Alice. Alice was capable of turning this whole thing into mockery. Instead he looked quickly toward the white-haired old man sitting with his sweet old wife beside the fire.

"Grandfather," he said and his voice was clear and distinct, "will you pray?"

There was the soft stir of garments as the family and house guests knelt. Greg kneeling beside Margaret gathered her hand in a close clasp and prayed in his own heart, "Oh, Father, control this situation!—Let it be according to Thy will."

Grandfather began to pray as only one who knows the Lord

intimately can pray, and he did not forget to include the strangers who had just come among them.

And those strangers who had come to make mockery sat there strangely stunned, their faces a study of fear mingled with scorn. But there was only one in the room who saw them and that was Nurse Gowen. Not being much of a Christian herself, and being deeply astonished and curious about the strange unworldly atmosphere by which she had found herself surrounded during the last few days, she felt herself privileged to pursue her investigations under all circumstances. Being a woman of keen perceptions and by reason of her calling skilled in judging humanity, she had immediately sensed the situation. Therefore though she knelt with the rest for the prayer she kept a calm furtive eye open for observation and lost nothing. Through her long lashes she saw the dull stupid stare of "Mortie" as he watched the kneeling act, saw the little shudders of dislike and terror creep over the group, saw the blank ghastly look on the face of the woman with the red lips who had called the host intimately by his first name. Saw her actually shiver and turn white beneath her rouge. Saw her look toward the door, measuring the distance like a hunted animal.

Nurse Gowen could not possibly know that there had been a day long ago in this woman's girlhood when she had once been in a Sunday School class of girls and heard this story of the woman at the well fully explained. She could not know how the story with Rhoderick Steele's clear comments cut deep into her own experience laying bare a heart that was full of sin. She only saw the fear in her eyes, the look of a hunted animal at bay, saw her eyes rest upon the girl in white kneeling there so quietly, her hand in her husband's; then saw a look of pain and jealousy writhe around her little red mouth. She saw her rise cautiously, tiptoe noiselessly from the room to the vestibule and opening the front door silently pass from view into the night. The others of her company, realizing one by one her absence followed her, Mortie stupidly bringing up the rear and stumbling noisily over Jane Garrett's meek little foot that happened to be in his way. And so they all disappeared, and the prayer went on following them into the Christmas night, under the Christmas stars, drawing their minds inevitably to one other Christmas star of long ago and what it meant today.

But Mortie had failed to latch the door as he stumbled out, and they could all hear a hollow, empty, gay little laugh ringing out on the cold air, before Nurse Gowen roused to her duty, went softly and gave the door a final closing. Even Grandfather must have heard that bacchanalian laughter, for he prayed more earnestly than ever for those lost spirits who had dropped in upon their worship and slipped away into their own darkness again.

It was very still when they rose from that worship and stood thoughtfully together, and then Rhoderick Steele quoted solemnly:

"When the enemy shall come in like a flood, the Spirit of the Lord shall lift up a standard against him."

Later when at last Greg and Margaret went to their own apartment, he gathered her into his arms tenderly and looked deep into her eyes:

"And to think," he said sorrowfully, "that I used to believe I cared for that girl! Oh, the Lord has been gracious to me to save me from her, and to give you to me! My precious Christmas gift!"

Novels of Enduring Romance and Inspiration by

GRACE LIVINGSTON HILL

☐	22940	**A NEW NAME**	$2.50
☐	22670	**HEAD OF THE HOUSE**	$2.25
☐	20286	**MAN OF THE DESERT**	$2.25
☐	20680	**RAINBOW COTTAGE**	$2.25
☐	20911	**MISS LAVINIA'S CALL**	$2.50
☐	22533	**DAPHNE DEANE**	$2.25
☐	20568	**TIME OF THE SINGING BIRDS**	$2.25
☐	20828	**THE SEVENTH HOUR**	$2.25
☐	20498	**THE SUBSTITUTE GUEST**	$1.95
☐	20374	**THE BELOVED STRANGER**	$1.95
☐	20044	**CHRISTMAS BRIDE**	$2.25
☐	20986	**CHANCE OF A LIFETIME**	$2.25
☐	20302	**THE PRODIGAL GIRL**	$1.95
☐	20448	**ASTRA**	$2.25
☐	14270	**MIRANDA**	$2.25
☐	12167	**THE OBSESSION OF VICTORIA GRACEN**	$1.75
☐	14457	**LADYBIRD**	$1.95
☐	20189	**THE TRYST**	$2.25

Buy them at your local bookstore or use this handy coupon for ordering:

Bantam Books, Inc., Dept. GLH, 414 East Golf Road, Des Plaines, Ill. 60016

Please send me the books I have checked above. I am enclosing $_____
(please add $1.25 to cover postage and handling). Send check or money order
—no cash or C.O.D.'s please.

Mr/Mrs/Miss_____

Address_____

City_____State/Zip_____

GLH—2/83

Please allow four to six weeks for delivery. This offer expires 8/83.